CURSED TO LOVE

CURSED TO LOVE SERIES
BOOK ONE

KJ WARAWA

MYSTIC
CITY
PRESS

DEDICATION

For DBW
I'll be forever grateful you opened your heart to give me a second chance.
All my love, my laughter... my life. /k

CHAPTER ONE

Friday, August 9

For the thousandth time that week, Blake Akerman wished he could roll back the clock. Several weeks would be ideal, but six days would be enough. He would hug his mom and tell her he loved her, and he wasn't angry at her anymore. Maybe convince her to change her plans so she wouldn't have been on the road that day.

Blake had felt so justified in his anger for what she'd done shortly before her death. He'd stewed in his annoyance until he finally reached out to talk to her. Her latest incident hadn't been the sole reason for his frustration, but after a year of her uncharacteristic nagging and meddling, it hadn't taken much to push his anger over the edge. He didn't know what had flipped the switch in his mom to make her act irrationally.

Digging his heel into the porch's floorboards, he pushed off to set the swing into motion. After he'd seen the last mourner to the door, the swing had called to him.

He sat and stared out at the street, not focusing on anything, as the afternoon sunlight slowly waned. If he closed his eyes for a moment, he could push away his pain and play a movie in his mind of a time before his mom had changed. When his dad had been alive, there'd been so many happy times when she'd loved and laughed. They had been the ideal he aspired to. They loved each other completely and passionately.

A couple of times in his teen years, he'd caught his parents in compromising positions. At the time, he'd been embarrassed for both their sakes and his, but he still knew that he wanted that type of love one day. The kind that had kept them best friends and passionate even after five kids and a couple decades of marriage.

Images of his mom flickered in his mind, one after the other. One image of her with tears streaking down her face after his dad's sudden death surfaced. Lost without her husband, she had become a shell of her former self. They'd *all* been lost without him. Zachariah Bartholomew Akerman, Zach to his friends, had been the best father and husband in the world.

Blake had stepped up to take over the business, but he couldn't replace his mom's best friend. Eventually, she'd picked herself back up, but she was never quite the same.

It wasn't until several years later that Blake had an inkling of his mom's loss. Losing his father left a hole in his life, whereas losing a partner left him bereft in a different kind of way. With his mom passing, all his major losses felt fresh again, as if his heart needed to remind him of losing his dad —and of losing Paige.

His thoughts drifted back to all the dominoes that had toppled, eventually bringing Paige into his life. His dad had groomed him to one day be CEO. He just never expected to be thrust into the role at eighteen.

To balance work and school—something he hadn't always

done well—he had skipped a lot of the typical college experiences like parties.

Not long after the start of his junior year, his best friend, Jake Young, had marched into Blake's office on a Saturday, demanding he go with him to a party.

Blake would never forget that night because that was the night he'd met Paige. Nor would he forget the night almost eight months later when she went back to her old boyfriend. That was the night he got a small taste of what his mom must have felt when his father died.

Paige had come to Akermans to break up with him in person. She'd stood with her arms wrapped around herself, tears streaming down her beautiful face.

"My ex-boyfriend, Craig, wants me back," she'd said, choking on her words as she tried to explain. "I-I never—" She wiped the back of her hand across her eyes. "I never get to see you. You're always so busy with school and running the business. It's like you don't care about me." She paused for a moment, then shook her head and continued. "Craig says he loves me."

Blake had loved her too and wanted to tell her. But he didn't. Neither of them had said those three little words to each other yet, and in that moment, he didn't see the point. She had already made her choice.

When Paige continued to stand there, huddled into herself, he knew she wanted him to say something—to fight for her. But he didn't. At twenty-one and with the weight of the world on his shoulders, he wanted her to fight for him too. Couldn't she see how much was already being demanded of him? It wasn't fair of her to ask for one more thing from him without being willing to give the same. If she really loved him, he thought then, she wouldn't be able to dismiss him so easily.

The moment Paige turned her back on him and walked away, a burning sensation rose in his throat. It was then he knew that losing love—by death or choice, it didn't matter which—could break you.

"Hey," Jake said, pulling Blake out of his thoughts. Chewie, Jake's St. Bernard, sauntered over and nudged Blake's hand with his head.

Blake rubbed both sides of Chewie's head in his hands. "Hey, boy, I bet you're glad everyone's gone." Chewie always seemed to know when someone needed comfort, and today was no exception. Blake let him go and wiped off some slobber on his pant leg.

"Cade said he's ready to read the letter from your mom," Jake said.

Blake didn't know how much more he could take today, especially if his mom had left a goodbye letter, but he knew he needed to hear it. "You staying?"

"If you need me to, sure." Jake called to Chewie and then opened the door.

Blake nodded and followed his friend inside. His brothers and Jake had cleaned up while he'd been on the porch—there wasn't a casserole dish or paper plate in sight. Since his house wasn't big, every room including the back deck and front porch, had been packed with people. They had supplied some snack food and drinks, but luckily most had only stayed long enough to drop off a dish and pay their respect. "Thanks," he said, nodding to them as he took a seat on one of his two couches.

Jake sat beside him, across from Cade and Dane on the other couch, with Ford in the armchair. Only Gage was missing. He'd taken off right after the funeral, no surprise to anyone, even though his not staying during this time hurt them all.

A sense of unease settled in. Cade, a year and a half younger than him, had dealt with the paperwork, while Blake had been the shoulder to lean on in the five days since they'd learned their mom had been in a car accident. The other driver was distracted while texting and had gone through a red light, T-boning their mom's car on the driver's side. She died instantly.

As their company lawyer and the executor of their mom's will, Cade had said everything was in order. His shoulders, tense and climbing to his ears, seemed to indicate otherwise.

"Cade, you going to read the letter?" Blake asked, when his brother didn't get right to it like he expected.

"Yes." He reached into his briefcase and pulled out an envelope.

"Aren't you going to read the will too?" Ford asked.

Cade rolled his eyes at their younger brother. "No, dumbass. They only do that TV. Besides, everything in the will is exactly as Mom said it would be, except we'll have to decide what to do about her house."

"Not yet," Dane said quickly. "Can we wait?"

Blake wasn't ready to deal with the house yet either. "Sure." He gave Dane a nod. "Cade," he prompted, wanting to get the letter over with.

As the oldest and the CEO of Akerman Contracting, his brothers usually deferred to him for major decisions. He usually had no problem taking the lead, but not this time. Legal stuff was Cade's area of expertise, and even if it wasn't, Blake didn't want to read his mom's final words while remembering some of his last words to her—listening would be hard enough.

Cade pulled a single piece of paper out of an envelope and began to read out loud.

"Dear Blake, Cade, Dane, Ford, and Gage,

My hope for all five of you is that you will each find that special someone and experience the kind of soul-deep, magnificent love your father and I shared.

If that day came before each of you turned thirty, I would have ripped up this letter, and one day during a family dinner, I would have told you a crazy story about one of your ancestors."

Blake swallowed, already not liking where this letter was going. It sounded as strange as his mom's behavior had been over the past year.

"Since you're reading this, I'm sorry I didn't get to see each of you find your true happiness.

As you've all grown into amazing men, I've wondered hundreds of times if I should tell you this story in person. I never did because I knew you wouldn't believe me. I eventually decided this letter would be just as important as having a will—something I didn't want to have but knew was necessary just in case I would not be there to guide you through what was about to come.

I've written so many versions of this letter, trying to figure out how to tell you what I must, but then I realized there is no good way. So I'll tell you the story as it was told to me.

This story has been passed down through the generations in my family. In the late 1500s, one of our ancestors, Eamon, was approached by a peasant woman. He was a prideful, influential figure in his village, and quite arrogant too. The peasant asked Eamon for food for her sick beloved. When Eamon turned the woman away, she revealed that she was a guardian spirit and said it was known throughout the land that Eamon wasn't kind, but she had wanted to see for herself.

Since he proved he truly didn't have enough love in his heart for those around him, the spirit cursed Eamon and all his descendants. Each person in his family line had until their thirtieth birthday to find love and have that love reciprocated. If they didn't, the curse would take effect.

The curse affects each person differently. My great-great aunt withered away within a couple of months, and I was told one relative lost her mind. Another lost all their memories. There are many stories like this in my family history. No one knows the exact day the curse will take effect. It could be the day after your birthday, or weeks later.

Please, my boys, I ask that you take this seriously.

Blake, I know you will be skeptical. I saw how you shut down after Paige broke your heart. It's time to let that go and love again. You always brushed me off, but I ask that you listen to me now.

Cade, you're my dreamer. You need to look deep into your heart and see the truth when you love.

Dane, stuck in the middle, you've always been our peacekeeper, but you will need to find your own peace before you can love.

Ford, there will come a time when you won't be able to hide behind your charm, and maybe then you'll see what has always been right in front of you.

Gage, it is time for you to forgive and love yourself; only then will you be able to find your true love."

Blake half-listened as Cade read the last few words. He didn't believe in curses, but his mom obviously did, and now everything she'd done over the past year made so much sense. If only she'd told him. He could have gotten her some help to see that it was just stories.

"Blake? Were you listening?" Cade asked.

"Yes," he lied, knowing he'd have to read the letter again at some point since he hadn't been fully paying attention.

Dane snorted. "Is this a joke?"

Cade shook his head. "No."

Dane continued as if his question were rhetorical, and Cade hadn't spoken. "I never would have thought you'd do something like this, Cade. Did you forget we buried our mom today?"

"Of course I haven't! Who on earth do you think helped Blake make the arrangements to bury her?" Cade exploded.

The tension rose. Normally Blake would cut in, but he was still processing his mom's words. Why would she write something so outrageous? Maybe it was tied to her strange behavior and he had missed the signs she needed medical intervention.

"Woah." Jake strode in front of Cade, facing the rest of them. "Calm the fuck down." Chewie stood beside Jake, rubbing against his leg.

Jake looked over at him, and he read his friend's unspoken message loud and clear—he had to get a grip. His brothers needed him.

Blake looked at Cade. "Do you believe what Mom wrote?"

Cade ran his hands through his hair. "I'd like some evidence, but I don't have any reason not to believe it."

Jake moved back to the couch, Chewie following him. "Your mom was one of the kindest people I've ever met. Making up something like this, especially for you to hear about upon her death, doesn't make sense. Am I wrong?"

Blake shook his head. "You know you're not. You saw her almost as much as we did. But she'd been acting so strangely. Maybe this was a delusion."

"You think Mom was delusional?" Dane asked.

Ford thwacked Dane's arm with the back of his hand. "Of course she wasn't. But if not that, then what is this? A lie?"

His youngest brother looked to Blake for an answer, but for once, he didn't have one. "I don't know. Cade, was there anything else with her will?"

"No." Cade ran his hands through his hair again, pulling at the strands.

"Man, if you don't stop pulling your hair, you won't have any left. You'll look old before your time," Ford teased.

Cade dropped his hands, but ignored Ford's teasing. "No, nothing else. I'm surprised too. I had expected this to be a goodbye letter."

"This is crazy. We're not cursed." Blake stood and headed toward his kitchen. Not in the mood for one of the many casseroles that mourners had brought, he pulled out his phone. "Anyone want pizza?"

There was agreement all around. Dane walked into the kitchen and opened the fridge. "Who wants what to drink?"

Blake ordered pizzas and took the drinks from his brother, handing them through the passthrough into the dining room to Jake.

The action reminded Blake of a conversation he'd had with his mom right after he bought the house. The living room and dining room were like one big room, but because the house was old, there were walls on either end, closing the space in. She'd told him the house wasn't big enough for a large family. He told her again he never planned on having a family of his own—large or small—and the house was big enough for just him.

It had been one more bone of contention between the two of them.

"Root beer or beer-beer?" Dane asked him.

Root beer was his pop of choice, but tonight called for something stronger. "A beer. Thanks."

Shaking off thoughts of his mom's disapproval, he walked into the dining room and pulled out a chair.

"You ever going to get rid of the moss green cupboards?" Dane asked, his tone mischievous as he took the chair beside Blake.

"I don't know, the color's growing on me." He hated the color, but changing it wasn't on his priority list yet because there was always something else to do.

"Hey, dude," Ford said as he came around the corner. "Is there something you need to tell us? Your spare room is all set up for kids. There's a crib, a child's bed, and toys in there," he told Blake as if he didn't know.

It seemed there would be no escaping thoughts of his mom's antics today.

"That was Mom," he told Ford. "Almost a month ago, I came home from work and Mom was here. I didn't want to see her because I dreaded another lecture about finding someone to love. I thought she'd be waiting in the living room, like she usually was, ready to pounce." He remembered walking in and looking around, surprised not to see her.

"Where was she?" Dane asked.

"In my spare room. She must have arrived as soon as I'd left for work that morning because in less than ten hours, she'd changed the room from an office to a room fit for kids, in case I meet someone who already has a child," he said, repeating her words. "She said it was gender neutral. Also just in case."

"Neutral is better than moss green," Cade teased.

Blake gave his brother the middle finger but appreciated him trying to lighten the moment.

"Yeah. She said since she didn't know if her first grandchild was going to be a boy or a girl, blue and pink weren't appropriate. I think she was hoping that if I saw the room set up for children, it might encourage me to start a family."

"Whether the curse is real or not, Mom thought it was," Dane said.

"She must have," Cade agreed. "What should we do about it?"

"You're serious?" Blake asked. "You actually think there's a curse?"

"Mom believed it."

"I'm with Cade," Dane said. "Since Mom was pushing Blake so hard to find love, she must have had a reason to believe it. Today's August ninth, which means—" he held up his hands and checked off his fingers to count "—you have twenty-three days until you're thirty on September first." He turned to Cade. "Mom said it would hit when we turn thirty, right?"

Since Cade looked at everything but the law through rose-colored glasses and wouldn't believe for a minute that their mom had been delusional or lying, and Dane was the peacekeeper of their group, Blake wasn't surprised they believed the curse was real.

"Correct," Cade said. "Find love and have it reciprocated by our thirtieth birthdays or the curse would take effect and we'd be cursed for eternity."

"I guess we only have to wait twenty-three days to see if it's real." Ford grinned. "Better you than me. And then—" he pointed at Cade "—I guess we don't have to worry about you, since, you're already *in love*."

Ford said the words *in love* like one kid teasing another, but before Blake could tell him to knock it off, his brother kept going. Usually the charmer, he seemed more like a shit-disturber today.

"Then you." Ford pointed at Dane. "We'll have almost three years to wait for you to be cursed, then another two for me and Gage, so…"

Ford trailed off, and Blake knew he was thinking of his twin. When Gage had shown up for the funeral, a renewed hope had lit up Ford's eyes, even in the face of tragedy. But then Gage left after the funeral without a word to any of them, and Ford deflated. A moment later, he appeared to shake it off and assumed his usual charming façade.

The doorbell rang, and Blake went to answer it. "This is crazy. We're not cursed," he muttered as he walked to the door for the pizza. He could only hope the curse wasn't real because he wasn't falling in love again—ever—let alone in twenty-three days.

CHAPTER TWO

Friday, August 9

Paige Goshko laughed when her daughter shot off her chair and jumped around, demonstrating something she'd seen that day.

"Emmie," Paige said gently, "Grandma and Grandpa can't see you unless you're in front of the computer."

Without missing a beat, Emmie climbed back onto her chair and continued her story. "He laughed and milk came out. Out his nose."

Paige listened as her daughter and parents chatted, clarifying when Emmie launched into the middle of a story without any context. At three years old, her daughter's speech was pretty good for a child her age. Much clearer than when Paige first started the weekly video chats almost a year ago after leaving her husband. With Emmie two and a half at the time, many of her words were more gibberish than English. Amazing what a difference a year made.

And not just for Emmie. After getting the courage to leave her emotionally abusive husband, Paige had changed too. Learning what she liked and didn't. How to stand up for herself and get back on her feet. It hadn't been a quick process, nor a linear one. It might even be a lifelong journey, but she wouldn't be reliant on anyone again—even if the journey turned out to be a lonely one.

A few minutes later when Emmie yawned, Paige looked at the clock in the corner of the screen. "Emmie, time for bed. Please say goodnight to Grandma and Grandpa."

"Bye," Emmie said with a wave as she scrambled off her chair.

"Go to the bathroom and Mommy will be right there."

Emmie raced toward the bathroom before Paige finished speaking. "One more story. Please," her daughter yelled as she disappeared from sight.

Looking back at the computer, she smiled at her parents. Her mom returned the smile, but it wasn't the genuine kind she gave her granddaughter. As a daughter who couldn't live up to her mother's expectations, Paige received a smaller, more polite smile—the kind she was used to getting from her mom.

"Didn't you do Emilia's nighttime routine before our call?" her mom asked, the words more like an accusation than a question. "It's late in the evening to start that now."

Paige resisted the urge to roll her eyes and didn't bother pointing out that Emmie had been in her pajamas. "She's bathed and ready for bed, and I read her several stories. I'll read her one more to get her settled down after our call."

"Good. So... I wanted to mention that Craig's mom emailed me the other day. We still keep in touch..."

Her mom was the queen of pregnant pauses. At one time, Paige would have jumped in to fill the silence with what her mom wanted to hear.

Not anymore. It had taken Paige the entire twenty-eight years of her existence to figure her mother out, but she finally had. An abusive relationship and a yearning for something more had finally woken her up.

"She said that Craig is starting to date again. You know, if you—"

"Kristie, that's enough. Paige and Craig are divorced," her dad said quietly, in a tone that brooked no argument. At least from most people.

Her mom gave him a glance. "Steve, you know I want what's best for my children. Paige, it's not too late. You could talk to him. You have history and a child together."

Paige held in her sigh, not wanting to appear disrespectful. She loved her mom, but there were days she didn't like her. "Mom, you know our divorce was finalized months ago."

Would her mom be pushing for a reconciliation if she knew about the debt Paige had walked away from the marriage with? She hadn't told her parents about it because she worried her dad would offer to help her out when they couldn't really afford to. He would offer anyway—even if it meant dipping into their retirement savings—so she'd kept it to herself.

"Yes, but that's no reason you couldn't try again. You know that no one in our family has ever been divorced before; it's like you just gave up." Her mother scoffed, obviously not worried about being disrespectful like Paige had been.

Paige crossed her arms over her chest as if she could hold in all her hurt and resentment against her ex-husband, and her feelings of failure. "I didn't *give up*, Mom. I got out. There's a difference. We've talked about this. Craig was emotionally abusive."

"But maybe—" her mom started again.

"Paige," her dad said, laying a hand on his wife's arm. He

looked at Paige. "We love you. Both of us. And we want what's best for you."

"I know." She sighed, no longer able to hold it in. "But that's not Craig."

"Well, thanks for calling," her mom said, giving her the polite smile again before disappearing from the frame.

Paige relaxed and smiled at her dad. "Still up for tea?" she asked him.

"You bet. It won't take me long to make mine, but don't rush; I'll be here."

"Thanks, Dad." Paige turned off her camera and muted the sound.

She and her dad had always been close. It could be because they were so much alike, always trying to keep the peace. Whatever the reason, she was grateful for their relationship. Especially now. During her years with Craig, she'd gradually lost her friends as he monopolized more and more of her time with his demands. If it wasn't for her dad, she wouldn't have a support system at all.

Paige loved her siblings, but she didn't speak to them much because they were always busy. Her brother lived in Italy. He had gone there to study under a master painter, found his soulmate, and never left. Her sister was a hedge fund manager on Wall Street with a rich fiancé from old-world money and seemed truly happy.

Thinking about her siblings always reminded Paige how much of a failure she was. She didn't have a successful career, or a loving partner she could lean on. Even a solid friend would be enough.

"I'm independent. No one will control me, and I won't become reliant on anyone," she whispered under her breath. Whenever loneliness crept in, she repeated the words like a mantra.

"Mommy! I have a book," Emmie shouted as Paige

entered her room. All thoughts of dreams and failures fled her mind for a while as she focused on her daughter.

Less than ten minutes later, Emmie was tucked into bed and Paige was back at her computer with a steaming mug of peach herbal tea. Looking forward to the chat with her dad, she turned her camera and sound back on.

"I heard everything about Emmie's day, which I live for," her dad said, smiling. "But what about yours?"

"It was Alex Akerman's funeral today," she blurted before she thought about it.

"What happened?"

"A car accident."

"Tragic. Standing room only at her funeral, I bet."

"Uh… I didn't go." She took another sip of her tea, hoping her dad would move on. She was an idiot for even mentioning it because of the conversation it would bring. Except, after learning about Alex's death, she couldn't stop thinking about Alex—and her oldest son.

"I thought you kept in touch with Alex over the years."

"Mostly Christmas cards. But when I moved back to this part of town, I bumped into her and Kelly Young. You remember Kelly, right? Jake's mom?" Her dad nodded. "We exchanged numbers, and I met them for coffee a few times. Kelly called to give me the details for Alex's funeral, but I didn't feel right going."

"Why not?"

Because I'm an idiot. "I haven't seen Blake in years and seeing him for the first time again at his mom's funeral would have been weird."

They both sipped their tea for a moment, until her dad broke the silence. "I used to think you would marry Blake."

She used to think that too. Had dreamed about a loving relationship where they treated each other as equals and raised a family together. Until Craig came back into her life and sweet-talked her like he always had. "Blake and I only dated for eight months," she said, trying to downplay their relationship.

"I know. But he seemed like a great guy, and you were happy with him."

"He was—well, probably still is—great." As for the happy part… she'd learned it was best to rely only on herself for her happiness.

More silence as they sipped their tea, but Paige knew something was coming because her dad's brows wrinkled. She'd always thought of it as his thinking face. "Paige… Your mom means well, you know?"

"I do, but Dad, she knew Craig was abusive, and she never once stood up for me."

"That's not just on your mom, Paige. I didn't do anything, either. I put blinders on and figured, as an adult, you knew what you were doing."

"It's okay."

"It's not, but it is what it is, and you can't change the past."

He took another drink as if he needed time to compose himself. Paige did the same, swallowing against the sudden tightening of her throat. Whether it was from her dad's love for her or from thinking of her own failures, she didn't know.

"Well, don't worry about your mom and her nonsense about Craig. You know she's never liked the idea of divorce, but that doesn't matter. It was right for you, so she'll come around."

"I hope so."

"She will. You always knew your own mind. Maybe you got lost for a while, but look at you now," he said with a chuckle. "You're a fancy real estate agent, and you're moving on with your life."

Paige nodded, relieved her dad didn't know the truth.

True, she was moving on, but she was a total mess, both emotionally and financially. She may have left her husband, but that hadn't fixed her life. Some days she felt like she'd gone from the frying pan to the fire. "Yes, I am," she said, forcing a smile.

"Plus, you've got an amazing little girl."

"I do, so I can't ever regret marrying Craig." That was another of her constant mantras. If she wished she'd never broken up with Blake and hadn't married Craig, she wouldn't have Emmie.

"True. Speaking of our little princess, you must be tired after working all day and looking after her. Same time next week?"

"You bet. Good night, Dad. I love you."

"I love you too."

Paige closed the video app and pulled up her financial spreadsheet. As much as she wanted to crawl into bed and ignore her current depressing reality, she couldn't. Sticking her head in the sand and pretending her problems didn't exist was what got her into her situation in the first place.

It didn't take her long to update her finances and check what was coming due. With her hand on the laptop's lid to close it, her gaze landed on her remaining debt amount.

The number seemed to mock her. If she hadn't been such an idiot to let Craig control all the finances and lie to her, her credit score wouldn't have tanked. Then she wouldn't have been stuck with half of his debt, or have had to take such a high-interest loan to get a car for her job and the money for a security deposit on an apartment. Needing to buy professional clothes to make herself look like a successful commercial real estate agent added even more to her debt. The clothes had succeeded at making her look professional, but she didn't feel it yet. She was still following the fake-it-until-you-make-it model.

Even with renting a one-bedroom apartment and sleeping on the couch to leave the bedroom for Emmie, she was just barely scraping by. She sighed and shut the computer. As her dad said—it is what it is. There wasn't any point in going over past mistakes, and she had to remember to be thankful for what she did have.

CHAPTER THREE

Sunday, September 1

"Happy birthday, big brother," Ford said, holding up his mug of beer after the server cleared away their plates and brought another pitcher.

Dane, Cade, and Jake chimed in as well, saluting with their mugs.

"Do you feel any older?" Dane asked. "I mean… wow, thirty. You're practically ready for retirement, man."

Blake turned one side of his face toward his brother and scratched it with his middle finger.

"Hey, I resemble that," Jake said mockingly.

Ford reached across the table and patted Jake's arm. "That's right… I forgot we celebrated your birthday last month. You've had so many I lost track."

Jake grinned. "That's right," he said, mimicking Ford. "I forgot how young you are. Just a baby. Blake, remember when we had to change their shitty diapers?"

Blake snorted. "Don't remind me. I'm still traumatized from the stinky little buggers."

"Hey!" Ford chucked a balled-up napkin at him, and Blake laughed, batting it back.

Dane grabbed the napkin, most likely to stop the game from escalating, and nodded at Blake.

Ford snatched the napkin back. "I can take a hint." He tossed it on the tray of a passing server. "Thanks," he told her, flashing her a smile, their gazes locking for a little too long.

"My pleasure," the server replied, her words breathless.

Cade gave Blake a sly smile. "Speaking of being old. The curse could start any time. Why aren't you dating?"

Dane snickered. "Awesome segue, man." He high-fived Cade across the table like they'd reverted back to being ten-year-olds.

"You're supposed to be looking for looooove," Ford added, drawing out the word like he'd become a child as well.

"Well," Cade prompted. "Weren't you dating someone?"

"Dating?" Jake pretended to choke as he said the word. "I don't think that's what Blake calls it."

Blake twitched a grin. "Ha. You're all a bunch of comedians tonight."

He could have used a few more balled-up napkins to toss and distract his friend and brothers. Instead, all eyes were on him, waiting for a response. "No, I'm not seeing anyone."

His most recent friends-with-benefits arrangement had been good until April began talking about more. He'd almost not broken it off with her because he'd enjoyed her company, and living on his own could get lonely.

Every couple of weeks, they'd meet up for dinner or drinks and enjoy some great conversation before the night ended with them in bed. No matter how good the company and sex were, it wasn't worth the risk it could bring. He'd never again expose himself to the type of pain he felt after Paige left.

He caught the look that Dane and Jake shared. "What?" he asked, looking between them.

Dane leaned forward, lowering his voice as he asked. "Seriously, what are you going to do about the curse?"

"Nothing." He still didn't believe there even was a curse, and changed the subject by asking Ford and Cade how the marketing campaign and revamped website were going.

Once they finished the last pitcher of beer, they abandoned their table and headed to the back of the pub for a few games of pool. Blake wasn't skilled at it, but it was a fun way to stand around, shoot the shit, and pass the time.

He conceded a win to Dane and leaned against the wall as his brothers trash-talked each other, when Jake ambled over.

"Any thoughts on replacing Stewart?" Jake asked as he leaned beside him. "We're too busy to leave that position empty for long."

"I know. I tried to convince Stewart to stay on for a few more months, but he said both his wife and his doctor say it's time for him to retire." Stewart had been the VP of commercial operations for as long as he could remember. He'd hoped he would stay until he had found the right person to fill the position.

"He did like to work, probably too much."

"True." With Stewart retired, Linda and Denise were the only ones left from the days when his dad ran the company. Twelve years. It was hard to believe his dad had been gone that long. He hadn't felt ready to take on the reins of the family business as CEO.

That time of his life was almost a blur. School and work had kept him occupied until he met Paige a couple of years later. He could still picture what Paige looked like the first time he'd seen her. Her long brown hair had laid like a messy, enticing halo around her shoulders, framing her beautiful face, her lips coated in dark red.

He shook the image of Paige from his mind but knew it would be back. He could sometimes go months without thinking of her, but thoughts of her had come more often since his mom's funeral. He hoped Paige was happy.

Jake bumped his shoulder. "Earth to Blake. You still with me, man?"

Blake looked over at his best friend. "Yeah, just thinking."

Jake chuckled. "Don't hurt yourself."

"Funny," Blake said sarcastically as he bumped Jake in return. Hard. He laughed when Jake stumbled but managed to catch himself without face-planting.

Jake leaned back against the wall. "Back to my earlier question. What are you going to do about the VP position?"

Blake watched his brothers joke around as they played pool. The problem was that one brother was still missing. He checked in with Gage often but still hadn't convinced him to come home. Nor had he mentioned the VP position to him yet, even though it would be perfect for him. "I want Gage to take it."

"Have you asked him?"

"No." He scrubbed his hands down his face, feeling everything from the last month catching up with him. "I've sprung enough on him lately between calling him about Mom and then having to tell him about the curse. Unless the VP position comes up in conversation, I'll coax him back here first and then ease him into it."

"Will it work?"

"Don't know."

"And until then?"

Blake didn't know about that either. "I'll take on some of the load and see if the senior project manager can handle a bit more for now."

"I'll help where I can as well."

"Thanks."

When he and Jake decided to call it a night, his brothers razzed him. Called him old for turning in when the night was still young. It was Sunday night, and he had a busy week ahead, but he didn't mind the teasing.

Once in his truck, he used the Bluetooth to call Gage.

"Hey, old man," Gage answered.

"I am to you since you're still such a baby," he threw back, but couldn't stop the corners of his mouth from turning up. It was good to hear Gage tease him.

"Did you go out?"

"Just heading home now. I met Jake and the brothers at the Kings Head Pub."

"I wish…" Gage paused.

"Yeah?"

"Nothing, I'm good."

Blake didn't push. Patience had never been his strong suit, but he'd learned workarounds worked better with Gage than pushing. They may not have been as fast, but they quite often had better results.

"Malcom's first birthday is coming up. Cade is throwing him a party a week from today. He call you?" he asked Gage.

"Yeah. But I'm on a big job…"

When Gage trailed off again, a habit he'd picked up as a teenager when he worried about saying what was on his mind, Blake held back from commenting on it. His time to say something to get Gage home might not be today, but it would come.

"I get it. Call me in a couple days?"

"Will do. And Blake?"

"Yeah?"

"Happy birthday, old man."

"Thanks," Blake said with a laugh.

By the time they finished chatting, he was only a few blocks from home. When he stepped from the garage into the hallway, he yawned. "Maybe I am getting old," he muttered to himself.

He got ready for bed and thought about reading for a few minutes, but he wouldn't be able to concentrate due to all the thoughts swirling in his mind. Instead, he turned off the light and let his brain run its course, hoping he would eventually fall asleep.

Hanging with his brothers and Jake was always good. However, it would be better if their family was all together again. With his plan to stay forever single, ensuring he would always have his brothers, and Jake, around him drove a lot of his decisions.

Calling Gage to let him know about their mom's death was the most difficult phone call Blake ever made. Telling all his brothers had been excruciating, but he'd known it was going to hit Gage the hardest because he still struggled with their dad's death, more than the rest of them. He might always.

Gage had taken off eight years ago, as soon as he finished tenth grade. Blake had itched to chase after his youngest brother and drag him back home, but his mom had convinced him that he would drive Gage further away if he did.

She said Blake would be better off keeping in touch with Gage and gently guiding him, so that's what he'd done. He still wasn't always as patient as he would like to be, but after seeing how much more effective patience was than pushing, he'd learned to work on it. At least his brother always answered his calls.

When Gage first left home, he settled in Salt Lake City, as if he needed to get away without going too far. Having him within driving distance had been reassuring. For the first year, Blake didn't push Gage to come home. He'd been there for his brother when he needed to talk, then even managed to talk him into getting his GED. He was still pleasantly surprised it hadn't taken months to convince him.

After that, Blake got hold of a contractor he knew in Utah who offered Gage a job. Gage didn't need to know that the contractor, an old friend of their dad's, called Blake regularly to let him know how things were going. Or that two years ago when a company in Green Springs, Colorado, was looking for a contractor, Blake told Gage's boss so he could encourage Gage to apply.

Green Springs was only a two-hour drive from their home in Blue Mountain, Colorado. Blake's next move was to get his brother all the way home. It was what both he and his mom always wanted, even though she had visited Gage as often as she could. He just wished he could have done it while his mom had been alive.

Yawning again, he closed his eyes. Just as sleep was pulling him under, his thoughts turned to the domino effect. If their dad hadn't died, his mom may not have been driving that day, and he wouldn't have been trying to run the company while going to college. He would have had time for Paige, and they might have stayed together.

None of that mattered, though, because his dad had died, and then Blake learned what heartbreak felt like. Something he refused to feel ever again.

Monday, September 2

THE DATE at the bottom of her computer screen—September 2— caught Paige's eye, as if she needed the reminder. The disappointment on her rental manager's face when Paige had handed her a check for only half a month's rent wasn't something she was going to forget anytime soon. It might not have been so bad if Paige hadn't been late on last month's rent too.

Paige glanced over at Emmie on the couch to check on her, then looked back at her spreadsheet like she expected the number to have miraculously improved. She knew it hadn't—she wasn't an idiot, even if she felt like one a lot lately—but that persistent, optimistic soul that lived inside of her wouldn't let her think her situation was hopeless.

Only this time, she couldn't see a light at the end of the tunnel.

Believing there was no way out meant all her struggles in the last several years had been for naught. Paige wouldn't accept that.

For seven years, she lived under Craig's control, first while dating, and then during their marriage. Because of that control, she lost her independence, and not only had she become reliant on him, she had also accepted his abuse as normal. In the beginning, his comments had been subtle. A small dig here, a backhanded compliment there, all in an attempt to make her a better person, he'd said.

Paige was a pleaser, always had been. It was part of her nature, regardless of the situation. She enjoyed making others happy, but problems arose when her overly optimistic soul made her ignore her own needs.

It had taken a grocery store aisle, a jar of peanut butter, and a brick of cheddar cheese for Paige to come to that realization.

A few months before her parents moved to Arizona, Emmie started walking. She got into everything. Paige had to watch her then-one-year-old like a hawk, and grocery shopping had become a nightmare. Emmie didn't want to sit in the cart and had no bones about letting the entire store know.

Thankfully, Paige's mom agreed to watch Emmie for a few hours, so Paige could go to the grocery store, drop Craig's suits off at the dry cleaner, and stop by his favorite bakery.

Paige loved staying home as Emmie was her top priority, but her second priority became keeping the peace. She walked on eggshells around Craig. He harped on her endlessly—she was uneducated, didn't bring in any income, and never did enough. Reminding him that she dropped out of college because of him wouldn't have netted her anything but ridicule, followed by days of the silent treatment.

For as long as she lived, Paige would never forget the epiphany that struck her while standing in the spreads and condiment aisle. She'd checked her list and then reached for Craig's favorite brand of smooth peanut butter.

That day, with the large jar cradled in her palm, Paige looked back up at the shelf. Even now, she couldn't say why she looked back. She'd never consciously paid attention to how many brands there were, always rushing and reaching for what Craig liked.

It wasn't just the brands that caught her eye. There were different types as well: chunky, creamy, dark roast, natural, organic, low fat, and low sodium. The shelves contained peanut butter flavored with honey, cinnamon, and chocolate too. Her gaze moved to the right, and she noticed cashew butter, hazelnut butter, sunflower seed butter. So many kinds.

The jar in her hand became heavy, pulling her gaze away from the shelves. As she stared down at the green label, she realized she didn't know what kind of peanut butter she liked. A part of her brain told her this detail mattered, but she shrugged it off. It was only peanut butter.

Aisle by aisle, as she pushed her cart through the store,

picking up items from her list, her steps became slower and slower.

Standing in the middle of the freezer section with Craig's favorite ice cream numbing her fingers, she stared at the dozens of varieties and blinked back tears. She wouldn't have been able to pick out her favorite flavor even if her life had depended on it.

By the time she arrived in the dairy department, her throat felt tight, and her vision was blurry with unshed tears. It wasn't about peanut butter anymore.

Her hand shook as she reached for Craig's favorite cheese —medium cheddar—almost afraid to lift the brick. That little part in her brain that voiced concern over the peanut butter was screaming and had been screaming at her throughout the entire store. The voice asked the same question over and over again: *What kind do you like?* It was a question she didn't have an answer to.

She knew what Craig liked, and by default, what his wife was supposed to like. Then she realized that sometime during her years with Craig, what Paige liked had become unimportant. Insignificant.

Paige had become insignificant.

That day had been her wake-up call. It wasn't until she'd wiped off enough of the grime and sludge from Craig's insults and belittling comments that he'd plastered on her self-esteem that she was finally able to see clearly, and she'd made a plan.

It had taken her two years before she had the resources and strength to enact that plan and leave Craig, but she'd done it.

After the divorce was finalized, three months ago, Craig threw another wrench into things—he stopped paying child support. He said if she hadn't divorced him, the debt wouldn't have come to light so quickly, and he could have paid it off. Now he was saddled with it, and he had enough of supporting her lazy ass. If she wanted him to continue to pay, she could take him to court.

It wasn't legal for him to stop paying, but she knew Craig. Without the money to hire a lawyer—something he was fully aware she couldn't afford—she couldn't fight him. Then he twisted his knife in her back a little more. He told her that if she did somehow take him to court, he would apply for full custody of Emmie.

There wasn't any doubt in her mind that Craig didn't want their daughter. He hadn't even asked to see her in the last year, but he was enough of a narcissistic asshole that he would fight for custody out of spite. No judge would grant him full custody, or allow him to miss payments, but she would bet Craig was counting on her not making a fuss. Making her reliant on him so he could control her had always been his ultimate game. She didn't know why, since he never seemed happy, even when he had control. And now that she was no longer reliant on him, he was trying to find other ways to control her.

"Mommy, a knock. I get it." Emmie asked, interrupting Paige's thoughts.

"No, sweetie. Mommy answers the door to make sure it's safe, remember?"

"Okay," she said, taking it in stride.

Paige looked through the peephole in the door, and all her guilt from yesterday pushed up into her throat.

"Hey, Susan, how are you?" she asked the building's rental manager when she opened the door. Maybe if she pretended like yesterday hadn't happened, Susan would too.

"Hi, Paige. Hi, Emmie. Are you having fun with your dolls?" Susan asked as Paige stepped back to allow her to enter.

Emmie nodded and held up a doll in each hand to show Susan. "See?"

Susan engaged with Emmie for a minute, but Paige saw the exact moment her demeanor changed.

Susan straightened, pulling her shoulders back. "I'm going to talk to your mom for a little bit, okay?"

Emmie nodded and picked up another doll.

Gesturing to the kitchen, Susan took the few steps away from the living room.

Paige hoped she could head off what she expected was coming. "Susan, I'll be getting two commission checks soon. The closing on the properties is just taking longer than expected but I'll have the half I owe you."

Susan's sigh said it all. "I'm sorry, Paige, but I'm going to have to evict you." She lifted up a piece of paper that Paige hadn't noticed she'd been holding. "You were late paying last month, and the rental company told me we're not a charity. You either pay the full month's rent today, or you've got to go."

"I don't have it." Paige's shoulders sagged, her lower lip quivering.

Susan put a hand on Paige's arm. "I like you, Paige, and you have the sweetest little girl, but I need this job, so I've got to follow orders."

Paige nodded and blinked back tears of frustration. Susan didn't need Paige's tears on her conscience.

"This is a copy of the summons and complaint, and the hearing's set for next Monday. If you don't win, you'll have only forty-eight hours to vacate the premises. If you'd like, I can tell the rental company that you won't fight the eviction, and I can give you two weeks to find something else. Would that work?"

Paige nodded again and walked Susan to the door, barely managing to croak out, "Bye."

She shut the door, leaned back against it, and closed her eyes. The darkness behind her lids foreshadowed the tunnel she could no longer see through. The little light that had been inside her was now gone.

"Mommy?" Emmie asked, tugging on her pant leg.

Paige crouched down in front of her daughter. The very best thing in her life. Somehow, she'd find a way to make everything work out. She wouldn't let Craig use this as a reason to take her daughter.

She drew from her inner strength and smiled at Emmie. "Mommy's all done working today. Want to go to the park to play on the swings for a while before bedtime?"

"Yay!" Emmie dropped her doll and raced to get her shoes.

Running away from her problems never fixed anything, but a little while playing with Emmie and reminding herself why she couldn't give up wouldn't hurt. Maybe it would even give Paige the energy she needed to find a solution.

She pushed herself up from her crouch, feeling far older than her years, and went back to the kitchen table. Reaching for her laptop to shut the lid, it pinged with a new email.

Her boss had sent her a new commercial listing. She scanned the details before closing her laptop, feeling a little lighter.

"Ready to go, Emmie?"

"Yes!"

As they walked the short distance to the park and Emmie chattered away, Paige thought back over the listing details, and an idea began to form.

CHAPTER FOUR

Friday, September 7

Blake walked into his mom's house and stopped when memories assaulted him. Since moving into his own house, he'd visited her almost weekly. The difference was that his mom wouldn't be coming out to greet him this time.

He looked around and spied the old ding in the front mantel over the fireplace that he, Jake, and Cade had made while launching their toy cars off a track they'd covered the room with.

The side wall didn't look like it had ever been anything but smooth, but he could still picture his dad teaching him how to patch the hole in the drywall made by a hockey puck. A smile tugged at the corners of his lips as he remembered his dad spreading the putty on the wall. His mom had been furious, and although his dad told them they needed to play hockey outside, he'd leaned down and whispered in Blake's ear how to catch the puck next time.

A cool breeze hit the back of his neck, pulling him out of

his memories, and he turned, noticing he'd left the door wide open. Blake shut the door and turned back around. Movement caught his eye, and he glanced over to see Cade on the stairs.

His brother descended the final stair. "I thought I heard you."

"Yeah, got caught going down memory lane."

"Good ones?"

Blake grinned. "The hockey puck."

Cade frowned in confusion before looking where Blake pointed. "Right." He chuckled and gestured to the hardwood floor at the base of the stairs. "Remember that?"

A gouge about four inches in length was barely visible in the wood. During a wrestling match, they'd knocked over a small credenza and a sharp edge from a handle that broke off in the fall gouged the hardwood floor. That mishap led to his dad teaching them how to sand floors. He also taught them to move all the furniture out of the way before wrestling.

"I think we learned a lot about construction from Dad teaching us to repair what we broke."

"Like replacing a window because you couldn't throw a baseball?" Cade teased.

"Hey, that wasn't me. That was Jake." It had totally been Blake, but he was sticking to his story; that was the pact he'd made with his best friend. Blake had taken the blame for the window they'd broken at Jake's house, so it had been Jake's turn to shoulder the blame here. Good friends were like that, and so was family.

And as the eldest two in the family, he and Cade now had a job to do.

"Ready for this?" Cade asked.

"No, but we don't have a choice."

"We do. I've had a company coming in and cleaning the house for the last month. We can continue to use them while

I hire another company to clear everything out and then put the house on the market. None of us will ever have to set foot in here again."

"Mom wouldn't have wanted that."

"No, but she's not here to argue about it."

Blake walked to the couch in the living room and flopped onto the big cushions. They looked like someone had fluffed them recently. He ran his hand over the arm of the couch, remembering when his mom had bought it. His dad had died about six months earlier, and his mom wasn't coping well. Then she decided that the old couch had to go, along with Dad's favorite recliner. She announced at dinner one night she had purchased a living room suite, and it would be delivered the next day. After dinner, he and his brothers had moved the old couch and Dad's recliner to the garage.

Blake looked at Cade, where he'd taken a seat on the arm of the loveseat. "What happened to Dad's recliner? I'm not sure why, but I don't think I ever asked."

"Jake's parents have it at their cottage. At the time you were busy with college and keeping the company running. I'm guessing, out of sight, out of mind. Besides, it was years ago. When winter came, Mom couldn't park in the garage because it was full of furniture. I convinced her to donate the living room set, but she wouldn't part with the recliner. I mentioned it to Kelly." He grinned. "I was still calling her Mrs. Young back then. Anyway, since Ian was Dad's best friend, I don't think he wanted to get rid of it, either. He said keeping the recliner at the cottage would be like having a little visit with Dad every time they went up there."

He heard the roughness in Cade's voice and knew they had to get moving or they'd end up like a couple of old seniors in a nursing home reminiscing. He wasn't emotionally ready for that.

"Where should we start?"

"You sure you want to?" Cade eyed him. It was a look he'd pierced Blake and their brothers with all their lives, making them confess to things they didn't want to. Blake expected it worked well for him in court.

"Still no, but I think we should."

"What would you think about packing up her clothes and personal things and leaving the house as is until Gage comes back?"

Blake widened his eyes at his brother. "Is there something you haven't told me?"

"No, but I know you've been working on Gage for years, trying to get him to move back home, and I think you may be close to succeeding. I expect that's why we still don't have a VP of commercial operations. You want him in the position."

"About that." Blake rubbed his hands over his face, needing a second to regroup. "I've decided to promote Henry into the position."

"Our senior electrician?"

"That's the one. He says Mike is ready to move into his spot."

"And what happens to Henry when you finally get Gage to come home?"

Blake smirked. "Henry will retire. He said he's been considering it, and doing the VP job will be a change of pace and give him some more money to add to his retirement account. He's going to give me a year."

Cade nodded as if processing the information.

After a minute, Blake stood, ready to get on with their task. "Let's deal with Mom's personal stuff and leave the rest. Besides your cleaning crew coming in, we can set up a schedule for all of us to check on the house once a week. When I think Gage is ready, I'll let him know the house is available."

Cade nodded again. "And tell him it's been empty too

long and it's expensive having someone checking on it all the time. That we need someone living in it."

They headed up the stairs. "I always knew you were devious."

"Not devious. Strategic."

Blake gave a short laugh. "Right, you keep thinking that. But I'll use your *strategy* if I need it."

At the closed door to their mom's room, they both hesitated. Knowing it wasn't going to get any easier the longer they waited, Blake pushed open the door and walked in. His mom's floral perfume hit him like a hockey puck to the chest. He didn't even know the name of the scent, just that it was "Mom."

Trying not to dwell on it, he did a visual inventory of the room. "You want the dresser or the walk-in closet?"

"I'll take the dresser." Cade pointed to some flat cardboard boxes leaning against a wall. "I put some in the closet already so you can get started."

"Three categories? Keep, give away, throw out?" They'd been through this before. Although last time they'd helped their mom sort through their dad's stuff, and now they were the ones making all the decisions.

"Sounds good. I left you some garbage bags and packing tape too."

"Thanks." Blake braced himself and walked into the closet, the light already on. The space wasn't as big as some in newer homes, but it was big enough, and his mom had filled it.

He looked at his watch—his dad's watch, one of the three his grandfather had passed down. His dad gave it to him on his eighteenth birthday, two months before he died. In the twelve years since, Blake had come to terms with his dad's death—at least as much as anyone could—so the watch didn't usually bring up memories. It was just a great piece that kept the time.

Being in his mom's house surrounded by memories was getting to him. He had to look at his watch again, because he hadn't registered the time when he first looked at it.

Since he and Cade had decided to work at the office in the morning before coming to the house, it was already after one in the afternoon. Determined to get the job done before the sun set, he grabbed a box. After taping the bottom, he put together a few more and labeled them with the thick, black marker sitting by the boxes. He had to appreciate his brother's efficiency.

Starting with the shoes, hoping it would be the easiest place to start, he placed most of them in the giveaway box. One pair, his mom's favorite slippers, went in the garbage bag. Looking back at them, he hesitated. His dad had bought his mom a new pair of slippers each Christmas. He hadn't been the most romantic guy, but he'd loved his wife fiercely. Since his mom's feet were forever cold, his dad said buying her slippers every year meant he always had a present for her he didn't have to think about.

Blake stared down at the slippers as he held the bag in his hand. They were the last pair his dad ever bought. By the looks of them, his mom had worn them until they probably no longer stayed on her feet. He couldn't imagine being so attached to something as ordinary as slippers because someone bought them for him.

Turning away from the bag, he grabbed the next pair of shoes—black and shiny with really low heels. He dropped them into the giveaway box, then paused. He hadn't grown up around little girls playing princess or pretend, but he'd seen Jake's sister do it, and she had a little girl. Her daughter wasn't old enough to play dress up yet, but she would be one day.

Picking up another box, he labeled it as dress up, and put the shiny shoes in the bottom. By the time he finished with the shoes, there were three more pairs in the box.

Blake moved onto the clothes hanging on the rod at one end of the closet. Some pieces conjured more memories and threatened to drown him, like the Christmas sweater his mom brought out on the first day of December every year, and the long coat he and his brothers bought for her the year after his dad died.

He decided it was time to be ruthlessly efficient. Taking each item off its hanger, he gave it only a cursory look before deciding its fate.

An hour later, three boxes of dress-up clothes were stacked beside one to keep and eight to give away. With all the clothing finished, he was ready to move onto the boxes stacked on a shelf above the clothing rod.

"You ready for a break?" Cade asked from the doorway. At his nod, his brother passed him a cold can of root beer. "I haven't restocked the bottles of water yet."

"Thanks." He cracked the tab and took a long drink. "Restock?"

"I come over here every few days to make sure the cleaning crew locked the door and there's no mail piling up. I put a case of water and some canned drinks in the fridge so the motor wasn't working to cool an empty space, and sometimes I stay and get a bit of work done because it's quieter than at home."

"I appreciate all you've done." Blake looked at his brother, hoping he heard the sincerity in his voice.

Cade nodded, then tilted his chin toward the high shelf. "You want help with that? I finished the bedroom and bathroom. There wasn't as much, and almost everything in the bathroom went in the garbage."

"Sure." He knocked back the rest of his root beer.

Cade picked up the garbage bag in the corner, about to put his empty bottle in it.

"Not that one," Blake said, reaching for the bag.

"Why not?" Cade raised a brow.

Handing his empty can to his brother, Blake reached into the bag and pulled out their mom's slippers. When it had come time to put more garbage on top of them, he hadn't been able to do it. "Keeping old, worn slippers isn't practical, but Mom always said—"

"That sometimes practicality was overrated," Cade finished for him as he grabbed a new garbage bag for the cans. "Why don't you put the slippers in one of the keep boxes so they don't get thrown out?"

Blake opened a partially empty box and placed them inside. Then, with silent agreement, they pulled down the boxes on the shelf and went through them. Most held more shoes and sweaters.

Cade took one of the three remaining boxes from the shelf. "Those two boxes," he said, lifting his chin to the last one, "hold all the stuff Mom collected while we were in school—artwork, trophies, that type of thing."

Not sure he could handle going down memory lane again today, Blake labeled the boxes without opening the lids. "What's in that last one?"

Cade sat on the bench and placed the box beside him. "I think it may be more things Mom collected from us, but I'm not sure."

Blake sat on the other side of the box, feeling drained from the emotions that had flooded him all afternoon.

The final box was a banker's box, like his dad used to store important documents in until Blake had everything scanned and they went digital. Cade removed the lid, dropped it to the floor, and picked up an album.

Still weary of more memories but wanting to see the

album, Blake picked up the lid and put it back on the box. "Put the album here," he told Cade, tapping the lid.

Cade placed it on the box and opened the cover. The album was the old peel-and-stick kind. Blake didn't recognize any of the people in the first eight photos. Judging by the clothes, he figured it was the 1970s. He looked at the four pictures on the next two pages. "Is that Mom?"

"It sure looks like her. She's, what? Maybe mid-twenties? Could you have been born already?"

Blake studied the pictures. "Maybe. She had me two months before her twenty-sixth birthday, so it's possible." He pointed to a picture of their mom with another young woman. "That could be her sister. But Mom said Aunt Chrys died when I was a baby."

Cade turned the page to more pictures of their mom with the woman they thought was their aunt. "Does it seem odd to you that there aren't any dates or names? Mom was a fanatic about that."

"I hadn't noticed, but you're right." Blake grinned at his brother. "Remember whenever we brought home something from school?"

Cade smirked. "How could I forget? 'Put your name and date on the back,'" he said in a high voice, doing a pretty good imitation of their mom. "'If you don't, I'll never know whose is whose.'"

"She loved to label everything—our clothes, photos, food in the freezer. She was so excited when Dad bought her a label maker."

"Right? I think Dad may have even more excited than Mom because he had something else to put in her Christmas stocking. Remember the year he individually wrapped ten label cartridges?"

"Dad was proud of filling up the stocking that year..." Blake let his words trail off, thinking about the bittersweet memories, and glanced back at the photo album. "Maybe there are dates on the backs."

Carefully peeling away a corner of the plastic film, Cade tried to lift one of the pictures, but it was stuck.

Blake pulled his truck keys out of his pocket and opened the pocketknife attached to the ring. "Try this."

"Thanks." After almost a minute of gently prying the knife under the photo and wiggling it back and forth to loosen the glue, Cade picked up the picture. "It's blank."

"Well, it was worth a try. Do you want to look at the rest?"

"Sure."

The rest of the pictures were more of the same. Some with their mom and her sister, and a few of their dad.

When Cade turned to the last page, Blake frowned, pointing at the lone picture on the page. "That's Mom, her sister, and me. I don't know who the little girl is, but that's definitely you. I was seventeen months when you were born, and you look like you're one or two in that picture. Is it possible that Mom lied to us about Aunt Chrys dying when I was a baby?"

"It's starting to look that way." Cade shut the album and put it on the floor before lifting the lid off the box and tossing it to the floor again. "Maybe there's an answer in some of this stuff."

The box held another album, two journals, and some papers wrapped in plastic. Cade passed the album to Blake and picked up one of the journals.

The album held more photos of his aunt and the little girl, but no more of him and Cade. Not great at judging kids' ages, he guessed the little girl was about five in the last photo of her.

Blake put the album back in the box and picked up the second journal. "The photos were more of the same. You find anything?"

Cade shook his head and picked up the papers. "Mom's journal when she was a teenager. It just felt weird reading it." He shivered; Blake understood— he didn't want to know intimate details about his parents.

Opening the second journal, Blake recognized his mom's flowery cursive. He skimmed a few pages. She mentioned meeting their father and how handsome she thought he was. Fearing she might have described sex with his dad on the later pages, he closed the cover. "Maybe we could get Jake's mom to read these to see if there's anything about Aunt Chrys."

The corners of Cade's lips twitched up with a laugh. "Find something you're going to need to bleach your eyeballs after seeing?"

It was Blake's turn to shiver. "No, but I might have if I kept reading."

"Got it." Cade lifted his chin toward the journals. "I'll let you give those to Kelly or Jake for him to pass them on to her." He held up an old and brittle-looking piece of paper inside a plastic sheath. "This is a letter dated 1924 and signed by someone named Martha."

"What kind of letter?"

Cade frowned. "I'm not sure. There's a lot of rambling, like the woman couldn't focus. She talks about her love for George."

"Are all those letters?" he asked, looking at the pile of papers Cade had placed on the bench.

"I don't know. You want to read them?"

"No." Reading letters about undying love was the last thing Blake was in the mood for.

"Okay. I'll read them later, but I won't take them with me today."

"You don't have room in your vehicle?"

"No, I've got room. I'll take all the boxes for Goodwill and drop them off when I leave here. Then I've got to pick up Malcolm from daycare and I don't want to chance him getting into the papers. He's into everything these days. I'll come back and get them another time."

Blake gave his brother a sly smile. "Good. My birthday present will be perfect for him."

Cade groaned. "Did you and Jake even listen to me about buying educational gifts?"

"Of course. It says educational right on the box. It's good for cognitive skills."

It was also good for hand-eye coordination and hearing; it said so right beside the instructions for putting the drum set together. The same for the musical train Jake picked out. He and Jake had paid for the wrapping service, and while they'd waited, they had a good laugh, speculating how Cade would change the buying instructions for Christmas.

"We'll see," Cade muttered as they both stood and picked up some boxes.

Once the boxes were loaded and the house locked, Blake headed home. He couldn't get over the fact their mom had lied to them. Would they find evidence of more lies when they dug into the old papers?

CHAPTER FIVE

Friday, September 13

Paige stacked the last box on top of another one and locked the door behind her.

"Emmie?"

"I'm here."

She chuckled at her daughter's response. With the reassurance that Emmie was inside and safe—somewhere—Paige checked the blinds. She'd keep them closed at all times as an extra precaution. It would be dark in a few hours, and most people probably wouldn't question a light being left on if they saw it, but Paige didn't want to take any chances. The last thing she needed was someone questioning why they were there.

When her boss sent her the listing for an empty strip mall minutes after Paige got her eviction notice, it had seemed like fate. The idea to move into one of her property listings wasn't her brightest, but it would work for a while.

All the units had been vacant for almost a year, and although the owner wanted to sell, he was out of the country and leaving it in their hands. Her boss's notes stated the place hadn't been kept up and was going to need a lot of work. With the owner not budging on the asking price, her boss didn't think it would be easy to sell, but if she could manage it, the commission would be good.

The building held six side-by-side units, and Paige moved into the last one because the former salon and spa had a shower. A tall counter stood near the front door, with a few stray sticky notes and pens littering the surface. The entire space was a long rectangle. At one end, along the back wall, the faded paint showed silhouettes of where mirrors had once hung, the individual stylist stations long gone. The other end housed four small rooms; one, lined in wood, appeared to have been a sauna. Two others were empty but had likely been used for private treatments like waxing or massages.

When Paige had first walked into the final room—a fancy locker room—she realized her idea might actually work. Four stalls lined one wall, three of them toilets, but it was the fourth stall that clinched the deal. It held a large, fully functional shower stall.

From her notes, she'd known the owner had kept the utilities on to prove to prospective buyers that everything was in working condition. When she'd turned on the tap in the stall, the shower had started with ease. Within a minute, steam from the hot water had filled the small space.

Now, she and Emmie were moving in.

She was feeling pretty confident about their situation, except for one thing—her vehicle. There wasn't anything she could do about her car parked at the back of the unit. At least she was the realtor on file for the strip mall. If she had to, she could come up with an excuse as to why she was there.

"It will have to do," she muttered to herself and got to work moving the last of the boxes to a room in the back.

She'd given Emmie the last room before the locker room, keeping her as far from the front door as possible. The former sauna would be for storing her boxes, and Paige would sleep in the room between the sauna and Emmie.

Looking around the place, she wondered how she'd gotten to be where she was—a single, divorced, homeless mom. She never would have imagined this would become her life. "Temporary," she whispered.

"Mommy, come see!"

Paige smiled. That little voice was the reminder she needed that every sacrifice she made was worth it.

Standing in the doorway to Emmie's room, she grinned as her daughter bounced around the small space. First thing that morning, Paige had taken apart Emmie's bed, brought it over with a couple of boxes, and then put it together. The next trip contained the rest of Emmie's things, including all her toys, her small dresser, and a nightstand.

Emmie already had all her stuffed toys and dolls lined up on the bed.

"That looks lovely, sweetie."

"They're playing," Emmie said as she picked up two different dolls.

Her daughter had such a vivid imagination and Paige loved that for her. Paige sat on the end of the bed and listened as Emmie told her a story about each toy.

When Paige had moved out of Craig's house in the beginning of the year, she'd rented a small storage locker and used it to store several boxes of clothes, toys, and books. At the time, it seemed like a good idea, at least until she could afford a larger apartment. Several months back, she'd debated moving everything into her apartment just to save on the monthly expense. In the end, she'd decided against it because it would have made her apartment far too crowded.

Now it was a blessing because she hadn't had much to move into the strip mall.

She'd advertised her couch second-hand as free a few days ago if someone would come get it. A couple of college students had gladly taken it off her hands yesterday. While they were picking it up, Paige also offered them the small kitchen table and two chairs. They were more than happy to take them as well.

That left only Emmie's few pieces of furniture, a TV, and the small unit it sat on. Not wanting to spend money on a dresser for herself when she'd moved into the apartment—not that there had been room for one—she'd kept her clothes in rubber storage bins, so they'd been easy to move.

Everything fit into her SUV in three trips—another blessing. She'd chosen the SUV so she could look the part of a successful realtor and feel safe with Emmie when driving on snowy roads. If she'd gone with something smaller, her car payment would have been lower, and she may have been able to pay her bills for another month or two. But then she wouldn't have been able to move Emmie's furniture. Her life seemed to be full of irony.

A little while later, she showered with Emmie. It was her daughter's first shower because up until now they'd always had access to a bath and Emmie liked to play in the water.

Paige had turned each one of the day's new experiences into an adventure. For Emmie, every day was a grand adventure, and she loved it all. Even hearing that their new *apartment* was a secret and she couldn't tell Grandma and Grandpa was exciting to Emmie.

With all the changes in the past year, their lives seemed to be full of adventures too. Irony and adventures. Not perfect, and not exactly legal, but she was making it work, and she'd done it all on her own.

BLAKE LOWERED the weight to the thick rubber mats covering the floor. Grabbing his water bottle, he chugged a good third of it and mopped his face on the shoulder of his shirt. He'd hoped the exertion from heavy lifting would empty his mind. No luck.

Flopping down onto the bench, he stared at the blank screen of the large TV on the wall, wondering about the curse. He still had no reason to believe it was real, but every day Jake or one of his brothers asked about it. And with it now being Friday the thirteenth, their teasing had been relentless.

Out for a beer with them after work, he'd sat back as they speculated about the curse. Their mom had said it could take effect any time after his birthday, so he hadn't been surprised when Cade started a betting pool to guess when it would happen. The dates were spread out until the end of the month. Cade had even called Gage to place a bet. Jake picked that night—because it was Friday the thirteenth, he'd said.

Ideas about how it would manifest had ranged from a dream, to ghosts showing up to teach him a lesson like they had with Scrooge in Dicken's *A Christmas Carol*, to him being overtaken by aliens who just wanted some love.

Which of course led to talk about his love life. Dane and Ford thought he should call up an old girlfriend and confess his love. Move her into his place and woo her until she fell in love with him.

As funny as the teasing had been, there'd been an underlying current that maybe the curse was real. He'd left an hour later and had been pumping iron for another two. Now, sweaty and exhausted, he still couldn't stop thinking about the curse.

The possibility that his mom had just been screwing with them didn't make sense. That wasn't like her. He wanted to believe the whole curse thing was shit, especially since it had been almost two weeks since his birthday and nothing had changed.

It was his mom's behavior in the months before she died that made him hesitate to dismiss the possibility of a curse so easily. She'd pressured him excessively to date and find someone to love, which hadn't been like her.

On several occasions, she'd brought up Paige too. Said she'd bumped into Paige, who was now divorced and had moved back to this part of town. And that she even had a little girl. Was seeing Paige the reason his mom had redecorated his spare room?

Blake shut off the lights in the basement and walked upstairs. Drawn to his spare room by the thoughts of his mom's decorating, he stood in the doorway and flicked on the light, taking it all in. He'd always considered himself sensible and pragmatic, which was why he was having trouble believing in the curse. It was also why he should hire someone to redecorate the room since it wasn't useful to him as it was.

At least he wouldn't have to repaint the walls since his mom hadn't changed the original white, but now gold star decals were spread across the wall at the back. He'd been so angry when he realized that not only had his mom changed his office into a children's bedroom, she destroyed his closet doors. They were now covered in chalkboard paint.

Entering the room, he slumped onto the rocking chair in the corner and stared at the toys, without really seeing them. All he could see was the look of hurt on his mom's face when he'd told her how upset he was with what she'd done. That was the last time he'd seen her.

For a full week, he'd stewed in his anger before he called

to apologize. When he asked why she'd done it, all she said was that he had to be ready because the woman he fell in love with could already have a child.

His mom died three weeks later.

Maybe she'd been talking about Paige again.

For a fraction of a second, he wondered if his mom and Paige had worked together to try and manipulate him. He threw out the thought as quickly as it came to him. His mom had mentioned Paige, but she'd left it up to him to pursue. As for Paige, regardless of the years since he'd seen her, she wouldn't manipulate a man. After all, she'd stood in front of him, heartbroken, waiting for him to make a move, never trying to force his hand.

Blake scrubbed his face and dropped his hands to the arms of the chair. Planting his feet on the carpet, he started the chair in a slow rock.

As he rocked, he pictured Paige the last time he'd seen her. He recalled other images of her too. Happy ones. Like all the weekends they'd studied together in his mom's basement. They'd discovered they had a shared love for jazz music, so whenever they took a break from studying, they played some jazz in the background and partook in a rousing game of backgammon. Paige rarely beat him at the game, but when she did, she'd rub it in. She'd stand up and pump her fists and then straddle him, bragging about her win, and kiss him. Soon after, their clothes would be in a discarded pile, and they'd be making love in a frantic rush. She always worried one of his brothers would catch them, yet every time she won, she'd do the same thing. He got to the point that sometimes he'd *let* her win, claiming her skills were improving. Whether she caught on to *his* game or not, she never said.

The picture of Paige morphed again, but this time, he hadn't consciously called up a new one.

One after another, visions flashed in his mind, and a tightness overtook him. He became completely immobile, unable to move or speak, as if he'd lost control of his own body.

The air shifted. It felt different, like he was in another place and time. The rocking chair's hard surface under him was the only reassurance that he hadn't physically left his home.

The flashes of images slowed. They rearranged themselves into a line, then, like he was stepping into a movie, a scene played out in front of him.

A man knelt on a hardwood floor in a large room. He wore jeans and a long-sleeved buttoned shirt. A paintbrush lay loosely in his hand as he stared at a canvas on an easel in front of him. Scents of paint, oil, and turpentine were so thick Blake's eyes watered. He realized that where he now was, he again had full control of his body.

Blake could hear a radio host announce "Too Young" by Nat King Cole before the first notes of the song began.

Shafts of sunlight poured in from a domed skylight centered within exposed beams in the ceiling, highlighting dust motes dancing in the air. Dozens of canvases covered with splashes of bright paint leaned against white brick walls, some piled two and three deep.

The year was 1952, and the man, Peter, was quickly becoming a well-known abstract expressionism artist in New York City. Originally from California, he'd moved to New York several years earlier, following his girlfriend, also an artist, to the city. As a sculptor, Alice's preferred medium was clay.

Blake had no idea how he knew any of that. He just did.

He took several steps closer to the easel, but Peter didn't notice him. Blake reached out and touched a canvas. It felt as real to him as the smells in the room did. He was in the studio with the painter, and yet he was only watching what was transpiring as an unseen observer.

"Peter," a woman's voice called. A moment later, she ran into the studio. Peter stood and caught the woman as she ran right into his arms. He held the paintbrush away from her body as they hugged and then kissed.

The kiss became passionate and long. Their breathing became louder and his own heartbeat sped up. He feared he was about to become a voyeur to something he had no interest in seeing.

Finally, the couple separated, and Blake let out his breath.

The woman glanced down at the easel. "Oh, Peter. It's beautiful. I love your use of bright colors. Just the way they dance…" Her voice trailed off as she studied the painting.

Peter put his arm around the woman and tugged her close to his side. "It's all because of you, Alice. You're my inspiration."

Alice turned to face him, and they kissed again.

The air shifted once again and the scene changed. He was still in the studio, but something was different. It was quieter, the smell of paint and turpentine muted.

Peter paced in front of his easel. He stopped and pulled back a shirt cuff to check his watch, then continued to pace.

A minute later, Blake heard footsteps on the wooden floor and turned to see Alice walk in. She didn't rush this time.

"Alice. Thank goodness. I was becoming worried," Peter said as he walked toward Alice and opened his arms.

She gave him a quick hug but didn't linger. "I needed some air."

Peter frowned. "Is everything alright?"

Alice strolled around the studio, looking at the canvases. "I think I need to focus on my own art more," she said without looking back at Peter.

A burst of cold air hit Blake as the scene shifted again. The light in the studio was dark; clouds covered the skylight overhead. Blake rubbed his arms against the room's chill.

Alice stood several feet from Peter. She wore a heavy wool coat buttoned up to her neck, and a bright scarf covered her hair.

Peter reached for Alice, but she took a step back. "Don't," she said quietly.

"Please, Alice," he pleaded. "Don't leave. We can work this out. I came to this city for you. I paint for you, but most importantly, I love you."

Alice flung her hands out to the sides. "See? That's the problem. I can't be your reason for everything. I've told you this a dozen times, but you never listen. It's too much pressure."

"I thought you liked being my inspiration. My muse."

"That was before. I've found someone else and I don't love you anymore."

Blake felt a tightness in his chest, his mouth dry as he and Peter watched Alice turn around and leave. When she disappeared from sight, Peter dropped to his knees. His sobs stayed with Blake as the air shifted again.

When the new scene settled, the studio was stifling hot, a vast contrast from the cold Blake had just left. He pulled at the neck of his T-shirt to create a draft of air.

The once overpowering scents of paint and turpentine were now a subtle background against cigarette smoke.

He looked toward the room's interior, expecting to see Peter at his easel, but the painter wasn't there. Blake let his gaze wander around the studio. Canvases still leaned against the walls, but most were bare. Only a few were painted, all of them with dark strokes.

Not in a million years would Blake consider himself an art connoisseur, but even he could tell the difference in mood between Peter's original paintings and these new ones. These had come from a place of anger or sorrow.

"Why is this so hard?" Peter yelled.

Blake searched for Peter and walked into the middle of the room, slowly turning around. It was then he spotted an open doorway tucked into a corner.

The door led to the roof. The day was overcast, and a soft breeze blew, alleviating some of the oppressive heat. Peter sat at a small metal bistro table, a pile of smashed cigarette butts at his feet.

A cigarette in one hand and a paint brush in the other, Peter stared at the canvas on the easel in front of him. "Paint," he muttered to himself. "You don't need Alice."

Peter took another drag of his cigarette as he continued to stare.

Blake waited, willing Peter to paint. It didn't matter that this happened over seventy years ago. He needed Peter to find his muse. To move on from Alice.

A minute went by, and then two. Peter finished his smoke and reached for the pack. It was empty. "Need more," he said to himself, tossing his dry paintbrush on the table.

As Peter walked right through Blake, leaving the roof-top patio, the air shifted again.

Blake blinked against the change in light as he took in his spare room. He dragged his hands down his face, the movement rocking the chair beneath him.

"It was a dream," he muttered to himself—just as Peter had done—before heaving himself out of the rocking chair and turning off the lights. "A really fucking vivid dream."

He wanted to believe it, but knew he was lying to himself. Jake had won the bet.

CHAPTER SIX

Wednesday, September 25

Paige stopped at what felt like her ten millionth red light and blew out a frustrated breath. Of course she would hit every red light between Emmie's daycare and the strip mall—on today of all days. She was mad at herself for not taking the time to iron her blouse the night before. It had taken precious minutes she hadn't had to spare this morning.

Glancing at the clock on the dash, she made a calculation. It would be close, but as long as the client didn't arrive early, there would be enough time for her to get back to the strip mall to check for anything out of place before he arrived.

The client was someone from Akerman Contracting. Her boss had taken the call and said he didn't know who would be coming to tour the property because the person in charge of commercial operations had recently vacated the position. As the CEO, she doubted Blake would be the one to take the appointment, and maybe that was a good thing. A lot had changed, including her, in the eight years since she'd walked away from him in tears. She mentally crossed her fingers the person she was meeting wouldn't be Blake.

Paige hadn't mentioned her history with the Akermans since it had been years ago and didn't seem relevant. When she'd first left Blake, he was all she could think about, and she'd wondered if she'd made the right choice. She determined to do her best not to think about him, and as life went on, her thoughts of him became fewer and fewer.

It wasn't until she moved back into her old neighborhood that she ran into reminders of Blake.

A car swerved into her lane without signaling. Paige slowed, her grip tightening as she kept her gaze fixed on the space in front of her, both hands firm on the wheel. The first rush of reaction hit—the instinct to brace, to assume this was her fault somehow, to get out of the way before someone decided she was the problem.

Nothing happened. The other driver kept going, and the world didn't punish her for existing in the wrong place at the wrong time.

But Craig would have.

That was the part her brain still struggled with. With him, a small thing never stayed small. A dinner later than he wanted, a missing shirt, a bill that was higher than expected —anything could become proof that she wasn't careful enough, grateful enough, good enough. She had learned to move first and apologize later, even when she'd done nothing wrong, because it was easier than dealing with the look and lecture he gave her when he decided she'd disappointed him.

Even now, alone in the car, she could feel her body reaching for that old script: tighten, prepare, and then fix it before it got worse. Say the right thing, be smaller.

Paige loosened her grip one finger at a time. She refused to chase the fear or let it pull her into a spiral. She let the moment pass and kept driving, because Craig wasn't here.

He didn't get to take up space in her mind anymore. He didn't get to rewrite an ordinary mistake into a reason she deserved to be afraid.

By the time the strip mall came into view, her shoulders had dropped. She may be living in a strip mall and be in a financial mess, but she'd just ridden out an old reflex without giving it the keys. That had to mean she was doing something right.

That ease disappeared as she drove around to the back of the strip mall. A truck with the Akerman logo was parked behind the salon's back door, and Blake sat in the front seat.

Her contact was the CEO himself.

And he was early.

As she pulled into the parking space beside Blake's truck, he got out and walked around to the front of her vehicle and waited for her. She'd laid eyes on him for the first time when he'd offered her his hand to help her off the table at the party, and she'd been almost struck speechless by his good looks. Eight years later and he was still the most handsome man she'd ever met. The years had added maturity to his face, the light blond scruff he sported giving him a devil-may-care look. It was obvious he still worked out by the breadth of his shoulders beneath his suit jacket and the way it lay over his flat stomach. His hair was shorter than he used to keep it, but still thick and with just enough wave in it to give him a carefree look. She couldn't see his eye color from here, but she knew they were light blue, like a cloudless sky.

In lieu of the concrete suddenly opening up and swallowing her whole, she wished for three things when she got out of her vehicle to greet him. One—she wouldn't be struck speechless like in the past. Two—she didn't look like she'd pulled her clothes out of a box, and three—he wouldn't want to see all the units.

She threw her purse over her shoulder as she walked up to him. "Good morning."

"Good morning, Paige." His smile was genuine. Something she'd always loved about him. Since he hadn't hesitated at seeing her, he must have known who he'd be meeting.

She offered her hand. "Good to see you, Blake." *Oh, my god.* She should have made a fourth wish—that she wouldn't swoon when she smelled him. Just like when they were in college, he had an alluring fresh and citrusy scent.

He shook her hand, and if he held on a few seconds too long, she wasn't complaining. From the moment she'd first met him all those years ago, he'd felt like comfort and home. Not that there hadn't been lust—there had been plenty of that—but she'd never felt awkward around him. Until now. Her tongue had tied itself in knots. So much for wish number one.

"It's good to see you too. It's been a long time," he said.

Hoping her tongue would untie itself and not fail her, she forced out her words. "I'm really sorry to hear about your mom. I ran into her and Kelly when I moved into an apartment near her last year. We had coffee a few times. She was a lovely person."

His smile dimmed. "Thank you."

Paige felt uncomfortable for a moment, not like the confident twenty-year-old she used to be.

"Ready to show me the property?" Blake asked, gesturing to the units behind them. "I understand the owner didn't keep it up over the years."

Grasping onto Blake's suggestion, she got right down to business.

Starting with the first unit at the far end, they walked through each one, with her reciting the information she had about each space. Several times, their hands touched in passing, and she felt a tingling that only Blake had ever given her.

While leaving the last unit, he placed his hand at the small of her back. His old-fashioned upbringing, she told herself, trying not to read too much into the gesture.

They finished viewing five of the units and stood by their vehicles in front of the door to the spa and salon. She hesitated, and he raised a brow at her.

"Aren't you going to show me the last unit?"

Plastering a smile on her face, she walked to the door. "Of course."

Inside, she walked over to the front counter, dropped her purse on it, and leaned against the side of it. She'd learned that, depending on the client, it was sometimes best to let them explore on their own. Blake was just that type of client —he knew what he wanted to see and didn't need her tagging along. He'd always been confident like that. If he had questions, he would ask them.

As he wandered around like he'd done in the other units, she fought the impulse to go check the rooms for anything she and Emmie might have left out. The boxes she could explain away as the owner using the place as storage, and she'd locked the room Emmie used. If Blake asked to see it, she'd decided she would try different keys and say she didn't have the right one but would get it later.

She admired him as he walked around. Why was he still single? At least, she thought he was. He wasn't wearing a wedding ring. Not that a ring was always a good indication of commitment, especially if he'd recently become engaged. The last time she'd spoken with his mom several months back, she mentioned that Blake never dated anyone seriously. That had seemed strange as Blake had told her he wanted a large family. Maybe he'd changed his mind.

Blake gave her a strange look. "Paige? Don't you have the details for this unit?"

"Sorry, uh, yes." She let out a nervous laugh and fumbled with her tablet, almost dropping it before she pulled up the information.

He asked a couple of questions, then his body went stiff and his eyes closed.

"Blake? Blake, are you okay?" Putting her tablet on the counter, Paige walked over to him and laid her hand on his arm. "Blake?"

Paige had no idea what was going on. She doubted he was just lost in thought since he hadn't answered her. She had seen a few people having seizures on TV shows, but they didn't look the way Blake did now. Though the TV portrayals may not have been realistic, because the person always lowered themselves or fell to the floor.

Blake stayed standing. She didn't think he was in pain. Nor was he jerking or twitching. Since his eyes were closed and he wasn't talking, she couldn't tell if he was having a medical emergency.

"Blake?" He didn't do anything to indicate he'd heard her. She stayed by his side for another few minutes, and when he still wouldn't respond to her calling his name, she began to worry and went to retrieve her phone.

She had it in her hand when she heard Blake curse.

"Thanks, Paige. I've got to go. I'll let you know what I decide."

Blake strode out of the building without a backward glance. She had no idea what had just happened or why he would suddenly leave. Maybe he was embarrassed over her seeing him in that state.

Regardless of what had caused it, he had just left her standing there. Similar to how she'd walked away from him eight years earlier.

THE CURSE HAD TAKEN over Blake so quickly that even though he'd heard Paige call his name, there'd been no time to react.

When Blake felt the external control over his body free him, he blinked the salon into focus.

"Shit," he muttered, looking up to see Paige with her phone in her hand. Still swamped with the feelings from the woman in the curse, he knew he wouldn't be able to pretend like nothing had happened.

He thanked Paige and said he'd be in touch. Grasping for the door's handle, he pushed his way outside and was blinded by the bright sunlight. He stumbled forward, falling onto the hood of Paige's car. He straightened, saw a child's car seat in the back, and moved over to his truck.

Once inside, he took a deep breath to calm himself enough to drive, and glanced at his watch. Although he wasn't sure exactly what time the curse started, he estimated it had lasted for eight or ten minutes. He would need an excuse for his behavior, but that was too much to think about right then. Going into a trance and running out on Paige was not how he thought their reunion would go. Later, he would have to dissect what he'd been feeling, but not yet. He didn't have the bandwidth for it at the moment.

He checked his mirrors, backed out of the parking space, and pulled into traffic. Using Bluetooth, he put in a call to Jake.

"Hey, good timing. The inspector just left."

Inspector? It took him a moment to remember Jake's meeting. "Tell me later? I need you to meet me at my house."

"You okay?"

"Physically, yes. Ten minutes?"

"I'll be there."

He hung up and concentrated on his driving, making the short trip in good time, and pulled into his driveway. Jake pulled in right after him; neither said anything as they walked into his house.

After dropping his keys and wallet on the table by the front door, he made a beeline for the fridge. If it wasn't still morning, he would have reached for a beer to calm his nerves. Instead, he took out a bottle of water and drained it. His throat wasn't dry anymore, but his nerves were still shot.

Looking over his shoulder at Jake standing in the doorway and frowning, he asked, "Water or something else?"

"I'll take a water."

Blake passed him a bottle, and after tossing his empty one in his recycle bin, he took a root beer for himself. Popping the tab, he took a drink but didn't inhale the liquid like he had the water. Out of habit, they both moved into his dining room and sat at the table.

Jake put his bottle on the table and unscrewed the cap. "Tell me."

"I went to see some commercial property—it's Paige's listing. We'd been there maybe an hour, going from unit to unit. We were in the last unit—what used to be a spa—when my body froze. I got sucked in just like the last time, except I was standing."

"You think that being in the spa was important."

It wasn't a question. Jake knew him well enough to know if he mentioned seemingly unimportant details, they were relevant.

"Exactly. When I was in my spare room, it brought back memories of my mom and how she'd pushed me to find love. Not to mention what she'd done to the room. Maybe she did it because of Paige since she has a child.

"I figured something there triggered the curse. But this

time I was in an old spa with a salon in the front end. How could that have brought it on?"

"Paige is the only woman you've ever loved."

Blake ran his finger along the condensation on his can. "You think that would have been enough?"

"What makes you think it needs a trigger?"

"I don't know… I just… I don't know." Blake met his friend's gaze. "You don't think it does?"

"According to your mom's letter, your thirtieth birthday was the trigger. If that was the case, then the episodes could happen at random times."

"Fuck." Blake dragged his hands down his face.

"You want to tell me about it? If they're not random, we might be able to discern some clues about how to stop them."

"It's worth a try." Blake closed his eyes and pictured what he'd seen. He spoke out loud to Jake while he walked back through the episode.

When the images settled, Blake was in a large field with massive trees scattered throughout. It seemed to be a similar time of year to his own time. The leaves of the enormous oak trees had already turned a brilliant red. He wrinkled his nose as the smell of cow dung carried to him on a breeze. Still wearing the light coat he'd worn to tour the strip mall, he was warm enough but could feel a slight chill against his cheeks.

Less than twenty feet away, a couple stood at the base of a broad red oak. A fence made of interlocking logs only three high sat behind the tree and extended as far as Blake could see.

Blake knew he was in Massachusetts in the year 1778. He walked closer to the couple, hoping to hear what they were saying. Like the painter in New York, they didn't notice him, even when he was only five feet away.

The sun was setting, casting shadows over the couple.

The woman was crying, and the man used his thumbs to wipe away her tears. "Moira, please do not cry. I will come back."

Moira looked up at the man, her eyes roaming over his face as if she was trying to memorize his features. "You promise?"

"Of course. I could never leave the one I love," he said solemnly. "And until I return..." He put his hand in his pants pocket and pulled out something. "You can keep this locket as a reminder that I will come back."

The man picked up Moira's hand and placed the locket in her palm.

"Oh, Liam." The chain dangled down as Moria held the locket between her fingers and used her fingernail to open it. Her eyes widened. "A lock of your hair."

She threw her arms around his neck. "Thank you. I love you too," she whispered.

When the air shifted, Blake felt warm. He was in a formal sitting room with a fire blazing in the hearth.

Moira sat stiffly in a chair, her head bowed and one hand clutching something on a chain around her neck.

Another woman, almost a spitting image of Moira, only older, sat across from her on a couch.

"This is your duty, Moira," a man said as he stood by the fireplace. "As my daughter, you will do as I say. I have gone to great lengths to secure your future. Adam is a good man from a wealthy family. He will provide for you."

Moira looked up, dried tear tracks visible on her cheeks. "What about Liam? He's the one I love."

Her father scoffed. "Love will not feed and clothe you and your future children."

When the air shifted again, Blake stood outside a church. He watched as Moira, wearing a simple gown and a forced smile, exited the church on the arm of a man Blake assumed was the one her father had arranged for her to marry.

Before Moira and her husband reached the end of the short path, the scene changed again.

Blake found himself back in the field where he'd first seen

Moria and Liam, the scent of cows in the air. The same interlocking log fence still stood, now weathered from being exposed to the elements for years.

Not seeing anyone, Blake walked parallel to the fence until he spotted a man leaning against one of the massive red oaks. The man straightened, looking at something in the distance.

Following his gaze, Blake saw a woman walking toward them. As she got closer, he recognized her as Moira. He guessed a couple of decades had passed based on her aged appearance. He turned back to the man and realized it was Liam. His hair was longer, and a jagged scar that hadn't been there before ran along his right cheek.

"Moira, thank you for meeting me," Liam told her.

"Like last time, I should not be here."

"Then why did you come?"

Moira met his gaze while she clasped the locket at her throat. "Because I needed to tell you that you must stop asking your sister to bring me your notes."

"You still wear my locket."

"Yes. I will always keep it. Just as I will always love you, but I cannot be with you. I have children I must consider. I hope you find someone else to love, Liam. Goodbye." Moira turned to leave.

"Do you love him?" Liam asked.

She looked over her shoulder at him. "No. I had already given my heart to another. But it was my duty," she said, repeating her father's words.

Moira looked forward and didn't turn back again as she walked away.

Blake felt a bone-deep sorrow emanating from both of them, as if the loss of their love was his own.

He opened his eyes and blinked, trying to rid himself of the image of Moira in misery.

He glanced around his dining room as he grounded

himself in the comfort of his familiar surroundings before looking at Jake. "Thoughts?"

"All the love and loss you described… Was that how you felt when you had the first episode too?"

"Yes. Both times I could feel their love and then what they felt when neither of them could recover from losing it." Blake picked up his can of root beer and took a sip; it had grown warm in the time it took to relive the vision.

"I think you're seeing ghosts who have experienced failed love," Jake said.

"Failed love? In both… curses? Episodes? Whatever they're called. The love, on one side in Peter's case, and on both sides for Moira and Liam, was so strong I could feel it."

"And the love never waned, but none of them got to spend a lifetime with that person. In a way, both experienced failed love. Or perhaps they both felt unrequited love."

Blake slumped in his chair as he processed what Jake had said. Was the curse showing him failed or unrequited love because he hadn't found his own love? Or was it showing him that no matter how much one loved, failed love was inevitable? Was that what he had to look forward to? Would he eventually feel empty as he grew old? Would he choose to settle for a life less than he wanted if he didn't choose love?

The thought of suffering that type of sadness for the rest of his days was incomprehensible. "Do you think the curse is trying to show me my future?"

Jake shrugged. "I'm not sure. Your mom's letter just said that you had to find love and have it reciprocated before your thirtieth birthday."

Blake nodded for him to continue, knowing Jake was working through his thoughts out loud.

"But her letter didn't say when it would end," Jake said.

"Or even that it would end once it started." That was now Blake's biggest fear.

"How far apart were the episodes?"

Blake didn't have to look at a calendar to give him the answer; the days would forever be etched in his memory. "There were eleven days between my birthday and the first one and another eleven between that one and today. Not counting the days of."

"If they stay like that for now, it might not be too bad."

Blake snorted. "Says you who doesn't have to experience people drowning in their misery."

"Right. Sorry."

"Cade and I went through Mom's stuff a couple of weeks ago and found some old letters. I haven't talked to Cade about them, so I don't know if he's read them yet. He said he was going to give your mom some journals to look through."

"Maybe they'll have some answers." Jake pulled out his phone and checked the time.

Blake smiled at the normalcy of his friend's gesture after feeling so much heartbreak. It was a long-running joke between them that Jake had always asked him for the time until he got his first phone. "You got to go?" Blake asked him.

"No. Tell me about the property. Think it's viable?"

Welcoming the change of topic, Blake launched into his thoughts about the strip mall. By the time they finished discussing its possibilities, Blake's mood had improved.

After Jake left, Blake pulled out his laptop and did some work from home. Since he'd only had two episodes and they'd been eleven days apart, he wasn't concerned about having another one so soon, but he was tired from the emotional wear and tear of the morning. He worried if he went into the office and someone said the wrong thing, he'd chew their head off. The week before had been bad enough.

He opened an email from Paige with the particulars of the property. She hadn't mentioned him going into a trance, nor his abrupt departure. Still not knowing how he could explain it to her, he just replied by thanking her and saying he'd be in touch.

Seeing Paige again brought back so many emotions he'd buried for a long time. At one time, he'd cared so much for her he had begun to think about a future with her.

He snorted softly and revised his last thought. Well… probably as much as any twenty-one-year-old could think about a future.

Now, if he didn't find a way to stop the curse, he wouldn't have a future at all.

CHAPTER SEVEN

Saturday, October 5

$\mathcal{P}$aige slumped against the bathroom counter as she waited for her tea to steep. She'd set up both her Keurig machine and the microwave between the sinks on the long counter. Like everything about her situation, it wasn't ideal, but having her morning coffee and evening tea were necessities. It also meant she didn't have to spend money buying a coffee each morning. She hadn't spent money on takeout or going to a restaurant either. With only a microwave, their dinner choices were limited, but luckily, Emmie hadn't yet tired of nuked mac and cheese.

When her tea was ready, Paige removed the tea bag and took her mug back to her bedroom. That's what she'd started calling the storage room with a mattress on the floor and boxes stacked all around, to normalize the situation for Emmie.

She sat with her back against the wall and placed her mug on the floor. Her laptop rested on a box in front of her. She checked to make sure the virtual background she had

"

selected was behind her and turned her monitor and sound back on.

"Hey, Dad. I'm back." She loved chatting with him every week, but she hated lying to him. The week before, she'd been nervous the entire call, waiting for him to figure out that they weren't in their apartment.

"Hey, kiddo." Her dad frowned. "Didn't you get tea?"

Shit. She and Emmie had always sat at her small kitchen table while video chatting, with her mug visible in front of her. Picking up her tea off the floor, she raised it enough for it to be seen. "Yup, right here."

She'd bought Emmie a low stool so she could kneel like she'd done on the kitchen chair, making sure nothing looked out of the ordinary. That had been the easy part, although she'd forgotten about the tea.

Listening to Emmie's every word, ready to jump in if she said anything about where they were living, had put her on edge the entire call. Paige had been filled with guilt because of her lies. Last week everything had been new—a novelty for Emmie—but this week she'd been fidgety and too full of energy.

Several times Paige had to redirect Emmie before she said something about the strip mall. After the third time, Paige cut the call short, saying Emmie was wound up and it would take time for her to calm down and fall asleep.

Her dad frowned. "Kiddo, talk to me. What's going on?"

"What do you mean?" she asked, hoping none of her swirling anxiety was clear in her tone.

"What's with the background? Last week you said you used one because your apartment was messy... I didn't believe it then and I still don't. Even as a kid, we didn't have to nag you to clean your room. Your brother and sister? All the time. But not you."

It was true. Dusting wasn't her thing, but she'd been neat

and organized even then. She hated not being able to find things or having to step over items strewn on the floor. Every single day she had her bed made within ten minutes of getting out of it. She could leave a tidy pile of books on her nightstand and another one on the floor in a corner, but her bed had to be made.

"I broke my kitchen table," she blurted, her lies adding up. In for a penny... "It was old, and I leaned on one side and the leg broke. Now we're sitting on the floor and I have my laptop on one of my boxes I didn't unpack when we moved in."

"Why didn't you just tell us?"

Paige sighed. Even though she'd sold her table instead of breaking it, the result was still the same—she didn't have one. "Because I'm an adult and I don't have a kitchen table. It's embarrassing."

"No, it's life. Things happen." Her dad smirked. "Did I ever tell you that your mom and I stacked milk crates to use as a table for three months before we could graduate to a card table?"

Paige laughed. "Really?"

"Yep. The card table lasted six months before we found a solid oak dining room table in a garage sale. The owner had used it for an art desk. I swear it took me more than twenty hours just to sand the thing. Then there was the time we needed a new bedframe. Someone had given us an old one— you know, one of those metal frames close to the ground where the legs unfold. Well, one day we woke up with a start because all the screws had worked loose. I decided I could build us a bedframe. Now, let me tell you how that went..."

For twenty minutes her dad regaled her with stories of him and her mom being newlyweds and then young parents who were barely getting by. It was a side of her dad she didn't get to see often.

By the time she hung up, she felt a bit lighter. She pushed herself to standing and stretched. Maybe she'd get a low chair so she could reach her laptop from its position on a box. Sitting on a concrete floor wasn't fun.

Once she'd washed her mug and checked on Emmie, she went back to her "bedroom" and looked around. Her mom and dad may have had some hardships while raising three kids, but they'd never been reduced to living in a strip mall.

She flopped down onto the air mattress. "Ow," she muttered and lifted her butt to rub it. In all the months she'd slept on her couch, she'd never thought she'd miss it. Turned out there were worse things to sleep on than a couch.

Too wired to sleep after a full mug of tea, she leaned back against the wall and closed her eyes, relaxing.

Like they'd done a hundred times in the last week, her thoughts wandered to Blake. She hadn't heard from him since his weird zombie episode, but she'd left a message for him on Thursday. Now, she expected that if she heard from him at all, it wouldn't be until Monday.

He looked a lot like he had years ago, only better, and with more delicious muscle. At twenty-one, Blake had been good-looking, but now he was drool-worthy. If she was ever in the market for a man again—which she wouldn't be— Blake would make a fine partner.

Or maybe not. He wouldn't be an ass like Craig, but Blake wasn't a pushover either. He was impatient and strong-willed. He hadn't tried to control her when they'd been together, but maybe that was only because she'd allowed him to make so many of the decisions. Where they went to eat or studied hadn't been important to her, so she'd deferred to Blake more often than not. But in the end, she hadn't been important enough to fight for. If they'd stayed together, he may not have treated her as an equal partner or valued her opinion. If that happened, she might have fallen into her old pattern of people pleasing, and that was something she never wanted to do again.

Pushing herself off the air mattress, she groaned, making a mental note to buy a foldable chair too. She checked her watch and groaned again. Only nine o'clock on a Saturday night and she was ready for bed. Pathetic.

After she brushed her teeth and washed her face, she went to the front of the shop to make sure all the blinds were closed.

She ran her hands along the slats on one to make sure they laid flat, then walked the blind's length to make sure they all did.

Back on her air mattress, she pulled up her e-reader and went through the new books she'd downloaded. She laid back and the overhead light shone in her face. Debating whether to get up and turn it off now or when she finished reading, the light pinged something within her.

Checking the blinds had been easy because she'd left a light on. *Shit.* She scrambled to her feet, almost toppling over several of her boxes. Once she had the boxes steady, she raced to the front of the shop and flicked off the light.

She'd only been back in bed a couple of minutes when banging on the back door made her jump.

"Paige! Open up!"

BLAKE TURNED in his truck seat, resting his arm on the steering wheel. "I'll wait until you get inside safely."

"You sure you don't want to come in?" Kyleigh pushed out her bottom lip in a pout. "It's still early."

He and Kyleigh had gone out on and off over the last few years—off when he'd been dating anyone else, but then they'd hook back up when he was single again. The dates had helped keep his loneliness at bay, and he liked her, but it just wasn't feeling right anymore. It wasn't her fault that every time he looked at her his mind wandered to Paige, as it had for the past week. And when he wasn't thinking about Paige, he worried about the curse.

"No. I'm going to head home," he told her, hoping that would be enough of an explanation.

Her eyebrows rose. "Next week?"

"I don't think so, Kyleigh. I like you, but—"

She held up a hand. "Don't say it. We agreed this would just be two friends scratching an itch. I guess I just want to scratch it more often than you do. Bye, Blake."

Kyleigh got out of the truck and didn't look back. He waited until she was inside her house before pulling away, thankful she hadn't made the situation worse. Like all the other women he'd dated, she'd find someone else who could love her and give her what she wanted.

At one time he'd wanted what his parents had—a loving partnership and a house full of kids—but not anymore. He'd doubted his change in plans a time or two or a hundred. Today had been one of those days where he knew his decision to stay single and only date like-minded women was the right one. And not only because he wanted to avoid heartbreak, but because of the curse.

He and Jake had been working on Jake's deck, trying to get it finished before it snowed, when another curse episode hit him. Jake was measuring and Blake had already turned the miter saw on and had the plank in place when the curse froze him.

If Jake hadn't noticed right away, Blake could have lost a hand.

Like all the other episodes, the curse had come on without any warning. Blake had found himself in the late

1800s. A woman had fallen in love with a man who was in a higher social class, but he didn't care about that. They proclaimed their love for each other and planned to marry. Soon after that, she misinterpreted something she saw, leading her to believe her lover was leaving her for another. But he had been asking a female cousin to help plan an elopement for his beloved. Before either of them could get to the truth, jealousy and distrust ate at the woman, breaking her heart. She spiraled into depression and neither spoke to the other again, both eventually dying lonely and bitter.

The feelings of loss and loneliness had stuck with Blake for the rest of the day. He probably should have canceled his date with Kyleigh, but he hadn't because he'd hoped going out with her would help him shake the feelings. It hadn't and now he really wished he'd stayed home.

He was beginning to think that if Jake was right and the curse was showing him failed love, it was also showing him that he was too late. That no matter what he did, any relationship he had was bound to end in failure. Would it even be worth trying to find love if it was doomed from the start? He'd already had his heart broken once and seen his mom living like a shell of her former self after losing the love of her life. Add to that all the suffering the curse was showing him, and he had no intention of falling in love only to have his heart broken anyway.

His phone rang. Gage's name flashed on his console and Blake pulled over. He was probably too distracted to talk and drive at the same time anyway. Once he talked to Gage, he'd head straight home.

"Hey, Gage," he said when he answered, happy to be able to focus on his brother and not his own problems. "Something wrong?"

Gage let out a short laugh. "Not really. But I must need to

phone more often if you think I call only when something's wrong."

"I'd be good with you calling more." He could probably count on both hands the number of times Gage had initiated a call in all the years he'd been gone and still have a few fingers left.

"I was, uh..." When Gage hesitated, Blake had to bite his tongue not to push him. He could picture his mom telling him to be patient—difficult at the best of times, but almost impossible today.

Finally, Gage spoke up. "Our birthday is coming up."

On October twenty-fifth, Gage and Ford would turn twenty-five. Blake knew there was a word for that type of birthday, but he couldn't remember what it was. Their mom would have known. Regardless, turning twenty-five was kind of a big deal.

The last time Gage and Ford celebrated their birthdays together had been their twenty-first. Blake, Jake, Cade, and Dane had decided to drive Ford to Gage and had taken them to a restaurant to celebrate and ordered the twins their first legal beer.

"Yeah?" Blake prompted, forcing his tone to stay casual as hope bloomed inside him.

"I was thinking I'd come and visit."

"Great. You want to stay with me?"

"I don't know."

"When you figure it out, let me know." Channeling their mom's patience, he didn't say anything more. God, he missed her. She'd be able to advise him about Gage and the curse. There'd only been nine days between today's episode and the second one, coming two days sooner than the last. He didn't know if they would start coming more often and what he was supposed to do if they did. He could only imagine how they'd interrupt his daily life.

"Blake? You still there?" Gage asked, bringing him back to the present.

"I'm here."

"Did you hear anything I just said?"

"Sure."

Gage laughed. "Yeah, right. No worries. I was just talking about the job. What's got you so distracted? A woman or the curse?"

"Both."

"Want to talk about it—er—them?"

"The curse hit again today." He gave Gage the highlights and tried to make light of it by mentioning he still had all his fingers.

Gage was quiet for a moment. "I guess you have to fall in love then. Now tell me about the woman."

"I saw Paige last week."

"Paige? The one you dated in college who crushed your heart?"

Blake snorted. "I wouldn't go that far."

"I would. Where did you see her?"

"She's the real estate agent for the strip mall we'd talked about looking at."

"Why were you—You haven't replaced the VP of commercial ops?"

"Not at the time. But Henry said he'd take the job for a year as a stepping stone to his retirement."

"Then you'll look for a replacement?"

Blake hadn't mentioned the job to Gage yet, but maybe this was the perfect opportunity. Gage wanting to come for a visit was a good sign he might be open to it. "I have someone in mind, but he won't be finished on another job for a year."

"Who do—Oh. We'll see."

"That's all I ask." Since Blake had zoned out while Gage had talked about his job, Blake asked him a few questions to cover what he'd missed. Before they ended the call, Gage promised to let him know about his birthday.

Back on the road, Blake headed home. Since Kyleigh didn't live in his stomping grounds, he was still a ways away. He was going to drive by the strip mall Paige had shown him.

The traffic light by the property turned red as he approached. Stopping, he glanced over at the strip mall and noticed a light was on. It was in the last unit—the spa. Paige must have forgotten to turn it off after she showed the property to another client.

As he turned back to check the stoplight, he saw movement in the window and then the place went dark. The blinds were already pulled closed, but he swore he saw someone walk by inside.

As soon as the light changed to green, Blake drove to the next street and turned to double back to the strip mall. The parking lot behind the property was empty except for a single car. It sat directly behind the last unit.

Blake pulled into the space behind it and got out. The car was the same model as the one Paige drove, so he looked in the back window. There was a child's car seat as there had been in Paige's car.

If Paige was inside, was she showing the property? Had he jumped the gun? Her car was the only one there besides his, but she could have driven the client to the place. Then why did someone turn the lights off? Something wasn't right.

He tried the door handle of the last unit. Locked. Pounding on the door with his fist, he yelled, "Paige! Open up!"

If she was with a client, he would come across as a crazy person, but he had an uneasy feeling about her being in there at night, especially in the dark.

He waited about twenty seconds and pounded on the door again. "Paige! I saw the light and your car is here!"

More seconds passed. Blake raised his fist to bang again when he heard the lock on the door disengage.

The door pulled inward, and he walked in. Silently, Paige moved behind him to close the door, then reached over and flicked on a light.

He blinked at the sudden brightness, then took in her appearance. Her feet were bare, and she wore lounge pants and a baggy sweatshirt with their college name written across the front.

"Is that my sweatshirt?" The words were out of his mouth before he even realized what he was saying.

"Uh, maybe."

She'd kept his sweatshirt all these years even after breaking up with him? He was about to ask about that when he spied the empty spaces behind what used to be the stylists' stations, bringing his thoughts back to the present.

"Why are you here, Paige?"

"I…" She looked around, and he knew she was trying to come up with a plausible lie.

He held up his hand to stop her, even though he'd asked her a question. She was dressed for bed. It didn't take a genius to figure out she was staying in the unit. Turning around, he strode to the back of the shop.

"Blake, wait. I can explain," she called after him.

He didn't say anything for fear it would be the wrong thing. Emotions swirled around inside him. Anger at whoever put Paige into a situation that forced her into living in a strip mall. Confusion about why she hadn't asked anyone for help. Guilt for not realizing she was living here when she'd shown him the place. And lastly, hope. That was the craziest of all the emotions he was currently feeling, but he couldn't dissect it. Not yet. There were other things to deal with first.

When he'd been there before, he hadn't made it down the

hallway. He pushed open the first door and flicked on a light. The wood-paneled room had been a sauna at one time, but it was now filled with boxes.

A light was already on in the second room. An air mattress lay on the floor, a discarded e-reader on top of the blankets. A laptop sat on one box, and several pairs of shoes and a suitcase were lined up against one wall.

Blake turned around and almost ran into Paige. Her hands were in the pockets of her pants as she lowered her eyes to the floor.

Going to the next room, Blake already knew what he'd find. He didn't turn on the light, not wanting to wake the child sleeping in the small bed. The light from the room Paige used cast enough light that he could make out the child-sized furniture set up in the small space.

Blake pushed open the door of the final room. As if his feet had a mind of their own, they carried him into the space that used to be a locker room before he could stop himself. The light came on automatically as soon as he entered. The last stall held a large shower with towels neatly stacked on a shelf.

Pivoting, he eyed the long counter with two sinks. A coffee maker sat between them, and a microwave took up the space on the far side. Two toothbrushes and a tube of toothpaste lay by one of the sinks.

His gut tightened.

He didn't know what had led Paige—the strong, independent woman he remembered—to squat in a vacant property, but he didn't need the reasons right then. He was more concerned about Paige and her daughter.

Paige wasn't in the hallway when Blake walked out of the bathroom. He looked in the rooms as he strode by them and found her standing near the blinds at the front of the shop.

In that moment, he knew he was about to make what

could be the biggest mistake of his life. But Paige and her daughter needed a safe and comfortable place to live. If he moved Paige in with him, he could easily fall in love with her, and that would give her the ability to crush him. Again. If she left him this time, he might not be able to pick himself back up.

He remembered his mom in the months and years after his dad died and then the feeling he'd felt when Paige had walked away, his gut tightening further. He'd sworn he would never put himself in that position again. But knowing that didn't change his mind. Even if he doomed himself, he knew what he had to do.

"I'll help you pack," he told her.

CHAPTER EIGHT

It was time to face the fire. She took a deep breath and turned around.

He didn't seem angry, but she couldn't tell what he felt. Pity, maybe? If it was, she didn't want that either. She had no idea where she and Emmie would go now that Blake knew what she was doing. They could stay in a hotel for a few nights, since she had some money. But staying for too long would deplete everything she'd managed to save that didn't have to go toward debt. Then she'd be in an even worse position than she was in now. Still homeless, but without even a strip mall to stay in.

Paige nodded and followed Blake toward the sauna room where her boxes were stacked. She'd felt shame at her failure from the moment she made the decision to move herself and Emmie into the strip mall. All her poor decisions seemed stacked up on top of each other, glaring at her more brightly than the bare overhead bulb. It didn't matter that she'd left Craig and was trying to forge ahead. Forcing her child to live in an empty strip mall, combined with her other failures, outweighed any pride she'd felt from finally being independent.

Even with all the shame and guilt on her shoulders, it was nothing compared to how she'd felt when Blake had looked in all the rooms and figured out she and Emmie were living there.

"We can load all these into the bed of my truck and anything else you'll need for tonight," Blake said. "I've got plenty of room to store them in my garage. I can come back tomorrow for your daughter's bed and dresser."

Paige nodded again, and then his words sank in and her head shot up. "Garage? What are you talking about?"

"You can't stay here, Paige."

"No shit." Her shame fell to the back burner as her anger took over. "You think I like having my daughter living in a strip mall?" She realized how loud her voice had become and lowered it, hissing the rest of the words at him. "I left a bad situation, and I'm doing the best I can. Are you going to report me to my boss? Is keeping my things in your garage your way of easing your guilt when I lose my job?"

"What?" Blake's shock seemed genuine. "I'm not going to tell your boss. I'm doing this because you and your daughter are moving in with me."

"No, we aren't." Her protest was automatic.

What she really wanted to say was *"Okay, and thank you for helping,"* but that was a slippery path to go down. Once she accepted Blake's help and lived with him, it wouldn't be long before she'd start to lose her independence. After all, he had just demanded that she move in with him. How long would it take before he was demanding other things, like that she quit her job so she could cook and clean for him? Would he then start finding fault with everything she did? She had already lived on a constant edge, afraid of doing something wrong, and she wouldn't do it again.

The logical part of her brain knew she was projecting Craig's behavior onto Blake, but she also knew no one was without faults. He had just acted like Craig, telling her to move in with him, without consulting her. Maybe he wasn't the same Blake she remembered.

"Bab—uh, Paige. Please, be reasonable. I have—"

"Reasonable?" she hissed again, hating herself for it, but she was too afraid that if she didn't, she would yell and wake up Emmie. "You think I'm being unreasonable because I won't let you come in here and tell me where I'll be living, without even asking me what I want to do?"

He held up his hands as if to fend her off. "No, I think you're being unreasonable because I have enough room for you and your daughter, and instead of accepting my offer, you're letting your pride rule you."

Paige felt like he'd slapped her in the face. For so long, her pride had been non-existent. It had taken a tearful walk through a grocery store for her to find some pride and self-worth. It felt like Blake was trying to wipe it all away with only a few words, but she wouldn't let that happen.

"You don't know anything about what I've been through," she spat at him. "Don't you dare judge me."

Blake scrubbed his face with his hands, a gesture he used to do when he was trying to rein in his frustration. Back when they'd been together, the frustration usually hadn't been aimed at her.

He dropped his hands and looked at her, his expression softer. "I'm going about this all wrong. I'm not trying to tell you what to do. I want to help you out, and I have the means. No strings, okay? Use my spare rooms for as long as you need. I won't get in your way, but I'll be there to help you out however you need."

The offer was too good to be true. He was handing her everything she wanted—someone to lean on and help her.

Maybe even love her. *No.* He hadn't promised her that, but the possibility was there to love him again. But it could come at the risk of giving up her independence. She couldn't become reliant on him, even if letting him take some of the weight off her shoulders would feel like heaven.

If it was only about her, she would refuse and tell him all her stuff would be moved out the next day, and he didn't need to know where. But it wasn't only about her.

She swallowed—not an easy feat as her pride threatened to get stuck in her throat. "Thank you, Blake. It's a generous offer and I accept."

He nodded at her and turned.

"Wait." She lunged forward and grabbed his arm, forcing him to face her. "This is only until I can get back on my feet. And you won't try to control me or tell me what to do." Even though she had a history with him, she still had to be cautious.

Blake frowned. "No. You're an adult." He looked around the space before looking back at her. "Like you said, I don't know what you've been through, but we used to be friends. Let me help you out until you're on your feet."

Years of manipulation had formed Paige's responses, though even recognizing that fact wouldn't make them go away overnight. She feared Blake had ulterior motives. Did he need a maid or a companion? The sex between them had been combustible from day one. Was that what he wanted, and he saw an easy way to get it whenever he needed it and maybe a maid and cook too?

It dawned on her she might not be the only woman living in his house. During their infrequent coffee dates, his mom had told her that he dated a lot. "You live alone?"

"I do. And I don't have a girlfriend."

This time, she nodded. As Blake had reminded her,

Emmie was more important than her pride; she only hoped she wasn't dooming her future.

BLAKE DIDN'T SAY anything as Paige followed him into the first room, where he picked up a couple of boxes. He'd gone a bit caveman on her, but he'd begun to panic that she was going to refuse his offer. Just the thought of her continuing to live in a less-than-ideal situation without anyone to go to for help had him clenching his teeth in anger. Not at her, but for her.

Keeping as quiet as they could, not wanting to wake up her daughter until the last moment, he carried the boxes to his truck. It took several trips to load his truck, but if it was everything she owned, it wasn't much.

He had so many questions flying around in his head, like what had happened, and why her parents hadn't stepped in to help her. Or her friends. When they'd dated, she hadn't hung out with a huge posse, but she'd had two or three close friends. Where were they? Was she in financial trouble? She shouldn't be since she had a good job, or at least she seemed to.

Out of all his questions, the thing that concerned him most, even more than her not having a proper home, was her thinking he would control her or tell her what to do. Sure, he was decisive. It made him a good CEO, and a lot of people depended on him to make the hard decisions, but he never did it without the input of those around him.

The Paige he used to know hadn't exactly been a wallflower herself. The night he met her, Paige was the first person he noticed when he and Jake had walked into the house party. Standing on a low coffee table, her long, dark hair hung like a curtain down her back, swaying back and forth as she danced. A friend was dancing on the table with her, but at the time, Blake couldn't have even said the color of the other girl's hair, his eyes only on Paige.

She didn't have much rhythm, something he later teased her about. Paige had been caught up in the moment, enjoying herself. Her happiness had called to him. He'd known right then he wanted to be a part of it—not just to bask in it, but to contribute to it and ensure it was never stifled.

"This is the last box, minus the few things still in Emmie's room," Paige said, pulling him out of his thoughts. She stood beside him, a box in her arms. Taking it from her, he put it in the back of his truck and closed the tailgate.

"You still good with getting your daughter's furniture tomorrow?"

"Sure."

In the glow from the security light over the back door, he could see the hesitant look on her face, like maybe she didn't trust him.

He was an idiot. Why should she trust him? He hadn't seen her in years, and then he barged into her life and told her to move in with him. Leaning back against his truck to avoid towering over her, he feigned a casualness he didn't feel. All he wanted was to get Paige and her daughter inside his house where they'd be safe. Hell, maybe the strip mall was safe at night, but it couldn't be safer than his house.

"I should have mentioned I have a kids' room set up at my house. Your daughter… What did you say her name was?"

"Emmie, short for Emilia."

"Right. Emmie will have a brand-new bed to sleep in, so when we do come back for hers, we can store it."

Paige stiffened. "You have kids?"

"No." He winced, not quite sure how to explain the kids' bedroom in his house. Telling her about his mom's obsession for him to get married might not go over well, so he opted for a partial truth. "My mom was dreaming of grandchildren, and one day while I was at work, she decorated my spare room as a children's nursery, set up for a baby and a toddler."

When Paige's eyes widened, he realized he maybe should have told her his mom wanted him to get married too.

"It's neutral colors," he blurted. Like that would make it better. Once again, he felt like an idiot.

"Okay. As long as we're not putting you out."

"You're not."

It took Paige a few minutes to wake Emmie and get her shoes and coat on. It was almost eleven o'clock, and there was a definite fall chill in the air.

While Paige buckled Emmie into her car seat, Blake took one of the empty boxes leaning against a wall and folded the bottom together. Knowing what his nephew was like with his toys, Blake didn't want Emmie to be without her favorites.

Realizing he didn't know which ones to pack, he gathered up all the dolls and books from the bed and loaded them into the box, as well as the few toys that had fallen to the floor. On his way out, he turned off the lights and pulled the door shut, locking it.

Paige was standing beside her car, her arms once more crossed over her body. He wasn't sure if she was cold or if the position was a form of self-protection. Either way, he didn't like that she still seemed hesitant.

"I packed up some of Emmie's toys. You okay to follow me home?"

"Yes."

Exhaustion was clear on her face, and here he was standing beside his truck holding a box like a dumbass. She probably wanted to get to his place and get Emmie into bed.

"Good." She got into her vehicle, and he opened the door

of his truck, pushing the box across to the passenger seat, before climbing in.

All the way home, he kept glancing at Paige's car in the rearview mirror, to make sure they didn't get separated by a red light. The twenty-minute drive to his place felt much longer because he worried about her and constantly watched her.

By the time she pulled into the driveway behind him, he was already out of his truck and waiting to open her door. "I'll bring everything in after you get her settled."

He followed Paige around to the passenger side of the vehicle. "Will Emmie be okay if I pick her up? You look tired."

"Sure, that would be nice." She opened the rear door. Emmie opened her eyes but didn't really look awake. "Emmie, can Blake pick you up? He's got a fancy bedroom to show you." When Emmie gave her mom a sleepy nod, Paige unbuckled the car seat and stood back.

He cradled Emmie against his chest. Her hair, a tangled, bed-headed mess, brushed against his chin, sending her child-sweet scent wafting up to him. Like her mom, Emmie awoke something in him. He was startled by the sudden sense of protectiveness he felt toward this child he'd only just met.

She patted his cheek and then laid her head on his shoulder. He realized then that he was going to have to guard his heart against both mother and daughter.

CHAPTER NINE

$\mathscr{P}$aige followed Blake into his house and took a quick glance around. Her first impression, even in the dark of night, was that the house was welcoming. A swing hung from the large porch's rafters, and she could imagine herself sitting in it one day.

While she admired the house, the two sides of her brain were in the middle of a sparring match. One side believed she'd made the wrong decision in accepting Blake's offer because it would be too easy to become dependent on him. And the other side of her was full of hope for a cozy home and partnership.

Too exhausted to know if she was even thinking clearly, she shoved the thoughts aside. It was late and she needed to get Emmie settled.

Before she had a chance to check out the inside of the house, Blake walked up the stairs and into one of the open doorways.

"There's a small lamp attached to the wall above the twin bed," Blake whispered. Paige hurried past him, seeing the bed on one side of the room and a crib on the other with an identical lamp. Both lamps were secured a safe distance above the beds.

She reached up and flicked on one of the lights.

Blake stood beside the bed, rubbing Emmie's back in slow circles.

Paige pulled back the blankets, and he lowered Emmie gently to the bed. As if they'd done it a hundred times before, he removed Emmie's shoes while Paige got her out of her coat.

He pulled the blankets up to Emmie's waist as if passing them off to Paige, and she tucked them around her daughter's shoulders before leaning down and giving her a kiss. "Mommy loves you," she whispered, Emmie already sound asleep.

When she straightened, Blake was shutting a set of closet doors. "I put her coat and shoes in here," he said quietly.

She nodded and took a moment to look around the room. Random gold stars decorated the wall with the lamps, and Paige's lips twitched as she remembered how nervous Blake had been when he'd explained that the room was decorated in neutral colors. He'd been right—everything was neutral but inviting, from the rocking chair to the mobile above the crib to the rugs covering the wood flooring to the bookshelves and baskets filled with toys.

"I'll go get your things," Blake said and left the room.

Paige looked down at Emmie. She'd been through so much during the last year, and each time, she seemed to roll with the punches. But the apartment had been sterile and the strip mall even more so. Blake's house was a home. When Paige eventually had to rip Emmie away from it, it would hurt her if she'd become attached to it, like when they'd left the only home Emmie had known.

It didn't matter that she and Craig had to sell the house because of his debts; Paige had been the one to take Emmie away from it. Would her daughter start to resent her for everything she'd done? When Emmie got older, she likely wouldn't even remember this time in her life, but the effects could stay with her. This was a crucial time in a child's development, and she constantly worried that her decisions were ruining her daughter.

A year ago, Paige had been so sure that leaving Craig and standing up for herself would be best for Emmie in the long run. Now she wondered if all the upheaval was selfish on her part.

"Paige?" Startled, she turned at the sound of Blake's voice. "You okay?"

He stood in the doorway with a box in his hands.

At her nod, he came over to her and placed the box on the floor beside the bed. "Emmie's toys," he said.

He looked at her for a moment, as if trying to read her, before leaving.

Paige opened the flaps of the box, took out Emmie's favorite doll, and tucked it into bed with her.

She left the light on and the door ajar in case Emmie woke up, and went downstairs.

"Hey," Blake said as he walked into the foyer, placing the boxes in his arms on the floor. "Let me give you a quick tour so you know where things are."

"Sure."

"Obviously this is the living and dining room," he said.

The front door on her left led into a foyer and opened up to the living room in front of her that was home to two large, comfy-looking couches and two armchairs. A massive flat screen TV was above the fireplace and a large, molded archway led to the dining room, making it a semi-open layout. Three lamps placed in the corners of the living room glowed with soft light, and the only overhead fixture was the one above the dining room table.

He led her through the dining room and into the kitchen, then smirked as he gestured toward the cabinets. "As you can see, I haven't gotten around to renovating in here yet."

The room took up the entire back of the house, creating a long but spacious galley kitchen. The stainless steel appliances looked new, a big contrast to the cupboards that looked as if they hadn't been updated since some time in the 1950s, but they gave the whole space a homey, retro feel.

Blake pointed to a door with a large inset window covered by frilly curtains. "That leads to the patio and the backyard. I keep it locked, but just in case Emmie manages to get outside, the yard is fenced and the lock on the gate is up high so she won't be able to reach it."

Paige leaned forward to peer out the curtain, hoping she hid her shock. Blake had known Emmie less than three hours and he'd shown more concern for her well-being than her own father ever had. "Thanks, good to know."

He pulled open a door. "A bathroom."

Once Paige poked her head into the two-piece bath and stepped back, Blake opened a final door. "This leads to the basement." He flicked on the light, and Paige followed him down the stairs.

Considering the age of the house, she was surprised when Blake led her into an area that took up almost the same amount of space as the upstairs. The floor was covered with what looked like high-end laminate, and the entire space was drywalled and painted in a soft green. Even the ceiling was finished, with pot lights spaced throughout.

The area directly in front of them was set up as a bedroom. A king-size bed sat against the back wall with a nightstand on either side, and a large armchair and bookshelf sat in the corners at the end of the bed. A dresser and armoire provided a visual separation from the rest of the room.

Paige followed Blake to the other side of the bedroom space to an area with rubber mats covering the floor. A workbench, treadmill, and weights filled the area. "I always keep the door at the top of the basement stairs locked because my nephew Malcolm is walking now, so you won't have to worry about Emmie exploring.

"That door," Blake said, pointing to the first of two doors on the section of the basement furthest from the bed, "is a bathroom with a shower, and the door beside it is the laundry room. Use whatever you need."

She followed Blake as he opened the doors to each room. Her brain was still coming to terms with Blake taking children's safety into account like it was no big deal. It was a huge deal to her.

"Come on, let me show you your bedroom. I probably should have saved this tour for tomorrow after you've had a chance to sleep." Blake must have mistaken her shocked look for tiredness because he ushered her up the stairs, locking the door behind them.

Back on the second floor, he pointed to the door beyond the one where Emmie was sleeping. "That's the bathroom and it's got a separate shower and a bathtub. I'm guessing Emmie still takes baths."

Paige felt her face heat with guilt. "The strip mall only had a shower, but yes, Emmie loves baths."

Blake reached around her and pushed open the remaining door. "This will be your room."

Paige walked into the bedroom. It smelled just like Blake, fresh with a hint of citrus. Most houses built in the early

1900s had small bedrooms compared to modern homes, but this one was spacious and had probably been two at one time.

The bed was a simple design made of high-gloss wood, with nightstands holding stylish lamps on either side, and there was a door furthest from the window, most likely to a bathroom. Slowly turning, she gasped when she noticed the entire wall opposite the window had been turned into a doorless closet made of the same dark wood as the bed. Shirts and jackets hung on a rod and shelves filled with baskets lay underneath. Beside that, another rod held longer clothing items. Other shelves held shoes and folded clothing, and much of the unit was filled with drawers.

As realization dawned, she turned to Blake. "This is your bedroom. I can't sleep here."

Blake took a step into the room. "Yes, you can. It's across the hall from Emmie so you'll be able to hear her."

Paige glanced back at the bed. Did he expect to sleep with her? Her body tingled at the thought, remembering how easily he used to make her come. Something that hadn't happened in a long time. And unfortunately, it likely wouldn't happen for another long while.

"Where will you sleep?" she asked, hoping her question sounded like only mild curiosity.

"In the basement. I'll take just what I need for tonight and I can move more tomorrow." He gestured toward a bench at the end of the bed. "Your things are there."

Only moments later, Blake had a toiletry bag and some clothes in his arms. "I'll leave the door open so Emmie can find you if she wakes up," he said as he left.

When he disappeared from view, she realized she hadn't even thanked him for moving her and Emmie into his house and giving up his bed for her. She and Emmie were there for only as long as it took for her to get back on her feet.

Rifling through her things, she found what she needed and headed to the bathroom. For the second time that night, she went through her nighttime routine, just a shorter version, and then climbed into bed.

Surrounded by Blake's scent and enjoying the feel of a bed for the first time in more than a year, she decided to put her worries aside for the night and let sleep take her under.

Sunday, October 6

BLAKE LEANED against the kitchen counter while he waited for the coffee maker to finish brewing. It had been after one in the morning by the time he'd crawled into bed, which was amping up impatience for coffee.

The night before had not gone the way he'd expected when he'd left for his date, but he didn't have any regrets.

As the last drops sputtered from the coffee maker, he thought about the plan that had begun to form last night. He and Paige had been friends once and hopefully they could be again. Then he'd approach her about staying on indefinitely. As roommates.

Living by himself could get lonely. It would be nice having someone around, especially someone he already knew he liked. How the curse would play into that, if it continued, he didn't know. All he could do was take things day by day.

Blake didn't move from his spot against the counter as he enjoyed his coffee. He had just about finished his first cup when he heard Paige and Emmie moving about upstairs. A warm sensation—and not from the coffee—filled him; he'd been right to set his alarm for six o'clock that morning in anticipation of Emmie waking early.

A few minutes later, he heard someone in the front room. He was on his second cup of coffee and had the machine set up for one for Paige. Leaning down, he looked out the passthrough and saw Emmie standing there with a doll clutched in one hand.

"Good morning, Emmie."

Her eyes went wide. "You're in a hole."

"See the door beside this hole?" He waited until she nodded. "Push on it."

Emmie came into the kitchen and looked around. "A secret."

"The kitchen?"

"I couldn't find it."

"I normally leave the door open, but it must have fallen closed. I'll make sure it's open from now on."

Blake set his coffee on the counter and crouched in front of the little girl. Her hair was in two ponytails, one on each side of her head, and she wore jeans and a sparkly blue shirt with the blond character from the movie *Frozen*. He wasn't exactly sure where the expression "cute as a button" came from, but it was the first thing that came to his mind.

"There isn't a table in here, but you can sit on the counter while I make breakfast. Can I pick you up, Emmie?"

"Yes—my dolly too!."

"Of course." Blake lifted Emmie and placed her on the counter, making sure she wasn't too close to the edge so she wouldn't slip off. He knew firsthand that little kids could wiggle a lot. When he'd been seven and Ford and Gage were three, he'd helped them climb onto the dining room table so they could watch him and Jake play a game, and Ford had slipped off the edge, landing on his butt on the floor. Luckily, he hadn't been hurt. Blake had learned a lot of life lessons from having four younger brothers. Many that he was thankful for now that Emmie was living with him.

Emmie sat still as she looked around the kitchen.

"Do you like eggs?" he asked her.

"I like pancakes. And waffles."

Blake suppressed a laugh. "You do, huh… Which do you like more?"

"Pancakes."

"I think I can do that. Would you like to help me?"

"Yes." She dropped her doll on the counter and moved forward.

Blake's heart entered his throat as he lunged for her and lifted her up. "Let's get you a chair so you can be my helper." He set her on the floor and grabbed a chair from the dining room.

When Blake had Emmie kneeling on a chair, he pulled out a bowl and the ingredients he needed. During his college years when his mom was struggling, he'd learned to make pancakes because it was a way he could feed all his brothers without a lot of fuss.

He measured all the ingredients and put Emmie in charge of stirring.

"Is this good?" Emmie asked while he was preheating the griddle.

Blake smiled. "You're a good helper. Do you think you can smash a few more lumps?"

She pushed her rubber spatula into the mix, splashing some onto her shirt. Usually, he wanted to get jobs done quickly, but with Emmie, he had a boatload of patience and just enjoyed seeing her help.

"Good morning," Paige greeted them.

"Mommy!" Emmie said at a decibel high enough to make Blake wince as she spun around, the bowl still in her hand. Blake dove for her and the pancake batter, catching them both. He set the bowl on the counter and lifted Emmie to her feet.

"Good reflexes," Paige said as she crouched down and Emmie launched herself at her.

"Thanks. They're getting a workout this morning." He pointed to the coffee maker. "It's all set up for you. Just lift the handle until the lights flash and select one."

"Thanks." She released her daughter and helped her back onto the chair. "What are you making?"

"Pancakes! I'm helping Blake!"

"That's great, sweetie. Anything I can do to help?" she asked, directing her question at Blake.

Blake gave Emmie a mock elbow jab. "No, we've got this. Right, kiddo?"

Emmie laughed. "Yep. We've got this," she mimicked.

Paige chatted with them while he cooked the pancakes and Emmie ran back and forth from the kitchen to the dining room, setting the table.

On Emmie's final trip to the dining room, he and Paige followed with their coffee and a pile of pancakes. "I'm going to need more sleep to keep up with her," he said, smirking at Paige.

She chuckled. "Don't I know it."

Blake enjoyed breakfast more than he could remember enjoying one in a long time. Paige reminded him so much of his mom when he and his brothers were younger, directing when needed, but not in a bossy way.

During the last year, his mom had been on his ass so much about getting married that he'd buried all the good memories, letting his annoyance take over. If only she'd told him about the curse… But, like she'd said in the letter, he probably wouldn't have believed her. He hadn't really believed any of it until he had experienced the curse firsthand. He couldn't change the past, but he would make it a habit to think about the good times.

"Penny for your thoughts? Or is it a dollar now?" Paige asked, her eyebrows raised.

"Just thinking about my mom. How you are with Emmie reminds me a lot of her."

"I'll take that as a compliment."

"I hope so."

"Mommy, I'm done," Emmie said.

Paige pushed her chair back. "Okay, let's get you washed up."

Blake followed them into the kitchen. "You can wash up in that bathroom."

"Thanks. Since you two were such great cooks, it's fair I clean up."

He hesitated, trying to come up with an excuse for why he needed to stay in the kitchen.

She must have sensed what he was doing because she asked, "Are we keeping you from something?"

"No. The only thing I had planned was a lazy Saturday."

She blushed. "Let us know if we get in your way."

"You won't." Blake wondered if she was thinking of all the times he'd woken her up early with his hands and mouth on her body.

During college, they'd both still lived at home, but his bedroom had been in the basement. One day when he was creeping into the house at oh-dark-thirty, his mom had been waiting for him in the living room. Since he'd never been one to stay out all hours, she figured he was trying to find time alone with Paige. Then she knocked the socks off his twenty-one-year-old self by telling him Paige could stay over as long as he was discreet around his younger brothers. Discreet became his middle name.

Although he wouldn't have that with Paige again, he would like having her around.

"Mommy, where are my toys?"

"Your dolls are in your room, but I think the rest are in the garage."

"They are." He held his hand out to Emmie. "You want to help me find them?"

"Yes." She put her hand in his. So trusting. Now he just needed to get her mom to trust him too.

CHAPTER TEN

*P*aige followed Blake and Emmie to where their boxes were neatly stacked in one corner of the garage. It wasn't everything she owned because of what was in her storage locker, but just seeing them stacked up, not taking up much room, made her feelings of failure rise to the surface, like they so often did. She should have a house of her own and belongings she was proud of by now. Maybe one day…

After some shuffling of boxes, Blake found several marked as Emmie's toys.

"I'll bring these in for you, kiddo." He straightened and walked toward another pile of boxes Paige hadn't noticed because she'd focused only on her own boxes. "Do you like playing dress-up?" he asked her daughter.

Emmie clapped her hands together. "Yes."

He grinned down at her. "Then I have something for you. Let's go into the living room. I'll come back for your toys." He lifted two boxes off a pile, and Emmie scampered ahead of him.

Blake set the boxes on the living room floor and knelt,

opening them. "When I was sorting through my mom's things, I found a bunch of stuff that I thought a little girl might like."

"I'm a little girl," she said, standing straighter.

"Yes, you are, and I think these will be perfect for you. Maybe you can dress up and play tea party with your dolls."

Paige sat on one of the couches and watched as Blake and Emmie went through the boxes. They pulled out shoes, dresses, scarves, and some fancy wide-brimmed hats that Alex must have worn to weddings.

When everything was laid out on the other couch, Blake went back to the garage for Emmie's toys. "What else do you need to have a tea party?" he asked Emmie when he returned.

"Teacups." She scrambled over to her boxes and rooted through them. "I found them," she shouted, holding up a plastic teacup in one hand and a saucer in the other.

Paige chuckled softly. "Inside voice, Emmie."

"Sorry, Mommy." She turned to Blake. "I need a table."

Blake pulled the coffee table into the middle of the room. "How's this?"

She set her teacup and saucer on the table. "Okay," she said, then after a beat, "A mirror."

"I think I have one downstairs." Blake left and came back a few minutes later with a full-length mirror.

He propped it against the wall beside the fireplace. "I'll leave the mirror here, but you have to promise not to touch it, okay? You can look into it, and if you need to move it, you have to ask me or your mom."

"I will." Emmie threw herself at Blake's legs, hugging him. "Thank you, Blake. I love them."

"I'm glad."

When Emmie began to play, he turned to Paige. "More coffee?"

"Yes, I'd love another cup." Paige stood, but Blake put his hand up to halt her.

"I'll get it," he said. "Then we can sit at the dining room table so we're close if Emmie needs you."

Paige watched him walk into the kitchen before turning back to Emmie.

She'd been watching Blake too. "Blake said it's not a secret. Don't close it."

"That sounds like a good idea." She smiled, imagining the conversation that had brought that up.

"Still take it with just cream?" Blake asked.

Paige laughed when she turned and saw Blake poking his head out the kitchen passthrough when the doorway was just as close. "Yes."

Sitting and letting someone wait on her when she wasn't in a restaurant felt strange. She couldn't remember the last time she'd been waited on. It could have been when she'd last been with Blake, as sad as that was.

She and Blake sat at the dining table drinking their coffees and watching Emmie for a few minutes. As an only child, Emmie was used to playing by herself and didn't seem to mind. But Paige did. She'd never wanted Emmie to be an only child.

By the time Emmie had been born, Paige knew her dream of having several children wasn't likely to come true. She'd even contemplated staying with Craig just so she could have more kids, but then she realized she was being selfish. She needed to get the child she had out of that environment, not bring more kids into it.

"Now a penny for you, or a dollar," Blake teased, echoing her earlier comment.

She looked across the table at him. His hair was messy from sleeping, but it was the kind of disarray that added to his looks, not detracted. She used to love looking at him in the mornings when he was all relaxed, the day yet to intrude with the million responsibilities he had on his plate.

"I was just thinking about Emmie playing by herself."

"Does she not normally?"

"She does. She has friends at daycare, but at home, unless I play with her, she's on her own."

"We can probably remedy that. Do you remember Linda and Denise?"

Paige narrowed her eyes, thinking back. "From Akermans? Oh, right. Linda was office manager and Denise was head of HR?"

"Switch the positions, but right. They're grandmothers now and both have their grandkids over a lot. They babysit together, and I'm sure we can arrange for Emmie to meet their grandkids for a playdate."

"I wouldn't want Emmie to be a burden."

"I'm sure she wouldn't." He snapped his fingers. "I just remembered... Akerman's annual Halloween party is on Saturday, October twenty-sixth. You'll be able to see Linda and Denise then. Talk to them and then make up your mind."

Paige nodded and ducked her head, taking another sip of coffee to hide her shock. Her eyes were probably as wide as saucers. October twenty-sixth was three weeks away. Last night she'd hoped she and Emmie would be out of his hair before the end of the month.

"I've been thinking..." Blake said.

She grinned at him. "Should I be worried?"

His smile was slow and wicked. Paige knew then that she should be the one worrying.

Blake laughed, relaxing his smile. "No, seriously. I was thinking about your situation and mine."

"What's yours?" She had no idea what his could be. He looked like he had everything he could want.

"I'd like to be friends again. We were once, and I think we could be again."

She hesitated for a moment. "We were more than friends."

"I know. But that was a long time ago, and it didn't end well." He held up his hand. "I'm not blaming you. Like I said, it was years ago and we've both probably changed, so let's get to know each other again."

Paige stared him in the eyes, not wavering. "It was my fault, Blake. I broke up with you and went back to Craig."

"It doesn't matter whose fault it was; it's done." He looked over at Emmie and then met Paige's gaze again. "Do you ever get lonely?"

"Yes."

"Me too." He paused as if he was trying to find the right words to continue. "I'm not looking for love. I don't plan on ever falling in love and getting married. I'm just telling you this so neither of us has any false expectations."

"Really?" Paige didn't know what else to say. It wasn't that she felt any different, because she wasn't willing to ever risk having a man controlling her or being reliant on one again. But Blake had wanted a big family. During one of their many deep conversations, he'd told her that he wanted a relationship just like his parents had, but something had obviously changed.

"Really."

He didn't say any more, and she couldn't help but think that his change of heart was her fault. If she hadn't broken up with him… She looked over at Emmie as her voice raised in excitement, talking to one of her dolls. If she had stayed with Blake, she wouldn't have Emmie, she reminded herself.

"I'm not looking for love either." She didn't tell him why, and when he smiled at her, it seemed like her statement was enough without an explanation. They were on the same page.

He extended his hand toward her. "Friends?"

She wasn't sure she could be only friends with Blake. At one time, she'd thought he would be her future. Now, she didn't know if she could even trust him. Physically, she knew Blake would never hurt her or Emmie, but emotions were something else. She'd had hers manipulated before, and if Blake had ulterior motives, her emotions might not be safe. She would just have to be extra cautious and look for warning signs.

After leaving Craig, she'd looked back over her years with him and saw hundreds of them. In the beginning, she had ignored every single one to keep the peace and please him. Never again. This time she would be more vigilant.

Paige shook his hand. "Friends."

"Good… I've been thinking about one more thing."

"Oh, no," she teased.

He gave her a mock scowl and then huffed a laugh. "Let's see how we do over the next few weeks, and if we get along well as roommates, I'd like you to think about you and Emmie staying here."

"Staying? For how long?"

Blake shrugged. "I don't know, and we don't need to worry about timeframes right now."

"Okay." Even as Paige agreed she wondered once more if she was making the right decision. Being friends was one thing, but staying here for an extended period and living like a family every day was something else entirely. She'd have to see what she could do to not only guard her independence but her heart as well.

Sunday, October 13

"THANKS," Blake said and smiled at the grocery store clerk as she handed him his receipt. He stuffed it in the bag before walking to his truck to head home.

He and Paige had been cooking together, taking turns coming up with what to have for dinner each night. Since he'd been in the mood for grilled steak, he popped by the grocery store and picked up the other items they needed as well. There'd only been a short, tension-filled conversation about who was going to pay before he went to the store. He didn't know anything about Paige's financial situation, except for her being homeless. That alone meant things couldn't be good, and as her friend, he wanted to help her. They'd finally compromised—he would buy the groceries, and if she needed anything extra for Emmie, she would buy it.

The week had been one of the best he could remember, and he wanted to keep the peace. He could live with compromise. His dad had told him when he was renovating a room—for the third time—that it was a small thing to keep his wife happy.

Every night he'd looked forward to coming home. They'd make dinner and talk about their days as they ate. Then Paige would give Emmie a bath while he cleaned up.

A few times, if he or Paige didn't have work to catch up on, they would all play a game together. He smiled as he thought about the day before. Emmie had asked to go bowling. She said a girl in her daycare went and said it was the *bestest*.

Blake wasn't sure if he agreed that bowling was the *bestest*, but they'd had a great time. After dinner, he and Paige put on a movie, some action flick she'd picked. It was one he'd been wanting to see, but if someone asked him what he'd thought of it, he couldn't have explained the plot.

He'd sat on the opposite end of the couch from Paige for

over two hours, her scent of vanilla and orange blossoms driving him crazy. It was the same scent she'd worn in college, and it had driven him crazy then too. The only difference was he could act on his feelings back then.

He probably hadn't been this sexually frustrated since he was a teenager, but he was loving their arrangement. He wasn't lonely, and he looked forward to coming home. Maybe he had been kidding himself into thinking that casual dates and hookups were enough. If he and Paige could stay friends and just be roommates, he would miss sex, but his life would still be pretty perfect.

Just thinking about Paige and sex in the same sentence had his cock hard and his jeans tight. He pulled into his driveway and turned off the engine.

Shifting to adjust himself, he blew out a breath, hoping his dick would behave by the time he walked into the house. As he reached for the door handle with one hand and the grocery bags with the other, a familiar tension took over his body. His hands dropped as his back stiffened against the seat.

Since he couldn't fight it, he closed his eyes and let the curse take over.

Images swam in his mind for several seconds before they slowed down, and he found himself on a fog-covered street in San Francisco beside the beach. He knew the year was 1924. The street he was on wasn't yet paved and the smell of salt water mixed in the air with horse manure.

A wind came off the bay, making him shiver as he stood alone in the fog. Just like he knew when and where he was, he knew it was early morning.

A deep sorrow crawled along his skin like it was his own. It wasn't grief like he'd felt when his parents died. More of a longing for something that would never be.

He turned slowly, trying to figure out where it was coming from. On the beach, he spied a man standing as if watching someone. Looking in the same direction as the man, Blake saw a woman walking toward him.

She was wrapped in a cloak, gloves on her hands. The hood of her cloak flew back in the wind, exposing her wavy, bobbed hairstyle. She looked like she was in her twenties, her face unlined and smooth.

Blake stepped off the street and trudged through the sand. He knew from the other episodes that it didn't matter how close he got to the couple; they wouldn't see him.

"Martha, are you all right?" the man asked. "You sounded urgent on the telephone."

"Thank you for coming, George."

Her voice was barely above a whisper and she didn't meet his eyes as she looked down at her hands fidgeting with the ties of her cape.

Blake moved in closer to listen.

Finally, she looked up at George. "Your friendship has meant more to me than you could ever know..." Her words trailed off, and George took a step closer.

"Martha, I have valued your friendship also."

She laughed nervously. "It has taken me years to muster the courage to say this to you, but I need to be honest."

"What is it? You know you can say anything to me, Martha."

"Can I?"

"Of course."

Martha's fingers continued to play with the tie of her cloak. "George." Her voice was soft, almost carried away on the wind, and again Blake moved closer so he could hear them better.

"George," she said again, her voice stronger. "I have loved you for as long as I can remember."

"I love you too."

She shook her head. "No, not like that. I am in love with you, George. I can't keep it a secret any longer, no matter how much it will change everything between us. I kept telling myself that if I loved you fiercely and long enough, it would be enough for both of us."

Her voice wobbled as she let out another nervous laugh. "But that's foolish, isn't it?"

Sadness came over George's features before he smiled softly. He lifted one of Martha's gloved hands and clasped it between both of his.

"Martha, I care deeply for you," he said, his tone reflecting the warmth of his words. "It is my fault that I did not say something sooner. I have known for a long time that your feelings for me were different than mine for you. I wish I could return your love, but I love another. I have decided to propose to Ruth, and I have her father's permission to marry her."

Taking a step back, Martha pulled her hand from George's and grasped her ties once more.

As the air hung heavy between them, neither of them saying a word, Blake felt a connection with Martha. It wasn't exactly the same as what he'd gone through, but he understood what it felt like to hear someone say they were in love with someone else.

Martha wrapped her arms around herself as if she could give her heart strength and protect it from shattering. "I see," she whispered, her voice huskier than before. "I'm glad you told me, and I'm happy for you and Ruth."

George looked down and kicked some sand with the toe of his shoe. "I wish things could be different..." His words fell flat; even Blake knew he didn't really mean them. "Well... I must be going, but we will still be friends and see each other. And you'll come to the wedding?"

Martha nodded and turned away, heading back the way she'd come. "I will never love another," she whispered to herself.

This time, the wind carried her words to Blake.

The air shifted, and Blake found himself in a well-lit ballroom.

A band played on a stage as George and his bride, both dressed in wedding attire, danced while everyone watched.

Blake looked for Martha but couldn't see her in the crowd. He walked through the throngs of people and shivered as his hand went through the arm of a guest.

He spotted Martha leaving the ballroom and followed her. She stopped an attendant and spoke too quietly for Blake to hear. A few moments later, a woman came back with Martha's cloak. Wasting no time, she donned it and left the building.

When the air shifted again, Blake braced himself for what he was about to see. He felt for Martha but understood George too. Love couldn't be forced.

Blake found himself in another brightly lit room, but this time it was a small kitchen, not unlike his own before the renovations.

Martha sat at a table, far older now, perhaps in her fifties or sixties, her hair almost fully gray. Her complexion was no longer one of youth, wrinkles etched into her skin.

She held a young child in her lap and laughed with someone.

Blake had hoped she would find love after George, but regardless of the laughter and child, a shroud of sadness hung over her.

"Thank you for stopping by," Martha said as she stood and handed the child to a much younger woman. "It's so nice to meet new neighbors. You're welcome to drop by anytime."

They said their goodbyes, and Martha closed the door behind the other woman.

Blake was ready for the next shift in the air. Instead of being transported to another time, a movie reel of Martha's remaining years flashed in front of him. She went about her daily life, connecting with people and sometimes laughing, but each night she went to bed alone, wrapped in her unrequited love.

A draft hit Blake as the curse released him. He still sat in his truck, all the warmth in the cab long gone.

He could picture Martha getting on with her life, but never quite feeling complete. A pall of sadness for her loss of love surrounded her for her entire life as surely as her cloak did.

Blake looked at his house and debated what to do. With Martha's sadness clinging to him, he wasn't sure if he should go inside. He could text Paige that an emergency had come up at work. That didn't happen often on a Sunday, but it was possible.

He took the grocery bag and got out of his truck. Hiding wasn't the way to go. He needed to stick to his plan to have a friendship, and only a friendship, with Paige. With each curse episode, he knew he'd made the right decision. He'd guard his heart at all costs to avoid the lifelong pain that came with heartbreak. Even the curse was showing him that was all that was possible.

CHAPTER ELEVEN

Wednesday, October 16

Sitting on top of the bed as Emmie cuddled in next to her, Paige read a book about cows and pigs dancing. She didn't even need to read the words as she'd memorized them a long time ago—that story and about a dozen others.

She finished and looked down to see that Emmie had fallen asleep. Laying the book on the stand between the bed and the crib, she carefully lifted herself off the bed while she laid Emmie flat and tucked the blankets around her.

"Mommy loves you," she whispered, giving Emmie a kiss.

Paige looked around to make sure everything was put away, nothing lying out for Emmie to trip on if she got up in the night.

After putting the books back on the shelf and a doll in a bin, she turned on the small light above the bed.

Flicking off the overhead light, she left the door ajar. She looked at her own bedroom and debated what to do. When Blake had returned from the grocery store the other day, something had seemed off with him. He'd said he was fine, but he'd been in a sullen mood all evening. She finally told him she was tired and would be calling it a night after Emmie was in bed. Living with Craig had given her enough moodiness to last a lifetime.

The next morning Blake had seemed fine, laughing with her and Emmie. She knew it couldn't have been him just not wanting to go to work on Monday, because he loved his job. One night he'd brought her up to date on all the changes he'd implemented at Akermans, and his excitement for the company was easy to see. She didn't understand why he wouldn't just tell her what was wrong, especially if he truly wanted them to be friends.

Her feelings seemed to be all over the place. That wasn't exactly uncommon for her, but she hated feeling indecisive. She wasn't exactly wavering on what she wanted, but sometimes she thought about having more with Blake. Then she would remember what it had been like living with Craig and she'd wonder if the living arrangement with Blake was a mistake. Could his shifting moods be an indication that she might have to tiptoe around him too?

If she left before she got another commission check and her debt still wasn't under control, she would be right back to where she'd been before moving in with Blake. Maybe worse because she wouldn't have the strip mall to fall back on.

Making her decision, she turned and headed downstairs, wanting to spend time with him despite all her shifting feelings. Maybe the mood thing the other day had been a one-off.

Even when she loved him years ago, she couldn't remember if she'd been as obsessed with wanting to see him as she was now. Not only see him but touch him too. Most nights lately she'd had to pull out her battery-operated boyfriend because Blake had the ability to heat her up, even without touching her.

At the bottom of the stairs, Paige heard jazz music playing softly, and it took her back to their time in college. She walked further into the room and a laugh bubbled out of her when she saw Blake.

BLAKE KNEW he'd been a bit of a moody ass on Sunday night. He did his best to shake off Martha's sadness, but it had stuck with him despite everything he'd done.

He and Paige were friends of a sort, but not like they used to be. They hadn't lacked for conversation, talking about Emmie and what they did each day. It was all superficial, but it was a start. Not that Blake always needed their conversations to be deep and philosophical because being sucked into the curse gave him more than enough deep emotions to deal with most days. But if he and Paige learned who each other was now, maybe trust would grow between them.

While he was thinking he sat at the table and set up the backgammon board. He heard Paige on the stairs and rotated in his chair to see her as she walked into the room. Dressed in yoga pants and a baggy sweater, her hair up in a messy bun leaving her neck exposed, made him want to kiss her. *No.* He had to remind himself that wasn't on the table. They were friends.

"Care for a rousing game of backgammon?" he asked, his face splitting into a grin.

"Absolutely." She pulled out a chair across from him and sat. "It's been a long time. I'm not sure I even remember the rules."

"No problem." He gave her a refresher and they launched right into playing.

The first game didn't take long. Blake sent her pieces back to the start so many times that he won handily. The second time wasn't quite so fast as Paige got the handle of the game, but he still beat her.

Paige groaned. "Let's talk while we play, and maybe it'll drag out the game so it will be longer between each ass-kicking you hand me."

Blake barked a laugh. "I'm game. No pun intended."

"Yeah, right."

Her eyes crinkled in the outer corners as she moved her first piece on the board, and he could tell she was holding in a laugh.

"We haven't talked much about our families and I'm curious what your brothers have been up to."

"You want an overview or the details?" he asked.

"Hmmm… how about somewhere in the middle?"

He eyed the board; he could send another one of her pieces back but chose a different move. At the rate she was going, she'd lose again, but he didn't want to clobber her every game.

"You know that Jake came on full-time as the VP of residential operations when we graduated college?"

"Yes, his mom told me one of the times we met for coffee. She said you expanded the company?"

"I did. Up to that point, we only had one operations division, so I split them into residential and commercial. Stewart stayed on as VP of commercial ops until he retired in June. Uh… you might want to rethink that move," he warned, looking at where Paige was about to place her game piece.

"What?"

"If you do that, you'll leave these two vulnerable." He

pointed out which ones. Chances were she still wouldn't win, but if she improved, they'd both have more fun.

"This okay?"

He smirked. "No." They played the next several moves with Blake talking her through each one.

"Thanks. I'll get better. Now, Jake is a VP; is he married yet?"

"No, but he has a dog. Chewie, a St. Bernard. And he's become a bit of a mountain man… Jake, not the dog. Ha, both, I guess. Jake has a huge beard and he wears flannel shirts." He chuckled just thinking how different Jake was from when he was in college. "You might not even recognize him now."

Paige captured one of his pieces and winked at him. "I'm sure I would." She paused and smiled. "I remember the first time I heard all about the notorious juniors—Blake and Jake. You were practically famous on campus."

"Come on, you're making that up. You never said you knew who I was when we met at that party."

"Of course I didn't. Before you arrived, there were a bunch of freshmen girls talking about how *hot* Blake and Jake were."

Blake moved his last piece, winning the game, and sat back, arms across his chest. He still wasn't sure he believed her.

"Did you just beat me again?"

"Yes. Another game?"

"One more. If we keep playing, one day I'll beat you."

And that was his plan. To improve her skills so she'd keep playing. And when he'd earned her trust, she would see they were good together and she'd stay.

"At least I get to keep going first since I lose every game." She moved her first piece. "I'm looking forward to seeing Jake again. He always seemed like your brother to me, but tell me about your real brothers. Wait… let me see if I can remember the order."

Blake smiled, knowing what she was talking about. His mom had loved the story of how he and his brothers were named and told almost anyone who would listen. Both his mom and dad had really long names. They claimed it was a pain to write them on documents and constantly having to spell them. They hadn't wanted any of their children to go through that, so they picked all single-syllable names and named them in alphabetical order.

Having Paige bring up happy memories was something he needed. He had promised himself he would make thinking of happy memories a habit and he hadn't. With Paige around, maybe it would be easier to remember the good times.

"None of your names begin with an A because of Akerman," she said like she was proud of herself for remembering. "So you're the B," she said, and held up her hand, ticking off one finger. "C is Cade, D is Dane, E… wait, there's no E. Why was that again?"

"Mom didn't like any of the boy names that started with E. Cade and I thought it would be a good idea to change Ford's name to Ernie… I think he and Gage were about four at the time. Of course, being older brothers, we wanted to do it to annoy him, but Ford said he liked Ernie because it was his favorite Muppet, so he was good with it."

Paige laughed. "I'm guessing you lost interest when it no longer annoyed him?"

"Pretty much."

"So no E. And since you said F is Ford, and G is Gage, you ruined my game," she said with a mock pout. "What were your parents' full names again?"

"My dad was Zachariah Bartholomew Akerman, Zach for short. And Mom was Alexandria Evangelina Montgomery, and then became Akerman."

"Those names are definitely a mouthful."

"What about your parents? Not their names... I know they're Steve and Kristie, but how are they?"

"Good. Both retired. They moved to Arizona last year just before my divorce. Emmie and I video chat with them every week."

"Did you chat with them on Saturday? Emmie mentioned the next morning that she told Grandma and Grandpa all about bowling."

A panicked look crossed Paige's face. "I wasn't trying to keep secrets from you."

He'd seen that look a lot over the last week and a half. He expected it had something to do with how her ex-husband had treated her. "Paige, you're an adult. If you want to keep secrets, you can. Although I wouldn't exactly call you not telling me about a video chat a secret."

"Okay," she said, but in a voice that said she didn't believe him.

"What did your parents say about you and Emmie moving in with me?"

"I didn't tell them."

"Why not?"

Her shoulders hunched forward and she picked up a game piece as if she suddenly found it fascinating. "I... uh... I told them we got a new apartment, but it's on a temporary lease."

He knew she didn't trust him, but it sounded like she wasn't even going to try. He tried to keep the hurt out of his tone when he asked, "You plan on leaving soon?"

"No... I don't think so. But what if this doesn't work out? Ah... you're good with that, right?"

In a heartbeat, their conversation had gone from laughing about his brothers to a palpable presence that draped over the room like a thick and suffocating blanket.

Blake hated the insecurity and nervousness he saw reflected in Paige's eyes.

He stood and walked around the table. Holding out his hand, he waited for her to place hers in his. When she did, he gently pulled her up and held her upper arms lightly. "I'm not mad and you can do whatever you want. I just like having you and Emmie here."

Her breath came out on a shudder. "Okay."

"Can I give you a hug?" he asked, looking into her eyes.

She nodded, and when he opened his arms, she walked right into them.

Blake felt like everything she remembered, plus more. His embrace was exciting and comfortable, familiar and new. He didn't hold her too tightly, but with the feel of his muscular chest underneath her cheek and his fresh, citrusy scent surrounding her, she wondered what it would feel like if he did.

During the week and a half they'd lived together she'd begun to want some of the closeness they used to have. But every time she thought about talking to him about it, she would panic and waffle like she had earlier in the evening.

She was so afraid of losing her independence that she wondered if in trying to protect it, she was losing other parts of herself. For years she'd identified as what she was to others—a daughter, a wife, a mother. Now she was a realtor, a friend, and a roommate. She used to be a sexual woman, but she'd lost that along the way.

Having sex with Craig had knocked down her self-esteem until she no longer felt pretty or even capable of anything, let alone like the sexual creature she used to be.

She wanted to be that person again. It wouldn't be easy, and she wasn't even sure she'd be able to confess to Blake all she'd been through and what problems she now faced. But if she tried and she still couldn't let go, at least she would have the intimacy she hadn't had in a long time. And it could be fun.

Digging deep for her courage, she pulled out of Blake's embrace so she could look him in the eyes. "Kiss me, Blake."

His eyes widened and he took a step back. "I wasn't asking for that, Paige. I just wanted to give you some comfort."

"I know." She licked her lips and Blake's gaze dropped to her mouth as she took a step toward him.

"Are you sure?"

"Yes. I want you to kiss me." She felt empowered by voicing what she wanted.

Paige moved closer to Blake and wrapped her arms around the back of his neck. Lifting onto her toes, she tilted her chin up and pressed her lips to his.

They were soft, and when his tongue touched hers, she opened her mouth, letting him in. Their tongues tangled in a slow, exploratory dance. And just like their very first kiss years ago, she felt a tingle in her core.

The sudden desire from such a simple touch surprised her. She hadn't felt anything like it in years.

Blake lightly bit her bottom lip before running his tongue along it and deepening their kiss.

His hands rested on her hips, but he kept several inches of space between their bodies.

Paige wanted more. Pressing against him, she could feel his hard length and knew he was as aroused as she was, but he was letting her set the pace.

The kiss went on for several more minutes until he lifted

his head. Their heavy breathing drowned out the sound of the soft jazz coming from the speakers.

A sexy smile graced his lips. "Wow. I wasn't expecting that."

She huffed out a small laugh. "It was good, wasn't it?"

"It was." A worried look replaced his smile, and he pulled back. "I'd like nothing more than to kiss you again, Paige, but I'm not the relationship kind of guy anymore."

She wasn't sure if she wanted to laugh at his arrogance or cry that he might not accept her next offer.

Getting into his space again, she walked forward until his back was against the wall. Blake had never been a pushover, but he was probably worried about ruining their friendship. Little did he know.

She poked him in the chest. "Awfully arrogant of you, don't you think, Blake? Did I say I wanted to get married? No, I did not. I will never get married again. Never. You got that?"

The corners of his mouth twitched slightly as if he was trying to hold back a grin. "No marriage. Got it."

"Good. Now, kiss me again."

His eyes widened with surprise. "Yes, ma'am."

Blake grasped her by the hips and flipped their positions so Paige's back was now against the wall. He planted one hand on the wall beside her head and cupped the back of her neck with his other. He leaned down so slowly, she felt her breath catch in anticipation and she parted her lips in invitation.

This kiss was different from the last—more sultry and exploratory—as he took his time.

When she gave his chest a soft push until he lifted his head, both of them were panting. With his hand still planted on the wall, he leaned his forehead against hers. That kiss was even better than the first. Maybe because it was still new between them. She figured that eventually their chemistry would level off, like it had with her ex-husband. Although she wasn't sure it had ever been like this.

Now that she knew they were thinking the same thing, she was ready to take the next steps toward rediscovering her inner sexual creature.

She pressed a little harder on his chest, forcing him back. "That was fun. We should do it again sometime," she said, wiggling her eyebrows.

Blake laughed. "I agree. Often."

Paige knew what she wanted to say, but that downtrodden person she'd become in the last decade hesitated, worried she would say the wrong thing.

When Blake turned toward the table to pack up the game, Paige dug deep to find the sultry side she used to have. Then she straightened her shoulders, pulling on the woman who'd had the courage to leave her abusive ex-husband and build a new life for her and her daughter.

"Blake?"

He turned around and faced her. "Yeah?"

"Do you think we're doing well as roommates and friends?"

"Yes. Don't you?" he asked, looking confused.

"Yes. Very well. Which got me thinking… what if we added something to our friend agreement?"

"Like what?"

"Some benefits." Paige smirked at Blake's surprised look.

"Benefits? Friends' benefits?… Just so I'm clear… Are you suggesting we have sex?"

Paige grinned. "Yes. Friends, roommates, rousing games of backgammon, and sex without strings."

He barked a laugh. "I accept." He stuck out his hand and they shook on it.

They worked together to finish boxing up the game "I had fun tonight," he told her.

"Me too. Want to go for round two tomorrow?"

Blake smirked. "Of what?"

Good question. They should probably clarify that. "Let me ask you a question first."

When he nodded, she thought about how to phrase what she wanted to ask. "You've had friends with benefits before, right? So when did you see them? On weekends?"

"Mostly."

"Then that's what we'll do. We'll save sex for the weekends."

"Sure. I can live with that. Saturday, then?"

Paige's inner sexy creature wanted to say yes, but the other part of her was still a bit cautious and wanted to make sure they were doing the right thing. "How about next Saturday? After the Halloween party? That will give us ten days to get tested and time to make sure it's what we both want."

"Agreed. And as much as I'm looking forward to our benefits, I want you to know that when I pulled out the game earlier tonight, I just wanted to get to know you again."

"I know." She was looking forward to the benefits too, and as long as she kept her independence, she might be able to have everything she wanted.

CHAPTER TWELVE

Saturday, October 26

Standing in the large foyer of Akerman Contracting with folding tables and chairs set up, Paige couldn't help but smile at Blake.

"Who wants a piece of cake?" he asked loudly, his voice full of excitement as he egged on the horde of children surrounding the table.

A chorus of *me's* and *I do's* responded.

Earlier in the day, Paige had worried Blake wouldn't be able to see where he was walking, let alone be able to do something like cut a cake.

"I've got it under control, dude," he'd assured her in an exaggerated tone, getting into character.

Blake, Jake, Ford, and Gage were dressed in elaborate Teenage Mutant Ninja Turtle costumes. Except for the colored masks over their eyes, they all looked the same to Paige, but Blake had informed her that he was Michelangelo, Jake was Leonardo, Ford was Raphael, and Gage was

Donatello. She learned later that Dane had drawn the short straw, so he was dressed as a rat named Master Splinter.

Their elaborate costumes came complete with molded turtle heads. Blake said they went all out every year.

This was her first time seeing all his brothers in years and the youngest ones as adults. As much as she would have liked to *see* them, she was having so much fun watching them joke around for all the kids.

Cade told her he'd opted out of the group costumes so he, Jessica, and Malcolm could dress up as a theme. Dressed as the characters from Toy Story, Cade was Woody, Jessica was Jessie, and Malcolm was the most adorable little Buzz Lightyear.

"Wait," Blake called out. "Where are my brothers?"

"We're here, dude," the turtle in the red mask answered. If she hadn't confused them, it was Ford. She'd made sure to remember that Blake's mask was orange; after that, it didn't really matter.

A photographer moved throughout the crowd, snapping pictures. When Paige pulled out her phone to snap some photos, Blake had told her he had it covered. He was true to his word. As soon as they arrived at Akerman Contracting, Blake guided them over to a large blowup pumpkin on the front lawn where the photographer was taking pictures of everyone. They took some together, some of her and Emmie, and Emmie on her own. Paige was dressed as Ana to match Emmie's Elsa. She'd parted her hair on the side and made two long braids to hang over her shoulders. The dress made up the rest of the costume, which Paige had been thankful for. No extensive makeup or awkward costume parts to worry about.

When the turtles and the rat posed for pictures together, they drew quite a crowd.

"Hey, dude, we were getting some pizza," the turtle with

the blue mask said, coming up beside Blake. Turning to the kids, the blue mask turtle, maybe Jake, put his hands on his hips and leaned back in an exaggerated pose. "All you dudes like pizza, right?"

The kids screamed in excitement. Emmie was right in the front, perched on a stool, her Elsa wig pushed back off her forehead. Blake had taken her around to all the games and made sure her treat bag was full, the two of them hamming it up and laughing all afternoon.

The turtles continued to talk to the kids, amping up their enthusiasm.

As if scripted, Master Splinter pushed between two of the turtles and stood in front of the cake.

"Now, my sons," Master Splinter said, his tone serious as he held up his hand. "It is time. Sometimes the path to the greatest joy is cake."

She'd never watched the show or read the comics, but judging by the chuckles from the turtles and some of the adults gathered around, Dane must be in character.

He turned to Blake's turtle. "Michaelangelo, cut the cake."

"Yes, Father," Blake said on a laugh. He raised his knife and then stopped midair. "Wait. We have one more cake." He turned toward a hallway off the foyer, and the crowds parted as two men carried in another large cake.

When they placed it on the table, Paige could see that the cake had a line of icing down the middle. One side was decorated like the red mask turtle and the other side like the purple mask turtle.

"We have two birthdays to celebrate today. Raphael and Donatello, come. Cut your cake."

One of the men who had carried the cake in handed a knife to each of the turtles.

"Let's sing hap—"

"No singing," the purple mask turtle said, cutting off Master Splinter.

Tension held in the air for only a moment before Blake moved to stand beside his brothers. "We don't need any singing, right, dudes?" Blake called to the kids.

"Right!" the kids yelled back.

Making a big show out of cutting the cake, Blake held the large knife up high and his brothers did the same. "On one. Three, two, one."

All three turtles brought their knives down, slicing through their cakes, and shouted, "Cowabunga!"

Paige laughed again, something she'd been doing all afternoon. She didn't think the turtles could have gotten the kids any more wound up, but they did. There were shouts of "cowabunga" everywhere.

Linda and Denise, who Paige had met earlier, elbowed the turtles to the side and took over the cake-cutting. When the first few plates held a slice of cake, they passed them to the turtles, who handed them out, while the ladies continue to cut more.

Paige would have offered to help, but there seemed to be enough volunteers already. Emmie didn't even need her help because Blake gave her a piece of the turtle cake and continued to check on her.

Blake came over and handed her a piece of cake before leaning against the wall beside her. "Can you hold my cake for a second?" he asked.

"Sure." She took his plate and waited while he pushed the molded head of his costume up enough that she could see his face. His skin was flushed. "Hot under there?"

A laugh rumbled up from his chest as he took his cake back. "You have no idea. I think I've sweated off a couple of pounds."

"Will you need to go straight to bed when you get home?" she teased.

His smile was slow and wicked as his gaze met hers. "First a shower and then to bed, but not to sleep."

Paige knew she was flushed now too. The last ten days had been sexually frustrating but still some of the best of her life. Each night after Emmie was in bed, she and Blake either played backgammon or watched a movie. Their conversations were easy and fun, but by the time they went to their separate bedrooms, there was underlying sexual tension. Her battery-operated boyfriend was getting a workout. It wasn't enough anymore, but it was at least taking the edge off.

Last weekend they kissed again but didn't go any further. It was an effort on both their parts to stop, but tonight they wouldn't have to.

"Did you get enough?" Blake asked, pulling her from her lust-filled thoughts.

She looked down at the forgotten cake in her hand. "Yes, thanks."

"Be right back."

Emmie was chatting up a storm, her face covered in green icing. As soon as she'd met Malcolm that afternoon, she'd taken on the role of big sister. He was sitting in a highchair beside her, babbling away.

Blake came back, adopting his previous position against the wall beside her, and handed her a bottle of water. "Figured you might need something to wash down all the sugar. I think I'll be buzzed all night."

"You and me both."

"Good. We won't be tired." He winked at her.

Feeling her face heat up again, she decided to change the topic or she would need to change her panties soon. "Why Teenage Mutant Ninja Turtles?"

"Because Gage said he'd be here and TMNT was his favorite growing up."

"He doesn't live close enough to get back often?"

"He does, but no, he doesn't come home much. I'm hoping that will change soon."

Paige wondered if Blake knew his tone changed when he talked about his brothers. His voice softened, similar to when he talked about Emmie and Malcolm. Family was important to him. It always had been, but she expected the increased need to have his family around him could be because he was the oldest and both his parents were gone now. Regardless of how many times he told her he didn't want a family, his actions said something different. Everything he did spoke to family.

Blake pushed away from the wall. "I think this will wind down soon so I'm going to get started on the clean-up."

"Do you need help?"

"No, we've got it covered. Besides"—he pointed at Emmie and grinned—"I think you'll have enough to clean up."

Blake laughed and walked off as Paige let out a small groan and headed over to her daughter.

"Did you have fun?" Paige asked Emmie as she washed her hands and face with wet wipes. Someone had brought out several containers of them and paper towels. This definitely wasn't their first rodeo.

"The bestest," Emmie said, smiling so wide her green teeth showed. "Did you see the dog? I petted Chewie. He's HUGE. Jake's his dad—he's a turtle. Jake said Chewie can come to our house. And maybe daycare too! For reading day!"

"We can talk about community reading time later. What else did you like?"

"I liked the big pumpkin and the cake. And the game with the bean bags. But not the scary house." Emmie shivered.

"Blake picked me up. I like Malcolm. He's a baby, but like a little brother. Can I have a little brother?"

"I think that's my cue," Cade said with Malcolm in his arms, coming up beside Paige.

"Thanks for the save," she whispered to him.

"Any time." He turned to Emmie. "You're going to have a sleepover at our house tonight."

Emmie's eyes widened and she bounced in her chair. "Yay!"

"Are you sure you and Jessica are still up for this?" she asked Cade.

"Yes, we'll be fine. We'll run them around a bit to wear off some of the sugar. Blake already put Emmie's bag and car seat in my SUV, so we're all set."

A few minutes later, Emmie and Malcolm were all buckled in the vehicle. Paige smiled at Cade and Jessica. "Thank you for this. Just let me know when I can return the favor."

"Definitely," Jessica said before getting into the front passenger seat.

After they drove off, Paige went in search of Blake.

She didn't have to look far. He, Jake, and his brothers were in the main foyer, discarded pieces from their costumes in a pile on the floor. They were laughing with each other, and she wondered if she should wait outside.

Before she could decide what to do, Blake noticed her and called her over.

"Paige, I'd like to re-introduce you to my brothers now that they don't all look like turtles."

"Or a rat," one brother teased.

Blake grinned. "Or a rat. That's Dane, Master Splinter."

"Dane is enough." Dane offered his hand to Paige. "Good to see you again."

"You too." Now that all the Akerman men were without

their costumes, she could fully take in their adult versions. They were on the tall side and good looking, but Blake was the only blond in the group. Dane's hair, like Cade's, was dark brown, but with blond streaks. Cade's was swept to the side and off his forehead, but Dane's would probably be considered a sexy mess. He had a few days' growth of beard and everything about Dane said relaxed and easygoing.

"You remember Jake?" Blake asked, pointing to the bearded man beside him. A dog sat at his side.

"You're right, I don't think I would have recognized him; he is kind of a mountain man," she said in mock seriousness as Blake and Jake both laughed. Beard or no beard, he was still a good-looking guy, but it was always his inner protectiveness that had drawn her to him. When she'd walked away from Blake, she'd left Jake and his family behind too. She offered her hand. "It's been a while."

"It has." Jake used her outstretched hand to pull her into a hug. "Glad you're back," he whispered against her ear before letting her go.

"This must be Chewie." She bent over and petted the St. Bernard to hide her flush from the emotions Jake's comment had brought to her cheeks. "Emmie was telling me all about him."

"Chewie is a better brother than Jake is," one of the brothers said, causing everyone to laugh.

That brother walked up to Paige. "Hi, I'm Ford," he said, flashing his pearly whites in his clean-shaven face as he stuck out his hand. "I was still in high school the last time we met."

Blake had said that Ford came across as the charmer of the group. When she asked what he meant by *came across*, he said that Ford was deeper than he looked. Paige shook his hand, responding, "Yes, I think so."

She turned to the last brother, once more offering her hand. "I don't think we've met before."

"No, I don't think so either. I'm Gage." He shook her hand and smiled, but it was more subdued than his brothers'.

Paige knew Ford and Gage were twins, but even with their similar coloring and facial features, they were easy to tell apart. Gage's hair was longer, several days of stubble covered his face, compared to Ford being clean shaven, and tattoos covered his arms.

With the introductions out of the way, Paige wasn't sure what to do next. It occurred to her that maybe Blake's brothers, except for Cade, didn't know she and Emmie were living with him. What if Blake wanted to keep their arrangement a secret? Should she leave now before it was obvious they were going home together?

She looked up at him as the familiar sense of doing something wrong swamped her. Craig had hated it when she hesitated to make a decision. He also hated it if she did something he considered inappropriate. It didn't matter that Blake and Craig weren't the same person; she'd lived in that environment for so long she couldn't always stop the thoughts before they got to her.

She was still second guessing herself when Blake walked up to Gage and gripped his shoulder. "Thanks for coming. You going to stay the night?"

Gage gave Ford a look Paige couldn't decipher. "No, I've got to get back. Ford and I are just going to go for a beer first."

Blake dropped his hand. "Talk soon."

"Ready?" he asked Paige.

They said their goodbyes and walked the few houses to Blake's. During the short walk, neither of them spoke. Paige wasn't even sure she could have said anything intelligent, her thoughts swimming with what was about to happen.

Blake unlocked the front door and waited for her to enter, then locked the door behind them. She kicked her shoes off and hung her bag and coat on hooks. Seconds later, Blake's hands were on her upper arms and her back against the door. His coat was already gone, and with the heat from his body so close to hers, her breath quickened with excitement. She was thankful their tests had come back negative, and she was on the pill, so they wouldn't need a condom, because she was ready and didn't want to mess around.

"I've been waiting for this moment," Blake said before his lips dropped to hers. There wasn't any of the sweetness of their previous kisses. He captured her mouth like he wanted to devour her. Good thing, because she wanted to devour him too.

Paige thrust her hands into his short hair, not wanting him to let go. He crushed his muscled body against her, his hard length igniting a sudden flood of wetness in her panties, unlike anything she'd felt in years.

She moaned, tightening her grip in his hair as he pulled back.

"Baby, I'm sweaty."

"I don't care," she said, her voice almost a whine.

"I know, but I've got something better in mind."

Blake held her hips as she let go of his hair and she gasped when he lifted her.

"Wrap your legs around me," he said. She did and he headed for the stairs.

"Oh, my god. This is so sexy." She ground against him, causing a groan to erupt from deep within his chest. "Just don't hurt yourself," she said against his jaw as she continued to kiss him.

Not even out of breath, he climbed the stairs like he did it with her in his arms every day. "I could carry you all the time, baby."

Swoon. As she felt herself melting into him, the annoying little voice in her head told her she had just given up control to Blake.

With the promise of amazing sex ahead, she shoved that voice down deep.

BLAKE LOWERED Paige onto the bathroom counter. "Don't go anywhere," he said, giving her a smirk as he leaned into the shower to turn it on.

"How about I get undressed?"

Just when he thought his dick couldn't get any harder, the sound of her husky voice proved him wrong. It had been years since he wanted a woman the way he craved Paige.

"No, I want to undress you. Reacquaint myself with your body." He was going to take his time, learning every inch of her all over again.

"Next time." Paige tugged up the dress she'd worn for her costume and pulled it over her head, sliding off the counter.

He feasted on the glorious sight in front of him. Her breasts spilled from a white, push-up lace bra, and all he could think about was getting his mouth on them. Savoring her naked body, instead of revealing one piece of her at a time, would work too. He was an adaptable guy. As long as he got to touch and taste her soft skin, he'd be happy.

Needing her, he trailed his fingers down her neck and onto her chest, eliciting a full-body shiver. Bending over, he filled his lungs with her vanilla and orange blossom scent. His lips then followed his fingers' path.

Pulling one bra cup down, he ran his tongue over her pert nipple. He nipped and laved at it before sucking it into his mouth. Urged on by Paige's small gasps, he lowered the other cup and took turns lavishing both her breasts with his hands and mouth.

He dropped to his knees, kissing down her torso, and reached for the waistband of her leggings.

"No." Paige pushed at his shoulders. "Uh, maybe later."

She pulled away from him and shimmied her leggings down her hips. That was the second time she'd stopped him. Could he have taken their agreement in a way she hadn't intended? For him, sex, even without strings still meant taking their time and enjoying each other. It didn't have to be rushed. Didn't Paige want that too?

Paige removed the rest of her clothes and added them to the growing pile on the floor, appearing unaware of the conflict warring within him. This was their first time together after years apart, and he wanted to relish every second. He shouldn't be unhappy with her fast and furious approach because he didn't want a commitment any more than she did, but something seemed off.

Not waiting for him, Paige pulled open the glass door and stepped into his massive, walk-in shower, right under the water. It cascaded over her body as she closed her eyes and tipped her head back. Her hands slicked through her wet hair.

Deciding to follow Paige's lead for now, he grasped the front of his shirt and pulled it off, dropping it to the floor. He watched her as he shucked the rest of his clothes.

When his briefs hit the pile of clothes, he ran his eyes over her, noticing the differences in her body. From the moment he had first seen her years ago, she drew him in, and he'd always found her beautiful. Now, he found her stunning —curvier and softer than she'd been before, radiating femininity. *Magnificent.*

His initial need to savor her intensified. Blake joined her in the glass stall, shutting the door behind him. He'd always been leery about having sex standing up on a slippery surface, but he could find other ways pleasure her.

Paige opened her eyes and met his gaze, a sly smile teasing her lips. "Took you a while. Second thoughts?"

"Never." Paige was offering him everything he wanted—a close friendship and sex without any complications. He'd be stupid not to take it. But it was the niggling feeling that something wasn't right that made him want to slow things down, even though he decided just to follow her lead.

Turning on the second showerhead, he quickly soaped himself up and rinsed before shutting it off. The costume had been fun but hot, leaving him a sweaty mess.

Paige watched him, her eyes running down his body. The tip of her tongue slipped out to run along her upper lip as she looked up at him with hooded eyes, like a siren's call.

He moved into her space. As he wrapped one hand around the back of her neck and the other at the small of her back, keeping space between their bodies, she placed her hands on his chest. Being naked with Paige felt like a dream come true. If he wasn't careful, he'd come like a teenager having a wet dream.

He lowered his mouth to hers, nipping on her lower lip like he had her nipple, then slowly ran his tongue over it. Their moans mingled as their mouths played.

Inching forward, he backed her against the wall. Placing his hands on the tile on either side of her, he trapped her hands between them. Finally, unable to resist any longer, he thrust his lower body against hers.

She arched into him. "Yes. More, Blake."

Her fingernails dug into his chest, sending zings of pleasure right to his groin. He dropped to his knees.

Determined to make it good for her, he trailed his lips down the front of her body while his hands explored her backside, continuing the journey they started before. He cupped her ass, pulling her closer as his mouth moved lower.

"No." She pushed on his shoulders the same as she had earlier. "Please, Blake, just fuck me."

Standing, he cupped her face, looking into her eyes, needing to see her reaction to his question. "You used to love it. What's wrong?"

"Nothing. I want you inside me."

Moving his hand to the back of her neck, he pulled her into him and kissed her. He couldn't shake the feeling that something was wrong, but he would take his cues from her. She wasn't being soft and gentle, so he responded in kind. He snaked his other hand down her body and dipped a finger inside her.

"Yes." She wrapped one leg around his hip, opening herself up to him. "Please, I need more."

Still kissing her, he inserted another finger and rubbed his thumb on her clit. He increased his pace, his fingers fucking her faster and deeper.

Paige moaned and thrust into his hand, working herself on his fingers.

"Yes, baby," he rasped. "Fuck yourself on me. I want you to come all over my fingers. I want to feel you squeeze my fingers like a vise. Then I'll take you to bed and fuck you again. Hard."

He rotated his fingers upward, searching for the spot that always set Paige off, while he continued rubbing her clit with his thumb.

Paige cried out and rocked against him faster.

He kissed her hard, remembering how she liked to be consumed by sensation.

She ripped her mouth away from his. "Yes," she yelled as

her muscles tightened around his fingers. She lowered her leg, and he kissed her softly, waiting for her breathing to come back to normal.

After they rinsed off, Blake took his time drying Paige, letting his hands linger on her skin. He wanted to please her, but he also wanted to know why she had faked her orgasm.

CHAPTER THIRTEEN

Paige rested her hand on Blake's shoulder as he lifted her foot to finish drying her off. He grabbed another towel and dried himself. He hung the towels on the rack and took her hand, leading her into the bedroom.

She chewed on her inner lip as guilt ate at her. Maybe she should have been honest and not faked her orgasm, but she worried about what he would think if he knew he hadn't given her one. It wasn't like she hadn't been turned on. She had, even more than she'd expected. Since he hadn't said anything, hopefully he didn't know she'd faked it.

She'd been so close to coming, closer than she'd ever been with her husband. Her orgasm had built and built, and when Blake had captured her mouth with his, there'd been a moment when she'd have bet money that her body was going to let loose with the kind of explosive detonation that she used to have with him. When it didn't, she'd been too embarrassed to explain that her body just didn't respond the way it used to.

Blake picked her up and laid her on the bed, then crawled up and planked over her. "You're so beautiful," he whispered.

She blushed. "You make me feel beautiful."

"Because you are." He caressed her cheek as he brushed the wet strands of her hair off her face. Their gazes locked like they had in the shower, and if she didn't know better, she'd have said he looked at her with love in his eyes.

Overcome with emotion and guilt, she stretched up and brushed her lips across his, needing his touch.

He lowered onto his elbows, still hovering over her as he kissed her. She wanted to spend forever kissing him. He made her feel more than she'd felt in years. The feeling was both glorious and scary. On one hand, she felt cherished when she was with him. But on the other, she still feared she'd end up being reliant on him for more than just a place to live. What if she was eventually willing to do whatever it took to please him? Would she lose herself again? Could faking her orgasm mean she was doing it already?

For a split second, she wondered if their friends-with-benefits agreement had been a mistake. Then he lowered his body fully on to hers and all thoughts fled. They kissed and rubbed against each other. Her mind finally shut off, and she was nothing but a mass of sensation—lips against lips, his callused hands along her skin, the rough hair on his legs against her smooth ones, his hard cock against her soft folds.

She roamed her hands along his sides and up over his back. Like a flashback hitting her, she remembered he used to like the sting of her fingernails dragging along his skin and wondered if he still did. Needing to know, she tentatively ran her nails down his back.

"Fuck, yes. That feels so good." He ducked his head into the hollow by her neck, melting at her touch. She did it again, enjoying the way he groaned and rubbed himself harder against her.

He lifted himself slightly away from her and gave her a

wicked, sexy grin. "More of that later. But now…" His voice trailed off as he kissed his way down her body.

The brush of his light beard as he dragged it along her stomach lit her up. She thrust up into him, getting wetter. Then she worried. She couldn't remember the last time she'd been so turned on. What if she was too wet? Would he think that was gross? Or if she wasn't wet enough, would he blame her?

When she'd been with Blake in the past, she hadn't been a virgin, but she wouldn't have called herself worldly when it came to sex either. She'd never orgasmed with a guy, until Blake. He used to love going down on her and using his fingers because he could make her come hard every time. Like see-stars-behind-her-eyes hard. Maybe she had nothing to worry about now that she was back with Blake.

She closed her eyes, trying to let the sensations take her again, but as Blake moved lower, the more up in her head she got. He rubbed his beard along her inner thighs, something she used to love, but now all she could do was think. She'd spent years walking on proverbial eggshells, especially in bed, and couldn't shake the feeling that she was going to do something wrong.

What if it didn't work this time? She felt herself get dry and stiff. Anxiety was such a bitch.

Blake lifted his head, looking up her body at her. "What's wrong?" He'd probably felt her stiffen.

"Nothing. I just want you inside me." It wasn't a lie, just not the entire truth. She crooked a finger at him, hoping her smile looked sultry and not crazed.

He crawled up her body, and she felt herself relax. He kissed her, then went back on his knees and grabbed his cock, giving it several long strokes. "This what you want?" he teased.

"Yes." She licked her lips and went on her knees too.

Grasping onto his thighs, she leaned forward and slowly lowered her mouth over his hard length. His hand dropped away and grasped the back of her head. He didn't push, just held her.

"Christ. Yes, baby."

Paige took him as deep as she could, then back out and swirled her tongue around his glans. Repeating the motion several times, she brought him closer to the edge. She loved hearing his groans, knowing he liked what she was doing.

Sliding her hands to the backs of his legs, she pulled him closer, giving him a silent signal.

"Christ," Blake groaned. "Are you saying I can fuck your face, baby?"

Paige squeezed the backs of Blake's thighs again in answer, his crude words turning her on even more. Even knowing the need to please had gotten her into trouble before, she wanted to pleasure Blake more than anything.

"Fuck." Blake pulled out of her mouth and lifted her toward the head of the bed. On her back once more, he planked over her. "As fabulous as that was, baby, I don't want to come in your mouth right now. I want to be buried deep inside you."

"I want that too." She reached down and guided him to her core.

He entered her in one long, slow stroke, sliding in deep. She arched into him, and her head fell back at the exquisite feeling of fullness.

"Paige, look at me," Blake demanded as he lowered himself onto his elbows, his body flush with hers.

She met his gaze. His blue eyes focused on her intensely, as if he could see right into her soul. In that moment she knew she couldn't fake another orgasm because it would be like lying to his face, but she would give him all of her that she could.

Wrapping her legs around him, she urged him deeper as he plunged into her over and over. His rhythm created just the right amount of friction, and she felt her orgasm build again, as it had in the shower.

"Oh, god!" she cried, hoping this time she'd be able to let go.

"Fuck!" Blake lifted up, sitting back, and grabbed behind her knees. Pushing them toward her chest, he opened her up. She grasped his biceps as he drove into her.

Her orgasm rode the crest. So close. She wanted to come so badly. "Yes! Oh, god!"

Blake dropped her legs and lowered onto her, taking her mouth in a savage kiss. He pounded into her again and stilled, his body a delicious weight on top of hers.

When he rolled over onto his back, he brought her with him and gently took her face in his hands, kissing her. It was soft and sweet.

"I'll be right back." He went into the bathroom and came back with a washcloth. She felt shy when he got back into bed, but he didn't let her pull away as he wiped her clean with the warm cloth.

He tossed the cloth on the floor and rolled onto his side to face her. "Paige?" he questioned quietly. "Why didn't you tell me?"

She tensed. "Tell you what?"

"That you couldn't come."

"I can." *With a vibrator*, she didn't add.

He pushed up on his elbow so he was looking down at her. "Then it was me. I didn't do enough."

"It wasn't you, Blake."

He frowned. "I don't understand. You used to orgasm when we were together before. At least… I thought you did. Were you faking it then too?"

That answered her question if he'd known about what she'd done in the shower.

"No, every orgasm I had with you before was real. I'm sorry for faking it in the shower. But I didn't just now."

"No, but you didn't come either."

She closed her eyes for a moment, his gaze too intense, and let out a slow breath. When she looked at him again, she detected only sincerity.

"My marriage wasn't great. It…" God, she felt like such a fool admitting her failures, but even if she and Blake never had sex again, he was her friend and deserved her honesty. "The sex with Craig was horrible, and he blamed it on me. I'd get so caught up in my head worrying that I'd do or say the wrong thing that I could never really relax. You…"

"I'm what?"

"You're the only guy I've ever orgasmed with," she said quietly as she watched his face. His eyes widened and then the corner of his lips twitched up into a smile.

"That's good news. Then I can try again." He ran his hand down her stomach.

"No." Paige sat up and scooted back against the headboard, pulling her knees to her chest and wrapping her arms around them.

Blake leaned against the headboard beside her. "I don't understand. Why not?"

"Because I'm not asking you to fix me, Blake."

"I won't try and fix you."

"Oh, come on, don't lie. Every time we have sex, you'll be trying to see if you can make me come. Neither of us needs that kind of pressure. Maybe it will never happen again, and then what? Both of us will be so tense it won't be any fun at all. I enjoyed what we did. Isn't that enough?"

"If you say it is." He pulled her down and spooned behind

her, wrapping his arm around her. "You'll tell me if that changes?" he asked quietly.

She grasped onto the arm he wrapped around her. "Yes. I'll tell you. But I did enjoy it."

He placed a soft kiss on her shoulder. "Okay."

Paige only hoped she hadn't thrown a wrench into their friendship or ruined their new arrangement almost as soon as it started.

Thursday, October 31

BLAKE LOOKED across the table at Cade. "You got everything you need?"

As an executive team, they'd agreed to buy the strip mall. Several of them, as well as the lead project manager, had toured the property. Once Jake and the temporary VP of commercial operations ran the numbers, everything had gone to Cade for a review, then to Blake for a final sign off. Akerman Contracting was a family-owned business and didn't have a board of directors, but Blake believed in involving his staff in the decision-making as much as possible.

"Yes, I'll finalize the offer," Cade said. "Let's do this the official way."

Blake gave his brother a nod, not needing an explanation. Cade didn't want Blake telling Paige about the offer until he had everything tied up legally. In case the deal, and her sale, didn't go through. Then he would inform the broker. As much as Blake wanted to be able to give Paige the good news, he would abide by Cade's wishes.

"Anything else?" he asked, checking in with everyone

around the room and getting a nod. "Thanks, that's all. Everyone can get home early to hand out candy."

As was their practice, Jake, Cade, Dane, and Ford would stay in the room once the others had left. As one-fifth owner of Akerman Contracting, Gage connected via video, his face projected on the screen on one wall, although he didn't make it to every meeting.

Once the door closed behind him, Blake sat back in his chair and relaxed. It wasn't that he was uptight around his employees, but he wasn't in his CEO role as much around his brothers. He was one of them.

"Anyone got any—" Blake's words cut off as the seventh episode took over his body.

He could hear his brothers call out to him, but he was unable to respond. His eyes closed of their own accord as images swirled in his mind.

The pictures settled and he saw a tall-masted ship through an early morning fog, ready to set sail. He was in England in 1802, but that was all the information the curse imparted.

The air smelled of saltwater, and Blake wasn't sure if he could truly feel the moisture on his skin or if it was part of the illusion. The cries of seagulls mixed with the excited voices of sailors preparing to embark on their journey.

His vision focused on a couple. Knowing now that he was meant to learn from the couples, Blake stepped closer, wanting to hear their words above the drone of the seagulls and other voices.

The man wore the same uniform as dozens of sailors around him and the woman's hair was covered by a bonnet tied under her chin. He held one of her gloved hands and used his other to gently brush some hair away from her face.

"Elizabeth," the man said barely loud enough for Blake to hear, "I vow to return, and when I do, I will make you my wife."

Elizabeth's eyes glistened with tears as she pulled her hand from his, dug into her coat pocket and pulled out a piece of cloth. "Take this," she said as she pressed the cloth into the sailor's hands. "It's a handkerchief that I embroidered with your initials so you'll always have something of me with you."

The sailor held the cloth to his chest. "Thank you. I will cherish it."

Elizabeth flung herself into his arms. Her body shook with sobs as the sailor held her tightly. After a minute he held her upper arms and pulled back from her. "I must go, but I will return. I love you, Elizabeth."

"And I love you, Christopher. I will wait for you."

When he reached down and picked up the bag at his feet and walked away, Blake noticed a man in the shadows. He had similar features and coloring to the sailor but wasn't dressed in uniform and watched the couple with a look of longing on his face.

The air shifted around Blake, the cries of seagulls replaced by the sound of horses' hooves on cobblestones, the shouts of vendors selling their wares, and people chatting in the streets. The smell of human waste and soot hung heavy in the air, forcing Blake to breathe through his mouth.

Like before, his vision focused on a couple. He recognized the woman as Elizabeth. One hand rested on her large belly, a gold band on her ring finger, while her other arm was locked with the arm of the man beside her.

It took a moment for Blake to place the man as the one in the shadows on the dock.

A shout caught Blake's attention, pulling his gaze away from the couple. A sailor, Christopher, stumbled down the street toward them. He clutched a cloth in his fist and held it toward the couple.

Elizabeth gasped and looked between the sailor and the man beside her.

"How could you betray me like this?" Christopher yelled at the other man.

"We had no word for the longest time, and Elizabeth feared you were dead," the man barked back, his tone defensive. "I didn't mean to steal her from you."

Blake felt uneasy listening to the argument, but even he didn't believe the man. He had an arrogance about him that belied his words.

"Betrayed by my own brother," Christoper hissed. He threw a punch, knocking his brother backward onto the dirty street.

Elizabeth screamed, but Blake didn't get to see what happened next because the air shifted again. When the images settled, Blake found himself in a home with stone walls and logs burning brightly in a fireplace.

A woman, her hair fastened up on her head, sat in a rocking chair, feeding a baby at her breast. A man sat in the chair beside her, staring at the fire. Two small boys rushed into the room and dropped the logs in their arms by the fire.

"Dad, will you tell us a story?" one of the boys asked.

The man adjusted in his chair to lift one of the boys onto his lap, and Blake recognized the man as Christopher. The years had not been kind to him. His face looked thin and haggard, and he didn't smile as Blake would have expected him to do with his sons.

He began to tell the boys a story and then the image changed once more. The air didn't change like Blake had come to expect. Instead, the scene sped up to show what he suspected was later in the evening of the same day.

Christopher and the woman were in bed together, her hair in long braids. "Will you ever love me?" she asked softly.

"Have I not provided for you? Given you a home and children?" Christopher questioned.

"Yes, but not your love."

"I told you when I asked for your hand that I would give you everything I was able to, which didn't include my heart."

The woman's lip trembled, and she nodded but didn't cry.

"I care for you, and I will always provide."

Christopher's voice held none of the passion Blake had heard while *he stood on the dock and promised to come back to Elizabeth. Christopher patted his wife's hand and rolled over, settling into the bed.*

When the air shifted again, Blake felt his body release from the curse's hold and opened his eyes to see Jake and his brothers staring at him.

"He's back," Ford said.

"Holy shit," Gage said through the speaker. "You were gone for over fifteen minutes."

Blake scrubbed his hands over his face, still feeling Christopher's detachment from his wife.

"Where did you go this time?" Jake asked.

Blake dropped his hands to the table. "At first I was on the docks in London in 1802. Then the vision fast-forwarded a few years, but I don't know how many."

Dane frowned. "How many days are in between the episodes now?"

"Four. The last one was the morning of our Halloween party." Blake walked them through what he saw and the emotions in each one. He always felt as if they were his own. He'd begun to think the emotions were more important than the actual events. Although he couldn't pinpoint why, he knew that during every single one, he felt a sense of hopelessness and despair at failed or lost love, which was why he wanted to avoid having those feelings himself.

"What I don't get," Cade said, "is how showing you all the misery is supposed to make you fall in love."

Blake didn't know either, and then he voiced a question that had been on the back of his mind. "What if it's not?

"What do you mean?" Dane asked.

"Mom's letter said the curse would take effect sometime after our thirtieth birthday if we don't fall in love by then, right?" Blake looked at Cade for confirmation, figuring his brother had memorized the letter.

At Cade's nod, Blake continued, not liking the conclusion he'd come to. "I didn't fall in love by the time I turned thirty. Maybe once the curse takes effect, it's already too late. It can't be stopped. Maybe it's trying to tell me that if I fall in love now, I'll only face heartache that will define the rest of my life."

"No," Gage said harshly. All eyes turned toward the screen on the wall. "You can't think that way. If you don't stop the curse you could end up in a trance all day long. There's got to be a way to stop it."

"Have you told Paige?" Jake asked.

"No, not yet."

"She needs to know what's happening because you could zone out in front of her."

Jake was right, but Blake wasn't ready to tell her. He'd been thinking a lot about her not finding release when they had sex, because he wanted her to enjoy it as much as he did. Telling her he was cursed without a way to prove it could sound like he wanted to get rid of her. At least that's what he would have once thought about a crazy story like being cursed.

"She could be the answer to breaking the curse," Ford offered.

Dane backhanded Ford's arm. "He can't force her to fall in love with him."

"I didn't say he could." Ford met Blake's gaze. "But maybe if it's meant to happen, you can speed up the process by wooing her."

Gage made a choking sound. "Wooing her?"

"Maybe Ford's right," Dane said, ever the peacekeeper, interjecting before Gage and Ford could start razzing each other. "Are you treating Paige the way she deserves? Showing her you're a half-decent guy?"

"Only half-decent? Thanks," Blake said, his tone dripping with sarcasm.

"Semantics," Cade said. "You know what he means."

"Woo, date, whatever..." Gage offered. "Just treat her right."

When Dane and Ford opened their mouths to add their two cents, Blake put his hand up to halt them. "I get it. I do. But Paige went through some shit with her ex. I don't know what, but I think he was a manipulative bastard and likely gaslighted her because she's always concerned about being reliant on someone and them having control over her. I don't want Paige to think I'm the same as her ex, and mentioning a curse I can't prove might not be the best move to earn her trust."

Cade stood. "We're not going to solve this tonight, and I've got to get going."

Gage said goodbye, and the screen went blank.

A few minutes later, Blake and Jake walked out of Akermans, leaving Dane and Ford behind to hand out candy.

Every year, one or two people took on the task since their building was a renovated house on a residential street. Blake was usually one of those people but he wouldn't be now that he had Paige and Emmie. Maybe one day Emmie would like to do it with him.

Jake looked at him with a serious expression when they reached their trucks. "Telling Paige about the curse might be tricky, but don't wait too long."

"I just need a few more days to figure out how to tell her."

Jake gave him a nod. "Okay. You and Paige going to bring Emmie by my place for trick or treating tonight?"

"That's the plan. See you in a while."

Blake was going to put the curse out of his mind and just enjoy his time with Paige and Emmie. If his time with them was limited, he wanted to enjoy it while he could.

CHAPTER FOURTEEN

Saturday, November 2

*S*aturday could just become her favorite day of the week. They were even better than lazy Sundays. Last Saturday hadn't gone exactly as she would have liked, but she'd had years of her body not cooperating with her. That didn't mean she couldn't still enjoy herself.

After taking Emmie out trick or treating on Thursday and showing a bunch of properties yesterday, she was tired. The entire week had been good but exhausting, and she and Blake hadn't spent as much time just relaxing in the evenings as they had the week before.

She loved the time she, Blake, and Emmie spent together, but she needed *mommy* time too. Evenings with Blake had become her favorite way to spend mommy time.

But could they have a deeper friendship without her falling into old habits? Without her falling in love?

Financially, she was already reliant on Blake. As much as that should worry her, it didn't because it was only temporary. With her latest commission check, she'd gotten a bit of reprieve from her debt, and as long as she was careful and Blake didn't make her suddenly leave, that trend would continue.

Being reliant on his friendship was something else entirely, and she knew all too well that emotional devastation could be just as bad as financial. But maybe it was too late to worry about that because she looked forward to seeing him every morning and evening. What if her heart eventually mistook this interim solution for the fairy-tale dream she'd had once upon a time?

In the past, Blake had gotten so caught up with school and work that he didn't have time for her. Even though school wasn't in the picture anymore, Blake had an entire company to run. And she couldn't forget that Blake didn't want more than friendship either. Would he eventually think she was too much of a burden? And what about Emmie? Would she come to expect time with Blake, and how would she feel if one day he was no longer in their lives?

Although Blake wasn't like Craig, she'd seen Blake withdraw several times. Needing time for himself was one thing, but if his withdrawals and moods were more than that, it could be a reason for concern.

For years she'd been afraid to speak up because Craig interpreted anything she said as criticism of him. He always found a way to spin it and place the blame on Paige until she became too fearful to say anything. She promised herself she would never live like that ever again, but she'd done nothing to prevent it from happening again.

Tonight, she would take control of her situation and talk to Blake. If she expected him to open up to her and be honest about what he wanted and why he'd been moody, then she had to do the same.

If that didn't work, then she would make plans to move out sooner rather than later.

Feeling good about her plan, Paige turned off the overhead light in Emmie's room and left the door ajar before heading downstairs. Emmie had only lasted for one book. Not surprising after the last couple of days and the game of tag they'd played in the backyard after dinner.

Emmie had been one happy but tired little girl, almost falling asleep in her bath. She'd been out like a light in no time. Now Paige could have some mommy time, something she'd been looking forward to all week.

Paige heard jazz music playing softly when she reached the bottom of the stairs. Only a floor lamp was on, casting a soft glow in the room.

She smiled at him where he lounged against the corner of one couch, two glasses of wine on the coffee table he'd pulled closer.

"She asleep?" Blake asked.

"Within seconds." Paige settled onto the other end of the couch and accepted the glass of wine he offered. "Thanks."

Blake played with the stem of his glass as if nervous. "This okay instead of a game tonight?"

"After a busy week and the game of tag tonight? It's perfect." She took a sip of her wine, relaxing back into the cushions.

For several minutes they drank their wine and listened to the music. Reluctant to break the comfortable silence, Paige almost didn't want to bring up what she'd been thinking about. Then the little nagging voice in the back of her mind spoke up. *That's what you did in the past—kept your head in the sand to keep the peace—and look where that got you.*

Paige put her empty wine glass on the table and sat back into the cushions. She pulled her socked feet up and wrapped her arms around her knees.

Blake set his own wine glass on the table and shifted so he faced her. "What's wrong? You look like you just withdrew."

"No." Protecting herself wasn't the same as withdrawing, so that wasn't a lie. She knew she'd pulled back to protect herself, not that her arms could shield her heart. "Maybe..." She took a deep breath and met Blake's gaze. The voice in her mind egged her on. *You can do this.*

"I want to tell you how I came to be living in the strip mall."

Blake nodded and reached for the wine bottle on the table. He filled his glass and lifted the bottle and his brows in question to her.

"Sure." Another glass of wine might help her resolve.

"Thanks." She accepted the refilled glass from him and took a sip. "I don't know if you remember, but Craig broke up with me the summer before I started college and you and I met."

"I do."

"When Craig and I met the winter before, he seemed like he was right out of a fairy tale—tall, dark, and handsome. He was four years older than me, and since I took time off after high school to work, he felt so much more worldly than me because he had already finished college and was working as an engineer. He seemed like he was all that and a bag of chips."

She let out a humorless laugh. "I didn't realize it at the time, but he was a narcissist. Actually, it took me years to see it... To learn that he didn't want me, but he didn't want anyone else to have me either."

When Paige had finally looked back at their time together, all the signs had been there. If only she hadn't been so young and desperate for a partner to love her that she'd turned a blind eye to everything she didn't want to see. She couldn't even pinpoint exactly why she had been that way, except perhaps to say that she had wanted to be recognized as someone special.

"After you and I started dating, I bumped into Craig a few times. He was best friends with the brother of one of my friends, so we were bound to run into each other now and then. The first time I saw him, you and I had been dating for about four months or so. He asked how I was. He was so good at faking kindness and interest… He still is, if he wants to… Anyway, I told him I was doing well. School was great, and I was dating you. I don't know if I was trying to rub it in his face or not. I had just turned twenty and wasn't as mature as I gave myself credit for, so maybe.

"We bumped into each other several more times. He was charming and kind, even more than he had been." She looked down at her wine, running her finger along the rim as she pictured Craig's face as he'd feigned interest, although she didn't know it was fake at the time. He'd continued to ask her out even though he knew she was dating Blake.

"Oh…" She flung her chin up and looked at Blake as something occurred to her. "I don't want you to think I cheated on you. I didn't. I never would have done that. But knowing Craig like I do now, I think he would have liked the thought of that so he could be the one who pulled me away from you. But every time he asked to meet with me alone, I turned him down."

Blake reached out and squeezed her free hand. "I know you wouldn't have," he said softly.

She let out a long breath. For all her mistakes, at least she hadn't made that one. Many of the things she'd done over the years to survive—like lying to Craig when she'd been studying to become a realtor and living in a strip mall—could be considered wrong or questionable in many people's eyes, but she'd tried to never hurt anyone.

Looking into Blake's eyes now, her throat began to burn.

She swallowed, trying to ignore it, and pushed through. It didn't matter if he thought less of her afterward; she had to get everything out in the open so their friendship could be based on honesty and understanding.

"I think I was falling in love with you," she whispered. "I wanted to be with you all the time. It was like I was depending on you for my happiness."

When Blake opened his mouth as if to say something, she held up her free hand to stop him. "Please, let me get this out."

He nodded, and she took a sip of wine to help soothe the burning before she continued.

"I've learned that the only person who can make me happy is me. Though I didn't know that then, and I was lonely. You were juggling school and work, and it felt like you never had any time for me. Craig kept showing up when I was with my friend, and I think he saw how lonely I was. Well… maybe not, that would have taken empathy on his part—something Craig has never had—but he may have seen how vulnerable I was, and he continued to push me. He told me he loved me and that he realized breaking up with me was a huge mistake. He promised to love me and always be there for me and I believed him because it was what I really needed to hear from someone. It was stupid to break up with you, but I don't regret it."

"Because of Emmie," Blake said, full of understanding.

"Yes, because of Emmie. I can't regret Craig for a moment because he gave me her."

"What happened when you went back to him?"

Paige drained her wine and set the glass on the table.

"More?" Blake asked.

She debated for a moment, then shook her head. Never much of a drinker, even though she enjoyed wine, she didn't want to use it as any more of a crutch than it'd already been.

"I was a mess of emotions. I missed you and was angry you didn't fight for me."

"For the longest time I regretted that I didn't fight for you either, and then it was just too late."

"So, why didn't you fight for me?"

He snorted a laugh, but there wasn't any humor in it. "My ego got in the way. And probably immaturity too. I was struggling with school and keeping the company afloat. So many people depended on me for their livelihoods, and I think maybe fighting for you felt like too big of an ask at the time."

He scrubbed his hands over his face and then met her gaze. "I wanted you to fight for me too."

Paige huffed out a humorless laugh. "Wow, what a pair we were."

"Yes, but no regrets, right?"

"Right." She thought back to that period of her life. "It didn't take me long to realize that so many of the lines Craig had fed me were only what he thought I wanted to hear. But I'd made my decision, and my pride told me to suck it up. Then… I guess… somewhere along the way, I became trapped. I had no money and no self-worth because nothing I did was ever good enough. Not how much I cleaned, or what I cooked. It didn't matter what it was. Eventually he wouldn't even allow me to adjust the thermostat."

Shame heated her face as she thought back to all the times she had to ask his permission to do something and how he made her reclean something because it wasn't up to his standards.

Paige expected to see a look of disappointment on Blake's face, but all she saw was understanding. She had to remind herself again that he wasn't Craig. She may have left her ex over a year ago, but the habits she'd formed to deal with him and survive hadn't just gone away. Several times over the last couple of weeks she'd found herself expecting a particular reaction from Blake and getting the exact opposite. It might even take months or years before she no longer projected Craig's habits and reactions onto Blake or any other man she ended up with.

"This is going to sound even more stupid…"

"No. Whatever you're going to say will sound like you did whatever was necessary to get through each day. That's not stupid."

She looked at her hands, fiddling with the cuff of her sweatshirt as she spoke, not able to look Blake in the eyes. "This next part… it wasn't about survival, it was just me being an idiot. I felt like I couldn't leave Craig because I was probably the best thing to ever happen to him. If I left him, he would never get anyone who would go out of their way for him like I did. But, on the other hand, he continually cut me down to the point that I felt worthless. I began to think that no one better than him would ever want me because I was such a loser. It was a trap of my own making."

Paige lifted her eyes to Blake's. "What a juxtaposition, huh?"

"Maybe, but it wasn't of your own making. Craig made it for you. You've always been a strong person, and that part of you was probably fighting with the part of you that felt less-than because of how he treated you." They were quiet for a moment before Blake asked, "What made you finally leave him?"

"What was my wake-up call? My aha moment? That all-important epiphany?" she asked, her tone dripping with self-deprecation.

The corners of his lips twitched up in a small smile. "Yeah, all that."

"A jar of peanut butter."

Blake barked out a laugh. "It must have been one hell of a jar."

She smirked and told him all about that fateful trip to the grocery store and how she realized she no longer knew who she was.

When she finished her story, she felt no less shame than she did every time she thought about it. This was the first time she'd ever shared her story with someone, and voicing it out loud made it even easier to recognize everything that Craig had made her believe.

"I didn't think I'd ever be grateful for a jar of peanut butter or a brick of cheese. But…" His smile sobered. "I'm thankful you were able to get out of your situation."

She lowered her eyes. "I was such an idiot. It's not like he hit me. I should have just stood up to him and walked away."

"Paige, look at me," Blake said.

He hadn't raised his voice, but she was powerless to refuse his gentle command. She met his gaze.

"You're not an idiot. You're smart and brave." He leaned forward, his face only inches from hers. She licked her lips, wanting him to kiss her so she could forget about all the stupid things she'd done.

Instead, he lifted her hand and held it. "What Craig did to you was emotional abuse. He belittled you and gaslighted you. Because it's insidious, it is just as bad as if he'd hit you. The damage is still there, you just don't see it coming. It's like death by a thousand cuts."

That's exactly how Paige had felt, but she'd never been able to put it into words. Craig had made her bleed in small ways every day until the day in the grocery store when she realized that she would lose herself completely if she didn't get out.

"Thank you," she whispered.

Blake dropped her hand and sat back. He looked almost as shaken as she felt.

"How did you get out?" he asked.

"With planning."

"It took me a long time, and I'm still learning who I am. Most days, I question my thoughts, wondering if they're really my own or from years of training." To lift the mood, she grinned and said, "But I do know I like organic cashew butter over peanut butter and mozzarella cheese over cheddar."

Blake barked another laugh. "Good to know."

His laughter made her smile, feeling lighter than she had since she started her story. But it wouldn't last. She had yet to answer his question.

"So… How I got out…" She was dragging it out, but it wasn't because she didn't want to tell him. Explaining would mean telling him one more way she was an idiot.

"I'd like to know… but only if you want to tell me."

"I do. I just… To do that, I'll have to tell you the first really stupid mistake I made." Maybe getting everything out in the open would help him see her triggers and where she was coming from.

"I…" She looked up at him through her lashes, wondering how she could face him while she spewed her failures. "I've never told anyone this before."

A softness came over his rugged, handsome features. "Maybe not looking at me while you're talking will help."

Before she could ask what he meant, he reached forward and grasped her hips, turning her around. With his back to the corner of the couch, one leg stretched out in front of him and the other knee bent, his foot on the floor, he pulled her into his body. Her back rested against his chest, his arms wrapped around her, his hands laying loosely on her stomach.

"Thank you," she whispered as she melted against him and placed her hands on top of his.

The position felt almost as intimate as when they'd had sex, just different. "Are you ready to hear how stupid I was? To know more ways I failed?"

CHAPTER FIFTEEN

"*Y*ou're not stupid." Blake turned his hand over and linked his fingers with Paige's. He hated that she kept saying that. "I expect you did the best you could in a shitty situation. I would never judge you."

He was already in awe of what she'd put up with from her asshole ex-husband. Besides stomping on her self-esteem and making her get all up in her head in bed, Blake expected that her being homeless had something to do with her ex as well.

In the time Paige and Emmie had been living with Blake, the guy hadn't reached out even once—at least not that he'd seen—which meant he wasn't even talking to his daughter.

"Okay," Paige said, her voice shaking. "The month after I broke up with you, I finished my first year and worked for the summer. Craig and I were both busy, and things seemed fine. I started my second year in August and then he proposed. I was blown away because I hadn't thought we were at that point yet. I'd even begun to doubt that we were a good match. But once again he told me he loved me and couldn't live without me. In the years since, I've wondered if he maybe felt as trapped as I did because he really didn't love me but still didn't want anyone else to have me, so he figured marriage was the next logical choice.

"Anyway… I accepted, and Craig left the wedding planning up to me. He wanted a big wedding, and although I would have preferred something smaller, I went along with it to please him. He told me to just put everything—the deposits, purchases, whatever—on my credit card and he would pay it off. For the first couple of months, I checked to make sure he was. One time when I checked, he'd only made a partial payment. I confronted him about it, and he said not to worry, he'd handle it."

Paige rubbed her thumbs along the outside of Blake's pinkie fingers. He wasn't even sure she was aware of what she was doing. She sounded lost in thought and rested her head back on his chest as if she no longer had the strength to hold it up.

"Like a total idiot, I trusted him. Then life got crazy busy, and I stopped checking. Every time the bill arrived in the mail, he would take it, saying he'd pay it. We'd been married for a few months and I'd already started my junior year when I realized he'd completely stopped making payments on the credit card.

"I had gotten used to giving him the credit card statement to pay, but since the wedding was over and it was still my card, I opened the next statement when it arrived. I felt like I was going to faint. The card was maxed out and the interest had been piling up. When I confronted Craig, he acted like it was all my fault and I'd been irresponsible by not paying the card off each month. He then said I needed to contribute to the household and not be a mooch.

"Since the house had been his, he was paying the mortgage and everything related to it—taxes, utilities, insurance. I used my savings from my summer job to pay for tuition and books and buy all the groceries. I still had to work part-time to make ends meet…"

Her voice trailed off, and Blake had to concentrate to make sure his hands stayed relaxed in hers. His first instinct was to curl his hands into fists and find something to punch to take out his frustrations on. Or better yet… find Craig to punch. It wasn't any wonder why Paige was worried about being controlled and reliant on someone. The asshole had used her for his own wants, then turned around and gaslighted her.

"What did you do?" he asked.

"I dropped out of school and got a job to pay off the debt. The only thing I ever wanted was to make him happy and have a family, so we had the big wedding, and then I had to pay off the debt. By the time it was paid off, I was pregnant. I wanted to be pregnant so badly, and I loved Emmie from the moment she was conceived. I…"

Blake turned Paige in his arms so he could see her face. Her eyes were shiny, but she hadn't shed a tear. "I'm in awe of you, Paige. You're strong and resilient. An amazing mom, and overall…" He searched for the right word. "Fierce."

She choked out a laugh. "Fierce?"

"Yes, fierce. Powerful and intensely passionate."

He kissed her lips lightly. As much as he wanted to do more, he knew she needed to finish her story. The problem was, just hearing all she'd been through made him care about her even more. Listening to any more of her struggles was going to make keeping his heart guarded almost impossible. But he would just have to.

Blake shifted, doing his best to ease the restriction in his jeans, and settled Paige's back against his chest once more. As if they'd done it a thousand times, he turned his palms up and she linked her fingers with his again, like they were meant to be together.

Trying to ward off any more encroaching feelings, he pictured how he'd felt when she broke his heart and how lost his mom had been for years after his dad died, but it was becoming harder and harder. Then his mind conjured images of Peter not being able to paint; Moira walking away from Liam, both of them unhappy; and Martha living only half a life, and he knew he and Paige could never be more than friends. But he'd be there for her while he still protected his heart, because the curse had already shown him any love he had was going to end in heartbreak.

"Finish your story," he said quietly against her hair, breathing in her vanilla and orange blossom scent.

"After that day in the grocery store, I knew I had to leave Craig. Not just for myself, but for Emmie. If I stayed, she would see that I allowed someone to treat me like crap. I couldn't have her growing up thinking it was okay for a man to treat a woman like that... or for anyone to treat another like that. The really stupid thing is that I almost didn't leave. I wanted more children so badly I almost stayed just so I could have more."

She sighed as if the burden of what she had considered doing weighed on her.

"I would have been teaching more children that it was okay to let someone treat them like garbage and manipulate them. Finally, I realized I couldn't do that and if Emmie is the only child I ever have, I'll still feel so blessed to have her. Once I'd made up my mind to leave, I felt like I'd started to take my life back. But, even after making that huge decision, it still took me almost two years before I could leave him."

Blake wished he could do more for Paige than just hold her. His only solace was that all this was in the past and now he could be Paige's friend and listen and help her if she asked. He wasn't so sure she would actually ask for help if she needed it, but one step at a time.

"How did you manage it?" he asked.

"When Emmie was born, Craig said I should stay home with her. Since I'd dropped out of school, the only jobs I'd be able to get would be crappy minimum-wage ones, making it not even worth putting Emmie in daycare. His words, not mine."

She let out a small snort. "It hadn't been worth pointing out to him that him wanting a lavish wedding and not paying the credit card off was the reason I had to drop out of school. He wouldn't have seen it that way.

"The diner I'd waitressed at before I had Emmie hired me back a few afternoons a week, and my mom agreed to watch Emmie. I didn't tell Craig, and he worked late a lot, so most nights he didn't arrive home until after Emmie was in bed. Which was a good thing because it gave me a chance to shower off the smells from the diner before he got home. The money I earned plus tips wasn't much, but it allowed me to save enough. I still had to buy our groceries, but I was using the money I'd made during the time between paying off the debt and having Emmie for that. Once that money was gone, Craig knew he'd be paying for everything, and believe me, he never let me forget. He tracked the account that money was in and every single penny I spent on groceries."

A part of Blake wished he'd known what Paige was going through so he could have helped her. But the other part of him knew she'd had to do everything on her own or she might not have ever realized what she was capable of.

"How did you manage to keep your earnings at the diner from him?" he asked.

"I opened an account at a different bank and used my parents' address for it. I left all my tips with them too. I gave my parents an excuse about keeping it all at their house because I needed to avoid the temptation to spend it. My mom didn't care what I did as long as I kept Craig happy, *because that's what a good wife does."*

Paige said her last words in an overly high-pitched voice, as if imitating her mom. Then she snorted, making him laugh, but he'd heard the underlying resentment in her tone.

"I told my dad I was saving up to take classes to be a real estate agent and I'd need some money to get started. I also told him I wanted it to be a surprise for Craig. I'm pretty sure my dad knew that for the lie it was, although he never said anything. As soon as I got my license, I asked Craig for a divorce. He was furious, but he didn't have a choice because I'd already gotten a lawyer."

"Did Craig drag it out?"

"He tried to, but then all his debt came to light. Turned out he had taken out a second mortgage on the house and maxed out several credit cards in both our names because he liked to play poker with some bigwigs. When we got divorced, I was left with almost half the debt."

Blake's urge to punch Craig ratcheted up a notch. He took a calming breath and focused on Paige's thumb rubbing softly along his hand. "To pay off his debt, he was letting you and Emmie live in a strip mall?"

She coughed a laugh. "If only that was it. When I left Craig, I rented a one-bedroom apartment for Emmie and me, the cheapest I could find that wasn't in a dangerous neighborhood. I was doing okay at first, but a couple things slowly sunk me. First, I needed a car for my job to get to properties, and I wanted one I'd feel safe enough driving Emmie in on snowy streets. But because my credit sucked and I had a lot of debt, I had to take out a really high-interest loan. Then Craig decided to stop paying child support."

Blake stiffened. "He can't just decide not to pay."

"I know, but I didn't have money for another lawyer, and

Craig threatened that if I did get one to go after him, he'd go for sole custody of Emmie."

"He is a vindictive fuck, isn't he?"

Paige laughed, a genuine one that shook her body in his arms. "He is that."

He forced himself to relax again. "What else?"

"As you know, I get paid by commission, and sometimes it's a while between checks. When I get one, it can hold me over for a long time, but with all my debt, Emmie's daycare, regular living expenses, and then Craig no longer paying child support, I was late on rent one month. Then I couldn't pay the following month, and I got evicted." She shrugged against his chest. "The strip mall wasn't great, but it seemed like a good temporary solution."

"You could have gone to your boss. I've known him for years and he's a good guy."

"He'd already taken a chance on me because I had zero experience. And because of that, he warned me when he hired me to make sure I had enough money to carry me between commission checks. I was too ashamed to go to him and confess all my debt."

"I get that." If even one of the shitty things in her situation hadn't happened, she probably would have been fine.

Paige turned in his arms and looked up at him, a sly smile curling her lips. "That's enough heavy stuff for tonight. So... *friend*," she said. "It's Saturday. The weekend."

He had to work not to smile as he raised his brow. "And?"

Paige faced him fully and went up on her knees. "I want my benefits," she whispered and leaned forward, placing her hands on his chest.

She wet her lips before closing the final few inches between them.

He kissed her, hauled her up into a fireman's carry, and she squealed when he raced toward the stairs.

"Shhhh, you'll wake Emmie."

"What about the lights?" she whispered.

"I'll turn them off later. I don't want to wait to touch you," he said stepping into their bedroom. *Her bedroom.* He needed to remember that. He lowered her feet to the floor and this time she let him remove her clothes, kissing down her body as he exposed it.

"Climb onto the bed. I've got something for you."

She laughed as she got on the bed. "Oh no… should I be scared?" she teased.

"No, I think you're going to like this." He quickly stripped off his own clothes and grabbed his phone and the headphones he'd placed on the dresser after dinner. He turned on the headset, already paired with his phone, and selected his jazz playlist from the music app.

He stood at the side of the bed and held out the headphones to Paige.

She frowned. "You don't want me to hear you during sex?"

His plan had seemed like a genius idea earlier in the week, but now he was beginning to doubt himself. "You said you get all up in your head and worry, so I thought this might help. At least for the first few times."

Paige grasped the headphones and looked down, but not before he noticed that her eyes had become glassy. He gently lifted her chin so he could look into her eyes. "What kind of tears are those?" he asked, too worried to even suggest an emotion that could be causing them.

He needed her to tell him, not confirm something he might have gotten wrong just to appease him.

She shrugged. "I'm not sure. Relief, maybe?"

Relief was okay. At least she wasn't angry. "Put them on. The volume is right here," he said, showing her how to adjust it.

When she had them on, he turned on the selected playlist and watched her face for a reaction. She smiled and laid back. He put the phone down and climbed onto the bed, planking over her like he'd done the week before.

He lifted one side of the headphones. "Close your eyes, baby. Just relax and let yourself go."

"What about you?"

"Don't you worry about me. I'll be having lots of fun."

She gave him a small smile, then adjusted the headphones back into position and closed her eyes.

Blake kissed her, loving that her lips parted for him right away and kissed him back. She tasted of wine and something uniquely Paige. He could kiss her all night, but he had other plans. She'd told him he couldn't fix her and that trying to would be too much pressure for both of them, and he agreed. But that didn't mean he couldn't want to pleasure her, whether she managed to orgasm or not.

He kissed down her body, using his mouth and his hands to bring her pleasure. His only worry was that he'd bring her right to the crest of her orgasm and frustrate her if she couldn't find her release. Then they'd both worry, and she'd likely believe that the pleasure she had found wasn't enough.

Fuck. Now it was his turn to get out of his head. He let out a breath and focused on pleasing Paige.

Exploring her body, he started with her neck, leaving no part of her soft skin untouched. He lavished attention on her collarbones and then her breasts, licking and softly biting her nipples until she was squirming beneath him.

He continued down her body until he reached her core. He slid his hands under her hips and cupped her gorgeous ass. She sucked in her breath but didn't pull away. Laying his body between her legs, he kissed up the inside of each thigh before kissing up the center of her folds. Then he ran his tongue up to her clit.

"Oh, god!" Paige arched into his mouth. "More. Please, Blake, don't tease."

A good sign. He draped each of her legs over his shoulders, and bringing his hands from underneath her thighs, he used his fingers to part her folds. He licked her again, going deeper, and her body bucked as she let out a moan. Laying one hand on her stomach, he held her down while he licked and sucked her, avoiding direct contact with her clit.

When her squirming and moans increased, he gently slipped two fingers inside her hot heat.

She reached down and gripped his hair. "Oh, god! More, Blake. Please!"

He thought it was cute that she was reduced to using the same five words when she was in the throes of passion.

Blake flicked her clit with his tongue and curved his fingers up to find that special spot. She bucked up against his hand and her cries of pleasure increased, then sounded muffled.

He looked up the length of her body to see she'd placed her hand across her mouth to stifle her cries. While still also using his fingers, he sucked her clit into his mouth. Her entire body stiffened and then convulsed as her cream flooded his mouth.

"Oh, god," she blew out on a breath, and her legs relaxed on his shoulders as if deflated.

He withdrew from her and placed her legs on the bed before crawling up her body. Paige tugged off the headphones, tossing them to the side of the bed, and reached for him.

"Thank you," she whispered against his lips before reaching for his cock. He groaned when she wrapped her fingers around him and guided him to her core. Knowing how wet she was, he entered her in one stroke, and she clenched around him. It felt like intense heat and pure ecstasy.

"Paige. You feel amazing. I'm not going to last long."

"Fuck me, Blake." She tilted her hips up, taking him deeper, and that was his undoing.

In a repeat of last week, he said the same words he'd used before: "Paige, look at me."

She opened her eyes, passion swimming in the hazel depths.

He lifted up and sat back, grabbing her behind the knees. He pushed them to her chest, opening her up. And just like last week, she grasped onto his biceps.

"See what you do to me? You are the sexiest woman I've ever met." Letting one of her legs drop, he rubbed his thumb on her clit and thrust into her over and over.

"Yes! Blake, I'm coming!" she whisper-yelled.

Her body arched as she clenched around him, ripping his orgasm from him. Pleasure, almost blinding in its intensity, rolled through him in waves.

When he felt like he'd finally caught his breath, he opened his eyes to see her grinning at him. "We did that," she said.

Lowering himself onto her, he snaked an arm under her and rolled them so they were lying on their sides facing each other. "Yeah, we did that," he huffed out and then kissed her. A slow, tender kiss.

"I'll be right back." He almost fell out of bed but managed to get his rubbery legs under him. She'd wrecked him, but in the best possible way.

He came back with a warm washcloth and cleaned her, thankful she wasn't as shy this time. "I'm going to turn off the lights downstairs." He gave her another quick kiss before getting up again. After tossing the washcloth in the clothes hamper, he went downstairs, turned off the lights, and checked that the doors were locked.

Back upstairs, he found Paige in the bathroom brushing her teeth. He did the same. It felt truly domestic, and for a brief moment, he wondered if they could be more than friends with benefits. Then he remembered the sailor the curse had shown him two days ago and he knew he should stick with his original plan to guard his heart. Although it might not matter because he was already doomed for heartache.

Tuesday, November 6

Paige listened to the manager list the property's rules as she looked around the two-bedroom apartment. It was bland but clean, and in a good neighborhood. Since it wasn't anything special, she didn't really need to tour it, but she walked through the bedrooms and checked out the bathroom anyway to show the manager she was interested.

She hadn't planned to look at apartments today. But after she'd shown one of her own clients a few properties, she'd gotten a text from Blake about dinner. He said he had a hankering for tacos—she'd laughed when she'd read it. The word hankering had been surprising, but when he said he'd pick up the fixings and they could show Emmie how to make tacos, followed by two lines of taco emojis, she felt her heart squeeze a little.

Blake had always been thoughtful. Whether they'd been studying or on a date, he'd always taken her thoughts and feelings into account. The only time she had ever felt neglected was when he'd been up to his neck in schoolwork while running the company. She was the one who should have been more thoughtful and done more to make his life easier. It was easy to see that now, but like she always said, she couldn't regret the path her life had taken since it had led to having Emmie.

Her daughter was one of the reasons she was looking at the apartment. Emmie was becoming so attached to Blake that she asked him to play dress up with her every day. She loved him reading her bedtime stories as well. He could make different voices for the characters, something Paige couldn't do even if her life had depended on it. Paige worried that Emmie would fall in love with him and start to expect him to always be there.

Like daughter, like mother. No matter how often Paige told herself to be careful and keep her independence, she was falling a little in love with Blake. Maybe even more than a little.

She still didn't trust him completely, but she was trending that way. Blake wasn't anything like Craig, and she'd begun to think that maybe it wasn't Blake she had to worry about, but herself. If she fell for him, would she also fall back into old patterns? Let Blake make all the decisions until she gave up all her wants for his? She'd readily agreed to go along with his plans for tacos. But maybe that was different, because, well… tacos.

Paige had just said goodbye to a client when she'd gotten the text from Blake. At first she'd laughed, and then all her worries swarmed to the surface like a bunch of angry bees. Their stings were a reminder she and Emmie could get in too deep and end up hurt.

She sent a text back saying yes to tacos, because… tacos… and pulled out onto the road, debating whether to drive back to the office or go pick Emmie up a bit early. Passing a newer apartment building, its large rental sign out front caught her attention, as if to say, *this is a sign.*

Making a spur-of-the-moment decision, she turned at the next street and doubled back to the building to see if any of the apartments fit her budget and needs.

"What do you think?" the manager asked when she walked back into the main room.

"I like it. You said you had four units like this available?"

He puffed out his chest. "Not anymore. I've only got this one and one other left. I'm sure they'll be snatched up soon. I run a tight ship, and I had to evict two units for constantly violating our noise rules. My units never stay empty for long because my tenants appreciate how I manage and take care of everything."

Paige felt like rolling her eyes. The guy definitely didn't have a self-esteem problem. "Yes, the apartment is very clean. I've got a few other places to check before I make a decision."

She said she would be in touch and left him to lock up. Back in her car, she turned it on to warm up but didn't pull out of the lot right away.

The apartment had been nice enough, but she wasn't so sure about the manager, as he seemed a little scary. And just the thought of moving again, and away from Blake, made her sad. She loved living with him. At times, it felt like the years that existed between their dating and now had vanished. They'd become more than just comfortable together. They'd become a family.

It was everything she wanted and everything she feared.

Thursday, November 7

"Ha! I beat you!" Paige jumped from her chair and did a little dance.

"Yes, you did," Blake said, grinning, glad she didn't notice he'd *helped* her along a little by not capturing some of her pieces when she left them wide open. "But you still don't have any rhythm."

Paige stuck her tongue out at him and plopped back in her chair. "I don't need rhythm when I beat you."

He raised his brows. "How'd you figure?"

"I don't know, but it sounded good."

"Sure, you go with that." They both reached for their pieces and set them back up again. Paige really wasn't good at the game, and on more than one occasion Blake had considered suggesting a different one, but changed his mind each time. She seemed to love the challenge, even if strategy wasn't her strong suit.

She lifted a piece to make a move, then wavered as if thinking better of it. The first move would have been better. He met her gaze and smirked.

For a few moves, Blake paid a bit more attention to where she placed her pieces on the board. Several times she almost put a piece down and then switched pieces. Perhaps she was more strategic than he realized. The last couple of times they'd played he'd begun to wonder if she was purposefully throwing a lot of the games. If that was the case, there was a good chance she was doing it for the same reason he made sure she won now and then—they both wanted to enjoy the game so they would continue playing.

Blake loved everything about having Paige and Emmie in his house. He backpedaled in his mind. Maybe he didn't love *everything*. The basement bedroom was fine, but he missed his bedroom, and on the nights he didn't sleep with Paige, he missed her too.

Since it was only Thursday, he had another two nights

before he'd have Paige in his arms and in his bed. Saturday had always been his favorite day of the week, but he started wondering if Friday could be.

The previous Saturday, after Paige had opened up to him, had been amazing. His ego had taken a boost when Paige had climaxed—more than once—but she was helping more than just his ego.

His eighth curse episode had struck the following day. With each episode, the days in between them had quickly decreased until there were only two days separating his most recent one and the one before it. But now he was on day four since he'd had one.

Paige must be the reason. He had racked his brain to think of another explanation and he'd come up with nothing. Maybe he and Paige caring for each other was enough— maybe they didn't have to fall in love to break the curse.

He didn't have a reason to believe the episodes would go away completely, but if they grew further apart, he might be able to live with them without going crazy. It was possible they could also grow so far apart that they eventually stopped, although he didn't think that would happen.

There were days when he was working in his office and his mind wandered to the scenarios that had played out before him. At moments like that, the sadness and desperation he felt from the people in the episodes clung to him like the fog that had surrounded Christopher and Elizabeth on the dock in London so long ago.

The more episodes he got sucked into and the more he witnessed lost love, the more the emotions settled upon him, taking longer and longer for him to shake them off.

"Hey." Paige squeezed his hand. "You okay?"

Blake blinked to focus his vision. He realized his hand hovered in mid-air, a game piece held in his fingers. "Sorry, got lost in my thoughts for a moment."

"Care to share?"

"It's nothing," he said as he clenched the game piece.

When Paige dropped her gaze, he knew he'd hurt her. She'd shared so much of herself last week, and he hadn't opened up at all. But he couldn't tell her about the curse because Paige would think he was gaslighting her.

Though he could bring up something else. Over the last two days—since their amazing weekend—a way to tweak his original plan had been brewing in his mind. He gave her a sly smile. "On second thought… Sure. I do have something I'd like to run by you."

Her face brightened with a smile. "Oh?"

"I'd like you and Emmie to consider staying permanently."

Paige choked. "What?"

"You and me can stay friends with benefits and as roommates. I can help out with Emmie more and you won't have a cloud of worry hanging over you, wondering when you should leave."

Paige didn't look convinced, and he feared he should have started with a more subtle pitch. Too late now, so he forged ahead.

"It's the perfect situation since neither of us wants to fall in love again. Money isn't an issue for me—" When Paige frowned, he felt like he was fucking things up even more. "I mean, I own the house and Akermans is doing well. So, it's not about money. We were both lonely and now we're not. And we get along really well."

She gave a single nod, but her pursed lips said maybe she wasn't completely committed to the idea.

He needed to seal the deal before he brought up the next part of the plan he wanted to tweak. "Why don't we try it for six months? That way you can make a big dent in the debt Craig left you with and not worry about a roof over your head. It will give you some breathing room."

"You really think this will work long term? Just being roommates with benefits?"

"Sure, why not?" Blake let the game piece slide back and forth through his fingers so he wasn't tempted to cross them in hope.

Paige smiled and held out her hand. "Let's give it a go."

He dropped the game piece and grasped her hand. He kept it in his as he stood and moved to her side of the table. Standing in front of her, he hauled her up and placed his hands on her hips, keeping a foot of space between them.

"There's one more thing I want to run by you."

Paige chuckled. "Does this have anything to do with the benefits part of the roommate agreement?"

He gave her his best salacious smile. "As a matter of fact, it does."

"Hmmm… why am I not surprised." She smiled up at him. "Okay, let's hear it."

"I think we were remiss in what we defined as the weekend," he said, almost failing at keeping a straight face.

"How's that?"

"Friday nights are technically part of the weekend, so benefits should start on Fridays."

She tilted her head as if mulling it over. "And end on Sunday mornings?"

"Ha! No way. Monday mornings start the work week, so they'll end on Monday mornings."

"At midnight?" she teased coyly, looking up at him through her lashes.

With his hands still anchored on her hips, he pulled her closer until their bodies were flush against each other. "No." He leaned down and nipped her bottom lip with his teeth. "Not at midnight."

He ran his tongue along her lip, soothing where he'd bitten her, and felt her gasp. "We start the night in bed, we finish the night in bed."

"Okay," she said, sounding breathless.

"And you know what?" he asked when he kissed her lips and then trailed his own to the sensitive spot near her ear.

"Wh… What?"

"Tomorrow is Friday." He ended the teasing and kissed her like he meant it.

She wound her arms around his neck, and he moved one of his hands to the small of her back, flattening her against him.

Several minutes later, when the seam on his jeans threatened to cut into him, he pulled back. "Tomorrow."

"Tomorrow," she repeated.

They packed up the game, and Blake watched Paige head upstairs before checking that the doors were locked and turning off the lights. If caring for and being friends with Paige—but without the risk of being hurt—was enough to hold off the curse, he'd be the happiest man alive.

CHAPTER SEVENTEEN

Friday, November 8

*E*njoying her coffee while Emmie ate her breakfast, Paige couldn't wipe the smile off her face, nor did she want to. She'd woken up with a lightness and joy she hadn't felt in a long time. Even when freeing herself from Craig's control, she hadn't felt as good. The debt and uncertainty hanging over her head at the time likely had something to do with it.

Now she had a safe place for her and Emmie to live, time to pay off her debts, and a growing friendship. It being Friday—the start of the weekend—also helped to broaden her smile.

She mentally went through her schedule for the day. Her morning would be busy, but since her afternoon was wide open... maybe she could treat herself. The last time she'd bought herself something sexy had been years ago. Shopping for new lingerie sounded like a good way to end the workweek.

Even while living at home, she'd always been careful with

her money, working to pay for tuition and books and anything else she needed. Since what she made during the summer didn't last throughout the year, she'd had to spend wisely.

That hadn't changed much when she moved in with Craig. As a splurge for their honeymoon, she had picked up a few sexy bra and panty sets and a few negligées that made her feel beautiful. Craig hadn't said much about them, more interested in getting to the act and pleasing himself.

Yet another red flag she should have seen, but she pushed that thought aside. Water under the bridge and all that. Thinking about past purchases, she realized that the lingerie she'd bought for her honeymoon was the last time she'd bought some.

Lingerie shopping it was. Red looked good against her light olive skin, so maybe she'd look for a red set. But black was considered sexy. Or maybe Blake would appreciate virginal and innocent white.

She snorted softly and covered her mouth. Virginal and innocent she wasn't, but that didn't mean her lingerie couldn't be.

"Mommy, more please?"

Emmie's question pulled her out of her thoughts of sexy panties. Leaning against the counter, her coffee mug in hand, Paige had zoned out.

Still smiling, she looked at her daughter. Only a small amount of some cereal-colored milk remained in her bowl. "Instead of more cereal, how about some fruit? We have bananas and oranges."

"Banana."

Paige raised her eyebrows and waited.

Emmie giggled. "Please."

"You bet." She grabbed a banana out of the bowl on the counter behind her, peeled it, and handed it to Emmie. She took the banana and barely got a "thank you" out before shoving it in her mouth.

Emmie sat at the small table Blake had bought for the kitchen, because he hadn't liked the idea of Emmie being out in the dining room by herself while they were in the kitchen getting their coffee or making lunches. Paige hadn't liked it either but had worried about saying something.

The kitchen ran almost the length of the back of the house, so it was longer than it was wide, but Blake had found a table that fit. One evening a few days after she and Emmie moved in, Blake walked in the house with the table. He'd acted like it was no big deal. He'd seen a problem and fixed it. But, like everything else he did to make them feel at home, it had felt like a big deal to her.

"Good morning," Blake said as he walked into the kitchen.

"Morning," Emmie said at a level loud enough for the neighbors to hear, drowning out Paige's own greeting.

He chuckled and came over to them. Standing beside Paige, his hand casually brushed her hip.

"It's Friday," he said in a deep voice, raspier than usual.

The sound of his voice sent a shiver coursing through her. "It is." She had to clear her throat after almost croaking out the words.

"What are you going to do today, Emmie? Climb a mountain? Traverse a jungle? Solve the world's problems?"

Emmie giggled. "Silly Blake. I'm going to *daycare*," she said, dragging out the word as if Blake had never heard it before.

"Daycare is good. I hope you have fun," he said to Emmie and then leaned closer to Paige. "Your mom and I are going to have fun later," he whispered so only Paige could hear.

He turned away from the table and wiggled his eyebrows at her as he walked around her other side to the coffee maker. His hand once more purposely trailed along her hip, and she couldn't hold back a shiver.

That joy she'd woken up with expanded.

She listened to Emmie natter on about what she was going to do at daycare and about it being reading day. She was usually excited on Fridays because someone from the community came in to read to them, and today was no exception.

Emmie's eyes got big and she looked up at Blake as she asked, "Blake, can you read to us?"

When Blake didn't answer, Paige turned around to look at him. "Did you hear her?"

Blake stood in front of the coffee maker, looking down at it, his hands braced on the counter. He wouldn't even look at her.

"Blake?"

"Mommy, can Blake come read?"

Paige turned back to her daughter. "I'm not sure, sweetie. Blake is thinking right now, so we'll get ready to go. You can ask him again tonight, okay?"

"Okay." Emmie scrambled down from her chair.

"Go upstairs and wash your hands and brush your teeth. I'll be up in a minute to help you."

"Okay," Emmie said again and raced out of the room.

When Paige heard her footsteps on the stairs, she turned back to Blake. "Blake, what's wrong? Can you please answer me?"

She bent around him to get a look at his face. His eyes were closed but his breathing was normal.

It was like when she showed him the strip mall—all of a sudden he just tuned out. During one of their game nights, she'd asked him about it and confessed she had begun to worry he was having a seizure.

Blake had brushed it off, saying he had been deep in thought.

She kept her eyes on him. "Don't ignore me, Blake. I lived with that once, and I won't do it again."

With everything she'd told him about Craig and after how loving Blake had been last night, she couldn't believe he was doing this.

When he still didn't say anything, she left the kitchen. If he didn't want to read at daycare or something else was bothering him, he should just say so. But he could keep his moods because she wasn't going to have any part of them.

Last night everything between them had been fantastic, and even this morning he seemed happy.

She didn't know what had suddenly come over him, but she refused to live in another house where she was ignored or she had to worry about everything she said or did.

Upstairs, Paige got Emmie ready for daycare and left her in her room with a book for a few minutes while she prepared herself for work.

When they came back downstairs, Paige went into the kitchen to check on Blake while Emmie sat on the floor in the foyer to put on her shoes. Blake wasn't there, and he wasn't in the basement either. He'd just left.

Paige felt the telltale burning in her throat, but she blinked back tears. Blake could do whatever he wanted, but that didn't mean Paige had to stick around to take it. Instead of lingerie shopping that afternoon, she would be inquiring about the apartment she'd seen.

BLAKE WIGGLED his eyebrows at Paige and purposely trailed his hand along her hip as he walked around her. Her shiver made him grin as he put a pod in the coffee maker. He could have sworn his fingers still tingled from their casual contact with her, and that was through her clothes.

Tonight, there wouldn't be any clothing. Excitement coursed through him like he was a teenager about to go on his first date. Sleep hadn't come easily the night before because he hadn't been able to stop thinking about Paige. He hoped the day ahead flew by.

"Blake, can you come read to us?" Emmie asked him.

When he'd sworn off falling in love and getting married, any possibility of having kids had dropped from his plans for his future. That realization had almost crushed him as much as his heartbreak had. But now, as long as he could guard his heart against Emmie too—in case things didn't work out with Paige and she left with her daughter—he could have a child in his life.

He looked down at the coffee maker to make sure it was brewing and was about to turn toward Emmie when the now familiar tension came over him.

His hands dropped to the counter—no longer under his control—as his body, stiff as a two-by-four, fell forward, braced on his outstretched arms. He struggled to break free of the confines, needing to answer Emmie, but like the times before, his efforts were futile.

Images swam in his mind, and his eyes fell closed.

Paige's voice came to him as if from far away, her words muffled, before they faded away completely.

The smell of smoke and body odor hit him first, then the melancholy soulfulness and passionate vocals of a woman singing jazz. He didn't recognize the song, but she reminded him of Nina Simone and the hours he and Paige spent listening to her.

When his vision focused, cigarette and cigar smoke drifted through the room like a visible presence. The singer stood on the stage, crooning into an old-fashioned ribbon microphone perched on a pole. Her lips were painted bright red, the color a perfect match to the long chain of beads around her neck that swung as she moved her hips.

If something in the curse hadn't told him he was in a Chicago speakeasy in 1928, the singer's sleeveless, gauzy dress alone would have made the decade evident. She looked like she belonged in any TV show or movie he'd seen set in that era.

Other women in similar dresses and men in three-piece suits swayed together on the dance floor and lounged against the bar. Some sat at small tables scattered throughout, a drink or cigarette in their hand.

In every other episode, there had only been one or two people for Blake to focus on. Now, he could have been sent to watch any of the dozens of people in the room. He chose to focus on the singer and wait for a clue to see who he'd been sent to see.

Watching wasn't a hardship. It was almost difficult not to focus on her because of her captivating voice. As the first song ended, her eyes drifted around the room and stopped for only a second, maybe two, on a young man sitting at a table in the front.

Blake walked between the tables and side-stepped dancers to get closer to the front of the room. Standing at the side of the dance floor, he could see both the singer and the young man, moving his head from one side to the next like at a tennis match, to see their expressions.

The woman stared ahead as she sang, sometimes closing her eyes, but every couple of minutes, she would look around the room. Her gaze landed on the young man every time.

By the end of the third song, Blake knew the singer and young man were who he'd been sent to see.

The woman finished her set. "Thank you. I'll be back after a short break."

A band started up as the woman left the stage from the side. She weaved through the tables and stopped to chat with patrons as if she had no destination in mind, but her eyes continued to stray to the young man.

When she reached his table, she leaned her hip against it, like she'd done with some others.

The man stood and gestured toward a spare chair. "Vivian, I'd be honored if you would sit for a moment."

She gave a delicate shrug. "I have a moment."

He pulled out the chair for her.

"You've been here every night," she said.

"I can't stay away."

"Is there a favorite song you're hoping to hear?"

He leaned forward. "Only the one you dedicate to me."

Vivian laughed. "And why should I dedicate a song to you? What makes you so special?"

"I'm not, but I'd like to be to you."

Her eyes widened.

"My name is Charles."

The smoke in the room disappeared as the air shifted. Blake took in a large breath of the fresh air. He stood in a park at dusk, blossoms on the trees visible in the fading light.

Charles and Vivian sat on a park bench only a short distance away. They were dressed similarly to how they'd been in the speakeasy, but now they both wore hats, and Vivian had a shawl draped around her shoulders.

"In New York?" he asked, not sounding pleased.

"Yes, can you believe it?" She lightly clapped her palms together, almost bouncing on the bench. "An offer to perform on a real stage, with real audiences..."

"What about us?"

She looked out into the park, not meeting his eyes. "Ah... you... you could come with me."

"You know I can't. My parents are depending on me, and I have the business. Can't you find something here?"

Vivian shot off the bench and whirled to face him. "Charles, this could be the big break I've been looking for. I thought you loved me and wanted me to reach for my dreams."

Charles stood. "I do love you. I don't want to hold you back, but I don't want you to leave either."

Silence hung heavy between them for several minutes.

"I've got to take this, but I'll keep in touch," she finally whispered.

When the air shifted again, Blake found himself on a train platform.

He looked around, not seeing Vivian and Charles at first. Walking around a family lugging suitcases, he spotted them up ahead. They stood facing each other but not touching, a suitcase at Vivian's feet.

"This is it? You're really going to walk away from our love?"

Vivian sniffed and brought a handkerchief up to the corner of her eye. "How can you say that?"

"Because that's what it feels like. You're picking your career over me."

Vivian straightened her shoulders. "Isn't that what you're doing, Charles? By staying here for the family business?"

"And my family. We're already established here and can have a good life."

Vivian bent down and picked up her suitcase. "I love you, but if I don't go, I'll always wonder what could have been."

"I'd rather have you wondering here, at my side, than not have you at all," he said, desperation in his tone.

"I love you, Charles, but sometimes love isn't enough."

"What would be enough?"

"Fulfilling my dreams." Vivian leaned forward and placed a soft kiss on his lips before turning away and boarding the train.

Charles didn't move.

When the train whistle sounded, the air around Blake shifted again. He was going to see misery and heartache he didn't want to watch, but he didn't have a choice, and like watching a car wreck, he couldn't turn away. Every episode showed him that love only ended in heartbreak and he knew this one wouldn't be any different.

He didn't need to see more to know it was true and that he had to continue to guard his heart with Paige. He just wasn't so sure he was doing such a good job anymore.

Blake next found himself in an upscale lounge in New York City in 1954. Vivian sang on a small stage in a subdued black dress this time, but there was no mistaking the power and passion of her voice.

He let his gaze wander amongst the tables but didn't see a lone man at any of them. Maybe he would only see Vivian. A sense of déjà vu settled over him as he wove his way through the tables to get closer to the stage.

"Are you going to talk to her?" a woman asked.

Blake looked to see who the woman was speaking to. Surprised to see her with Charles, Blake walked a few steps closer to them.

"I'm not sure," Charles said as Vivian finished her set and thanked the crowd.

Charles and the woman both watched as Vivian stepped off the side of the stage and walked through the room, stopping to talk with audience members as she'd done at the speakeasy.

"Charles?" she asked when she spotted him and the woman.

Charles stood and offered his hand. "Hello, Vivian. You sounded lovely as always."

Vivian hesitated for a moment before shaking his hand. "Thank you. I..." She gave a nervous laugh. "It's just such a shock to see you after all these years. How are you?"

"I'm good. Really good, actually." Charles turned and extended his hand to the woman. She grasped it and stood, coming alongside him. "Vivian, I'd like to introduce you to my wife, Evelyn."

"I'm pleased to meet you," Vivian said, but Blake sensed her words came more from habit than pleasure.

"Charles and I are just in the city for the weekend, but when we

discovered you were performing here, I just had to come. He's spoken so highly of you over the years. You have an amazing voice."

"Thank you," Vivian said, sounding surprised.

"How have you been? Are you married? Children?" Charles asked.

Vivian let out another laugh that sounded more forced than jovial. "No, no husband or kids. I'm married to my career."

"Well, it was really good to see you and hear you perform again," Charles said. "Will you be doing another set?"

"Yes, in a bit. Speaking of which... I should go get ready. Ah... it was lovely seeing you as well, Charles. And it was a pleasure to meet you, Evelyn."

Evelyn and Charles watched her go before he pulled out his wife's chair for her.

Evelyn put her hand on top of her husband's. "You okay?"

He turned his hand over and clasped his fingers with hers. "Yes. It was good to see Vivian, and I hope she found her dream." Charles leaned over and gave his wife a feather-like kiss on the lips. When he pulled back, love shone in his eyes as he looked at her. "I loved Vivian at one time, but she chose a different path. Would she and I have stayed together if she hadn't left? I don't know. But I do know that the day I met you became the best day of my life. I fall more in love with you every day, and I will love you until I take my last breath."

The shift of the air brought with it a stench of garbage so powerful that Blake's eyes watered. He heard what sounded like a woman crying before the scene came into focus.

He stood in a back alley, bags of garbage stacked along the outside wall of a brick building. Vivian leaned in a door frame, wiping away her tears with a tissue.

"Hey, sweetie, you okay?" a woman asked. She walked over from another doorway in the alley and took a drag on her cigarette.

"Oh. Hi, Lucy. I didn't see you there."

"I'm just taking a smoke break. The kitchen's been busy tonight."

"That's good, I guess. I'm... uh... just on a break too."

The woman tossed her cigarette on the ground and put it out with the toe of her shoe. "You okay?" she asked Vivian again.

"Yeah, just ran into an old flame. It took me by surprise, is all. When I saw him with his wife, I realized that could have been me."

"Is that what you wanted?"

Vivian shrugged. "At the time, I thought chasing my dream was the most important thing, but it can't love me and hold me during the night, ya know?"

"You have regrets?"

"I don't know, but I've learned something in the last twenty-five years... love is enough."

When the air shifted, Blake felt the stiffness leave his body. He didn't need to open his eyes to know he was in his kitchen. He could smell his coffee and the vanilla of Paige's lingering scent.

Emmie's giggle reached him from upstairs, but he couldn't face them right now—he didn't know how to explain what had happened. And even if he did try to explain, Vivian's last words were like an earworm that wouldn't leave his mind. Like she said, maybe love was enough, but what happened if that love left you?

He poured his lukewarm coffee down the sink and headed out. Maybe the day at work would bring some clarity. If it didn't, he didn't know how he'd get Paige to understand.

CHAPTER EIGHTEEN

$\mathcal{P}$aige had to read the document four times before she was sure she had filled it out correctly. She'd been distracted all day because of Blake.

Everything had seemed perfect last night and this morning. Blake had touched her and joked like he hadn't a care in the world. So seeing him standing in front of the coffee maker, his hands braced on the counter like he was steeling himself for something while blatantly ignoring Emmie, shocked her.

She'd run through their conversation a dozen times, looking for any sign that she had said something to piss him off or frustrate him. It hadn't been hard to set Craig off, so it got to the point that she rehearsed each sentence in her mind before she spoke. By the time she finally left him, she felt like she was a worried ball of nerves from morning until night. Always waiting for Craig to blow up, belittle her, or take something away because she said or did the wrong thing.

The rose-colored glasses she wore when she met Craig were easy to recognize when she looked back. She'd taken a while to mature and understand people, but she *had* learned.

It was one of the reasons her boss continued to expand her portfolio—that understanding meant she could tell what a client wanted. When to push, when to give them some space, and how to discern what they really meant when they said something vague. Her insecurities were still there, but she could fake it really well.

That's why she was so puzzled by Blake's behavior that morning. When she'd known him in college, he'd been distracted by his monstrous pile of responsibilities, but when they had seen each other, he'd been genuine. There wasn't ever any subterfuge with him. With Blake, you got what you saw, and in the month they'd been living together, there hadn't been any red flags that said he'd changed.

An image of him at the strip mall when she'd first shown it to him came to mind. He'd zoned out then too. And once when he'd come home from the grocery store, he'd seemed distant.

Holy shit. Was she falling back into old habits and ignoring what she didn't want to see? Blake would never be the asshole that Craig was, but maybe he was moodier than she first gave him credit for.

When he hadn't even acknowledged her that morning, he'd made her feel lower than if he had stood in front of her like a parent scolding a recalcitrant child. Criticism, even if not deserved, was one thing. But outright ignoring her made her feel like scum on the bottom of his shoe. If she talked with Blake, could they work on the moodiness thing? Could they still have everything they'd talked about? Or was she trying to sweep problems under the rug again?

If she put up with Blake ignoring her and had to start fearing what she said, or worse—spending hours going over conversations in her head, analyzing every word—she would be no better off than she'd been three years ago. She might even be worse off because she'd have broken a promise to herself. Everything she'd gone through to teach Emmie to be true to herself would have been for naught.

No. She couldn't go backward.

She picked up her phone and called the property manager of the apartment she'd seen. It had only been two days ago, so hopefully he still had a place left.

The phone rang twice.

"Broadview Properties."

"Hi, this is Paige Goshko. Is the apartment you showed me the other day still available?"

"No. I rented it yesterday and the other one this morning. I told you they would go quickly. I run a tight ship here. I—"

"Thank you," she cut in. She didn't need him to go into his spiel about how great he was. "Can you please let me know if another unit becomes available in the next month?"

"Sure. On this number?"

"Yes, thank you." Paige said goodbye and hung up. It was only one apartment; there would be others. Something she told clients all the time. She'd lived with Craig's asshole-ness for years, so she could put up with Blake's moodiness until she found a new place. As long as she didn't let him shake her resolve, she would be self-reliant once more.

Opening her browser, she began her search for an apartment.

After getting on some wait lists, she had picked up some moving boxes and Emmie, and they were back at Blake's house.

She wouldn't be able to move out that night, but she'd be ready as soon as something became available. With packing tape and boxes in hand, she started in Emmie's room. She would leave some of the boxes open on top so Emmie could take out something if she really wanted it, but at least the packing would be partially done.

"I don't want to move," Emmie whined from her perch on the rocking chair.

For Emmie's entire life, Paige had lived with guilt, always worried that she could never do enough for Emmie or was doing the wrong thing. Maybe guilt just came along as part of the birthing process. When you got a kid, you also got a pile of guilt—free of charge—and they both grew for the next eighteen years.

"I know, sweetie, but we're going to move into a great apartment." She only hoped Emmie was too young to know what actually constituted a great apartment. If Paige had to sleep on a couch for the next decade, she would. Providing for Emmie and being an example she could be proud of was all that mattered.

"I don't want an apartment," Emmie whined again, loud enough to make Paige wince.

"Why don't you go play dress-up and tea party? Everything is still in the living room."

Emmie sighed dramatically. "Fiiiine."

Paige bit the inside of her cheek to stop the laughter that threatened to burst out. More and more she was amazed by the things that Emmie said. She picked up new phrases all the time, and this time, she'd nailed the inflection.

She'd have to remember to write down that moment in a memo on her phone later. Hopefully, one day Paige would be able to look back at the entry and smile at remembering the adult phrase Emmie used, and not only the guilt of leaving Blake's.

"Bye," Emmie said, dragging out the word as she shuffled out of the room like she was heading off to a job she despised.

Paige wasn't sure whether to smile or shudder at thinking about what Emmie would be like as a teenager. Life definitely wouldn't be boring.

And as long as Paige did her best and gave Emmie lots of love—even if she wouldn't be up for a mother-of-the-year award—that would just have to be enough for now.

Moving for the fourth time in a little over a year wasn't something she wanted to do any more than Emmie did, but staying with Blake and being snubbed wasn't an option.

She wasn't looking forward to explaining to Blake they were moving out, but she didn't have a choice about that either.

"Blake!" Emmie shouted from downstairs. "We're moving. I don't want to. I wanna stay here—with you!"

By the time Blake was almost ready to head home, he still hadn't figured out what to say to Paige. They usually texted each other a few times a day, but it had been radio silence all day. On both their ends.

"Almost everyone is gone for the day. So let's have it," Jake said as he barged into Blake's office. He took a seat across from him, and Chewie lay on the floor beside him.

Blake took the box from under his desk and passed it over to Jake. With a practiced move, Jake took out a chew toy and passed the box back to Blake.

After giving Chewie the toy, Jake laid one foot on his other knee and crossed his arms. "You stormed in here this morning like a bull, and you've been an ass all day. I'm guessing you had another episode, so spill."

"We're just in time," Cade said as he walked into the office. He petted Chewie and sat in the other chair across from the desk.

Ford and Dane sauntered in next and leaned against the wall.

"Are you still in a shitty mood?" Ford asked him.

"Hey." Dane elbowed their younger brother. "Maybe he had a reason."

"Sorry," Blake said. "No reason is good enough for being an ass." Blake ran his hands down his face before dropping them onto the desk. "This time I was taken to the 1920s."

He told them how the morning had started off so great but left out that both he and Paige had been looking forward to tonight. Then he walked them through the episode and how he'd heard Paige and Emmie upstairs when he'd finally had control of his body again.

Jake looked incredulous. "You didn't say anything? You just left?"

He sighed, defeated. "I didn't know what to say."

"I thought you were going to tell Paige about the curse after the episode on Halloween," Cade said.

He hesitated, knowing he should have. "I didn't agree to tell Paige; you all did."

Dane smirked. "Yes, because we're smart and you're being a dumbass."

Blake scoffed as the others laughed. Whether he wanted to tell Paige about the curse or not, he wasn't sure he had a choice now.

Jake uncrossed his legs and leaned forward, piercing Blake with his gaze. "You need to tell her. They're coming every two days now?"

Blake hesitated again, not sure he should admit his suspicions, before he said, "I think maybe they're becoming less frequent."

"Do you love Paige?" Cade asked like he was cross-examining a witness.

Did he? He wasn't sure, but he didn't *want* to love her because then he would give her the ability to destroy him again. He couldn't afford to love her.

"No, but I care deeply for her. Maybe that's enough. When I first started experiencing the episodes, the time between each one lessened by one or two days. The seventh and eighth had only two days in between them, but it was four days between this morning's and the last one. Maybe that trend will continue." He heard the hope in his voice and wondered if it was wishful thinking.

Cade shook his head. "And what if they don't?"

"Way to be positive, Mr. Lawyer," Dane said.

Cade shot him a look over his shoulder. "It doesn't have anything to do with being positive. Blake needs to be realistic and be prepared in case the frequency doesn't lessen."

"I agree," Jake said and turned to Cade. "Did you get a chance to go through any of the papers you and Blake found? My mom read the journals and said there was only one reference to the curse."

Jake turned back to Blake. "Your mom said she was so in love with your dad that she didn't have to worry about the curse."

Blake scowled. "Lucky for her," he said before he could stop himself. Grimacing, he looked at each of his brothers. "Sorry. That wasn't fair. I'm glad Mom and Dad loved each other so much. For the longest time, I wanted what they had."

"You could still have it," Dane said. "You loved Paige once so you could love her again."

"He can't force it," Cade said as he stood. "I've got to go, but remember that letter we found from a woman named Martha?"

"Shit. I forgot all about that. Martha was in one of the episodes. Did she mention the curse?"

Cade nodded. "Almost all the old papers were letters from her and she does mention the curse in a couple of them. I scanned them all, so I'll email you the ones that might help you convince Paige the curse is real. I'll send you a copy of Mom's letter too."

"Thanks." Blake only hoped it would be enough.

Everyone left for the day, and Blake waited until he got the email from Cade before he headed home.

Paige's SUV in the driveway was a good sign. At least she wasn't avoiding him.

He walked into the house and barely had time to brace himself before Emmie launched herself at him.

"Blake!" she shouted, the high-pitch almost making him wince. "We're moving. I don't want to move. I want me and Mommy to stay with you."

The situation was worse than he feared. Paige *was* avoiding him, and she was not hiding the fact that she was moving out.

Hefting Emmie higher in his arms, he looked her in the eyes. "I'll go talk to your mom, okay? Maybe we can work something out." He wouldn't lie to her, but maybe some reassurance would work for now.

Blake walked into the living room and lowered Emmie to the couch. "How about a movie? Want to watch *Frozen*? I don't think your mom will mind since it's the weekend." He mentally crossed his fingers, hoping that wasn't a lie either. Paige limited Emmie's screen time, but they did watch movies on the weekends.

About to set up the movie, he paused. If Paige was angry enough to leave, she'd need to be able to let it all out so he could tell her about the curse and they could work through everything that had convinced her she needed to move out. They wouldn't be able to do that if Emmie was around since he didn't want her to see her mom get angry and yell at him, which he deserved.

Pulling his phone out of his pocket, he shot Cade a text. It was one of those emergency type of situations where you acted and asked for forgiveness later. Within seconds, Cade was responding.

Blake crouched in front of the couch. "Emmie, I need to talk to your mom. She's mad because I did something wrong."

Emmie patted his cheek. "Say sorry. Then it's okay."

If Blake wasn't so worried that Paige would never accept his apology, he would have smiled at the sage advice. "I hope so. Can you please put on your pink boots? My brother Cade is coming to pick you up so he can take you and Malcolm out for dinner. Cade even bought a car seat just for you."

Emmie scrambled off the couch and ran to the foyer. "Pizza?" she asked as she plopped onto the floor, pulling on a boot.

"I don't know, but you can ask him."

She hesitated and looked up the stairs. "What about Mommy?"

"I'll make sure your mom gets something to eat."

"After you say sorry."

"Right. Aft—"

"What are you doing?" Paige asked, her tone more accusatory than questioning.

He turned to look at her, mentally crossing his fingers she would hold in her anger until Emmie was gone. "Cade is coming to pick up Emmie to take her to dinner so you and I can talk. I have something to tell you."

"You can't just make plans for my daughter without me," Paige hissed at him.

"I know it was overstepping, but we need to talk," he repeated, hoping it would be enough, and took Emmie's coat off the hook by the door and helped her into it.

"Mommy, Blake was bad. He'll say sorry."

Paige's lip curled and her face reddened. He shouldn't have said anything to Emmie, but he didn't regret it because he would raise his kids to know that screw-ups happened and they needed to apologize. He planned for Emmie being his kid one day because he loved the little girl and her mom.

There was a knock on the door and then Cade walked in. He must have felt the tension in the air, because he turned right to Emmie. "You ready to go, Emmie?" He took her hand in his and headed straight through the still-open door. "What would you like to eat?"

"Pizza. Cheese—"

Blake shut the door, blocking out the rest of Emmie's words. He turned around, ready to face whatever Paige threw at him.

"Don't ever do that again! Don't send my daughter away!" Paige closed the short distance between them and shoved at his chest with both hands. He stumbled back into the door.

Her eyes widened and she took a step back. "Oh, my god! I'm sorry. So, so sorry." She stumbled over the couch and sat on the end, pulling her knees up to her chest and wrapping her arms around them.

Blake sat a few inches from her on the couch. "You have nothing to apologize for."

"I shouldn't have shoved you."

"I deserved it. You have every right to be angry. I had Cade pick up Emmie so you could yell at me all you want."

"You want me to yell at you?" Her lips pressed into a fine line.

"Not usually, no, but in this case, it might be good to clear the air. I'm not angry at you for shoving me, Paige, and I'm not going to react the way Craig did. Will you look at me?" He needed to look directly into her eyes when he explained everything so she'd see his sincerity.

She lifted her chin, and the hurt he saw in her eyes made him feel like the worst kind of friend. Since he couldn't erase the hurt from this morning, he forged ahead. "There's something I should have told you before you moved in and —" Her eyes widened again, and she opened her mouth.

He held up his hand. "It's nothing bad… well, not really. It's just something my brothers and I learned about when my mom died. I need to explain, and then my strange behavior this morning will make sense."

"I'm not sure any excuse will be enough. I won't put up with someone ignoring me and making me feel like garbage."

"You shouldn't have to."

"I'll listen, but I won't promise anything else."

"That's fair." Blake shifted so his back was against the couch and let out a breath. He still wasn't sure how to tell Paige he was cursed or if she'd believe him, but he would give it his best shot.

CHAPTER NINETEEN

"Our family is cursed. I'm sorry for not telling you sooner. I should have, but I didn't know how. The curse has been handed down—"

As his words fully registered, Paige felt her previous rage reignite. "That's your excuse?" She raised her voice, unable to tamp down her anger. "You're telling me your bullshit behavior is because of a curse?"

She pushed off the couch, but Blake grasped her wrist gently.

"Don't," she said, jerking out of his hold.

"Paige, please. You said you would listen. Will you let me explain?"

"You expect me to believe your family is cursed?"

"I understand your skepticism. I didn't believe it at first either." He patted the cushion beside him. "Please, sit down. I know it sounds crazy, but I can explain."

Having been fed so many bullshit lines by Craig over the years, she hesitated. It was only the suffering and sincerity she'd heard in Blake's tone that convinced her to listen. She sat back in the corner of the couch, her socked feet pulled up on the cushion so her toes wouldn't touch his leg, and nodded for him to continue.

"I told you my mom decorated my spare room as a children's room because she wanted grandchildren. That wasn't the whole truth, though my mom did decorate the room and she did want grandchildren. I came home from work one day and it was completely redone; even the chalkboard paint on the closet doors was already dry. I didn't know how to explain it to you."

Dragging his hands down his face, he let out a big sigh. "That was three weeks before she died. I didn't talk to her for a full week after she did it because I was so angry."

"Did she tell you why?"

"She said that I needed to have a room ready just in case I met someone who already had a child."

Paige gasped. "Did she think you'd just invite a woman with a kid over to live with you?" She snorted. "Oh, wow. You did. Was your mom psychic?"

Blake chuckled. "Not that I know of…"

He paused and his expression sobered. "Right after my twenty-ninth birthday, my mom started hounding me to find love and settle down. And when I say *hound*, I mean all. The. Time. No matter how often I told her I didn't have plans to ever settle down, she wouldn't let up. She called me a couple of times a week asking if I had any upcoming dates. In between the calls she would text asking the same thing, and then send me emails with articles."

"Articles about dating?"

"Yeah. You know the kind… "Ten Turn-offs You Must Avoid,' 'Seven Dating Rules to Follow,' 'First Date Dos and Don'ts'… that type of thing. She even tried to set me up on blind dates. I wasn't interested but I went on a couple hoping that would appease her. Instead, she just got worse."

"She wanted you to get married that badly? Why?"

"That's where the curse comes in. The thing is, she never told us about the curse, never mentioned it once in my entire life, just started with the crazy behavior when I turned twenty-nine."

He blew out a breath, his frustration almost palpable in the air.

"She left us a letter with her will. Cade knew about it because he was the executor of her estate, but he figured it was just a goodbye letter. The night of her funeral, Cade read it to us. Mom said that a relative of hers was cursed hundreds of years ago by a spirit because he didn't have enough love and empathy for others. The spirit said that if anyone in the ancestor's lineage did not fall in love and have that love reciprocated by their thirtieth birthday, the curse would take effect."

Alex had always seemed like a reasonable person, but maybe she'd developed early-onset dementia or something. Paige hadn't seen any signs of it on the few occasions they'd met for coffee, but then, Paige wasn't a doctor. Maybe there had been signs and she hadn't realized what they were. Or maybe Alex didn't exhibit them all the time.

"Your mom must have believed the curse since she was pushing you so hard. Decorating your spare room—as much as Emmie loves it—was kind of crazy. But... you don't actually believe you're cursed, do you?"

As much as Paige wanted an answer for why Blake had ignored her, she didn't believe in curses. And even if she did, she still didn't see how it would explain his behavior.

Blake took his phone out of his back pocket. He unlocked it and pulled something up before handing it to her. "Here's my mom's letter. Why don't you read that while I get us something to drink? Wine?"

She took the phone from him and stared at Alex's

handwriting on the screen. She'd only seen it a few times on cards, but it was distinctive due to all the curls. "Sure," she said as she started to read.

Blake came back just as she finished reading. She put his phone on the table and accepted the glass of wine he offered. "Thanks." She took a sip, letting it soothe her throat, dry from so many emotions.

"Your mom really believed… that this guy Eamon was cursed by a spirit, and now you'll be cursed for all eternity." She shook her head. "That's crazy."

She realized then that Blake hadn't answered her earlier question. Shock slid through her as she looked at him. "You believe it too, don't you?"

"I didn't at first. My birthday came and went, and nothing happened then."

"Your birthday is September first, right?"

His lips turned up into a small smile. "You remembered."

She shrugged. "I'm good with dates." While that was the truth, when it came to Blake she remembered so much more than just dates. She remembered the first time she saw him, the first time they kissed, and every time they made love. She also remembered how he'd shut down when she broke up with him and didn't fight for her.

He looked as if he was waiting for her to say something more. When she didn't, he continued. "Anyway… nothing happened until almost two weeks after my birthday. On the Friday two weeks later, September thirteenth, the curse hit me."

Paige scoffed. "Friday the thirteenth? Really? How cliché."

"Seriously. I was thinking about my mom, so I walked into my spare room. The curse pulled me in when I sat in the rocking chair. It took over my body. I couldn't move. Looking at me, you would think I was in a trance."

Going into a trance sounded almost crazier than a curse. The expression "stranger than fiction" popped into her mind. It was a saying for a reason, but could Blake's curse be one of those reasons? She remembered how scared she'd been seeing him standing in the middle of the empty salon, wondering if he was having a seizure, not knowing what to do.

"When I showed you the strip mall… that was the curse?"

As soon as she asked the question, she realized she'd phrased it as if she believed everything Blake was saying— that the curse was real. But there were no such things as curses.

"That was the second time," Blake said. "I'd almost convinced myself the first time had been a dream, even though I was awake. When it struck while I was with you, it freaked me out so much I didn't know what to say. That's why I rushed out. Again, I'm sorry for not telling you then. I was just too freaked out. Then, later, I didn't know what to say."

She wanted to say she accepted his apology, but it seemed too farfetched. "I've never heard of someone being cursed before." Maybe if she said it enough times, Blake would tell her this was all a joke. But then what would he come up with next to explain his strange behavior?

Blake put his wine glass on the table and picked up his phone. "When Cade and I went through our mom's things, we found old journals and letters. Some of them were photocopies, and some were the old and brittle originals."

He handed over his phone again. "Cade scanned that. A woman named Martha wrote it to her best friend, George."

"Did she ever send the letter?"

"No, and she wrote them later, after she told him in person that she loved him."

"She said that in one of the letters?"

Blake shook his head. "No. I know that because I was there when she said it. I heard her confess her love to him in San Francisco in 1924."

Paige almost dropped the phone. Fumbling with it, her wine glass started to tip.

Blake rescued Paige's wine and put it on the table.

"You were there?" she asked, her eyes wide.

He nodded, and she stared at him like she was searching his face for any signs he might be joking. He wished he was. The whole concept of curses and traveling back in time seemed ludicrous even to him, and yet the curse had sent him to the past nine times now.

As Paige read Martha's letter, Blake could picture Martha as clearly as if he'd really known her. In less than fifteen minutes, as he'd watched Martha suffer into her old age, she'd become real to him, as had all the other people he'd seen in the episodes.

No matter how much he thought about it, he still hadn't been able to wrap his head around how the curse was supposed to make him want to fall in love when all he saw was misery.

Or perhaps it wasn't.

Lately, as each new episode sucked him in to watch and experience another heartbreak, he wondered if the curse was punishment for not opening himself up to accept love. The more he thought about it, the more he believed the curse was telling him it was too late for him. But then what? Would he spend the rest of his life watching people suffer, sucked into misery after misery? He'd already suffered through his own broken heart. That was misery enough. If it was trying to tell him something else, he was clueless as to what that could be.

Paige looked up, her palm across her heart. "She watched him marry someone else," she whispered. "It's heartbreaking. She loved him so much."

"I know." He remembered how Martha had looked when she'd finally worked up the courage to confess her love to George. "I first saw her when she told George she was in love with him."

Blake told Paige about hearing Martha's declaration of love, then watching her at George's wedding and through the years after. As Paige listened, her eyes became glassy with unshed tears. "I don't think she ever stopped loving him," he said when he finished.

"It's sad."

He raised his brow in question. "That she never stopped loving him?"

"No… Yes, that too. But I meant that she was alone. She didn't have anyone to share her life with."

"She had friends." Just like Blake had his, including Paige, for however long it lasted. "That's all Martha needed, I guess," he said, although he didn't know if that was true.

Blake told Paige about seeing Liam and Moira in 1778 and how Moira was forced to choose security over love.

"Is that the couple you saw this morning?"

"No, I saw them when you were showing me the strip mall."

"No wonder you rushed out. It would have been a horrible thing to watch."

"It was, but I think I was more freaked out about going into a trance. That was the second time, and I didn't know what to do."

She brought her wine glass to her lips, then lowered it, letting out a short laugh. "It's empty."

"You want some more?"

"No, I'm good." She put her glass on the table. "Ah, do you want to tell me more?"

Good question. He hated remembering the sorrow from each episode, but eventually he would tell her all of them so she would understand what he'd seen. Unless there were too many to remember. And wasn't that an unpleasant thought?

"I'll tell you about each one if you'd like, but not today, if that's okay? There are more… Including this morning, I've been taken into the past nine times."

"Later is fine. But can I ask you just one more question?" When he nodded, she asked, "Is every one about people with broken hearts?"

"Yes, in some way."

"How do you stand it?"

"I don't have a choice." What he didn't tell her was the deep sorrow he felt for all the lost love. It didn't matter that what he saw took place so long ago; the stories were still heart-wrenching and felt like they had just happened.

"Each time the curse hits you, are you frozen like you were this morning and in the strip mall?"

He scrubbed his hands over his face again before meeting her eyes. "Yes. Since the last two episodes were further apart than the previous ones, I'm hoping that will keep happening. But… if it doesn't, I'm not sure what I'll do. If a curse comes upon me while I'm driving…" He shuddered.

"Blake, I—" The door opened, interrupting her.

"Mommy! Blake!" Emmie ran up to Blake and pounced on him, pushing him back into the cushions as he wrapped his arms around her. She patted his cheek. "Did you say you're sorry?"

He smirked. "I did."

Emmie turned in his arms to look at Paige. "Mommy, did you forgive him?"

She smiled at her daughter. "Yes, I did."

Blake expected that she might have, but he also assumed it would be a while before the idea of the curses truly sunk in. It had with him, and he was the one cursed.

"Paige," Cade said from the foyer.

She stood and walked over to him. Blake followed and helped Emmie take off her boots and coat.

"You believe it too?" she asked Cade quietly while Blake distracted Emmie.

"I do. And I thought you should know, but don't put any pressure on yourself."

Blake looked up, seeing Paige frown before her eyes widened. "Oh. Being in love and have it reciprocated," she whispered, repeating what Blake had told her.

"As horrible as this is for Blake, you can't force anything or…"

"Or what?" she asked.

"If the episodes become worse and something happens to him, you can't blame yourself. We'll all be there for him no matter what."

Paige's fingers flew to her parted lips at Cade's words, and as much as Blake wished his brother had kept his trap shut, Paige had to be ready for anything. There had already been so much for her to digest. It's only fair she should know what could happen if he didn't fall in love and have it returned.

Cade turned to leave, then turned back and smiled. "A warning… Emmie was falling asleep in the car. I think she might have just gotten a second wind." Cade waved and left, but Paige didn't move. He could only guess at the thoughts running through her mind, and not about Emmie's sudden burst of energy. It wasn't until Emmie tugged on her pant leg that Paige turned to her daughter.

"Mommy? Are you still mad at Blake?"

Paige crouched down in front of Emmie. "No. Blake said he was sorry, and I forgave him. I was just lost in my thoughts." She smiled, but he could tell it was forced.

"Okay." Emmie looked at her for a moment, and then, as if happy with the answer, turned toward Blake. "Can we play tag?"

Blake groaned and dramatically flopped onto the couch, throwing his arm across his eyes. "Oh, no," he said on another mock groan. "You've worn me out. How about we play a board game instead?"

"Chutes and Ladders!" Emmie shouted and ran to the sideboard in the dining room where her games were stored. When Paige and Emmie moved into Blake's, Emmie only had two games, but during the last week, he feigned surprise when several new games appeared as if by magic.

Paige had worried Blake was spoiling Emmie, but he confessed that it wasn't about Emmie at all. He'd told her that if he had to play the memory matching game or Go Fish one more time, he would go crazy.

She'd laughed and made him promise to lay off buying any more for a little while.

An hour and a half later, Emmie was in bed asleep. They'd played three games and given her a snack while he and Paige ate some sandwiches he'd thrown together. Then Paige gave Emmie a quick bath, and he read Emmie two stories. She was out before he finished the second one.

Paige had chosen to sit in the rocking chair to listen to him read to Emmie. By the look on her face the first time he took over story time, he may have surprised her with his superior acting skills. He liked that he could surprise her; it kept their relationship fresh. He realized the word he'd used to refer to them, but a friendship was a relationship.

"Mommy loves you," Paige whispered as she kissed her sleeping daughter before following Blake out of the room.

They stood in the hallway by the bedroom door.

Blake turned toward the stairs and hesitated. He turned back, wanting to say something, but unsure of the right words.

"I do forgive you," she said softly and walked right into his space. Wrapping her hands around the back of his neck, she pulled him down for a kiss. It wasn't passionate like the one from the night before. More of a getting-to-know-you-again kiss.

"Thank you." He rested his forehead on hers. "Tonight, I'd just like to hold you."

"I'd like that too."

He let Paige lead as she took his hand and pulled him into the bedroom.

Blake sat on the bed. "Would you like me to leave the door slightly ajar, so we can hear Emmie, since there won't be any hanky panky tonight?"

She chuckled like it was a tension reliever after the day they'd had. "No hanky panky, huh? Maybe tomorrow?"

"Maybe." He reached out and pulled her between his legs, hoping she would understand what he said next. "I'm not saying that to be coy. I want to earn your trust back, Paige. I'm sorry for not telling you about the curse earlier. I... I just didn't know how. I didn't want you thinking I was trying to gaslight you like Craig did."

"If you had told me earlier and I didn't see you in a trance like you were today, I probably wouldn't have believed you. Even with what happened in the strip mall."

After a quick kiss, Blake was true to his word and they got into bed. He wrapped his arm around her, pulling her into his side. She laid her head on his chest and lightly caressed his bare skin with her fingers.

When her breathing evened out with sleep, he thought about her reaction to what Cade had told her. And how dead set against love he'd been for so long. If he couldn't open his heart to love, would the curse eventually consume him? It was a chance he was going to have to take because he couldn't force himself to love her, any more than he could force Paige to love him. What they had would have to be enough.

CHAPTER TWENTY

Sunday, November 10

"One more, pl—" Emmie pleaded before her yawn cut her off.

Blake placed a kiss on Emmie's forehead and stood. "Tomorrow."

He raised his arms over his head and stretched. "You tuckered me out today." He had looked after Emmie that afternoon so Paige could pop out to show a property to a client who was only in town for the day.

Paige loved watching Blake and Emmie together. She still worried about being too vulnerable, and now she had the curse to worry about too, but Emmie was thriving with having a father figure.

Blake pretended to yawn, then faked a snore while standing up, making big snorting noises. Paige had to put her hand over her mouth to smother her laugh.

"Kay," Emmie said as she yawned again. "Good night. I love you, Mommy. I love you, Blake," she said as her eyes drifted close.

He leaned down and placed another kiss on Emmie's forehead. "I love you too, kiddo," he said on a quiet breath.

Loving a child was so much easier than putting yourself out there for a partner.

When Blake straightened, she wouldn't have noticed his slight pause if she hadn't been watching him. Should she reassure him that it was okay to love Emmie and that he didn't have to love her too because she didn't love him? She bit her lip, wishing she knew what to say. Why was it she always thought of what to say in certain situations hours or days later?

Blake took a step toward her, and she tensed. Then he winked as he walked by her. "Meet you in the bedroom," he whispered.

Paige blew out a breath, letting her tension escape with it, and made sure Emmie was tucked in. Even though Blake had already done it, she wasn't ready to give up on her nightly routines. She gave her sleeping daughter a kiss. "Mommy loves you."

Turning off the main light, she left the door ajar and hurried the few steps to Blake's bedroom. Only the lamps on the nightstands were lit, the drapes closed, giving the room a soft warmth. Seeing Blake sitting on the wooden bench at the end of the bed, she felt a sense of contentment and happiness she hadn't felt in years, if ever.

He held out his hand to her. "Come here."

Placing her hand in his, she let him pull her between his legs.

"It's Sunday." He wiggled his brows, making her laugh.

"It is. Hmmm… " She tilted her head as if pretending to think. "I believe the agreement said that Sunday is part of the weekend."

"It is."

He pulled her down for a kiss, and she fell right into his

lap, letting out a giggle. "You scoundrel," she mocked, waving her hand in front of her face like she was a fainting flower who needed fresh air.

"Well, ma'am. If I'm a scoundrel, then I think I've soiled your person, so now I must get you clean," he said in a horrible British accent.

Blake stood, cradling her in his arms. She let out a small shriek before slapping her hand across her mouth. "Shhhh, don't wake Emmie," he said as he strode into the bathroom, and bumped the door closed with his hip.

He slid her down his body, then reached for the hem of her shirt and pulled it over her head. She helped him with his, and they rid each other of the rest of their clothes.

Paige ran her fingers along his chest and turned toward the shower.

"Nope, not yet." He gripped her hips and lifted her, setting her down on the long counter. Another small shriek erupted from her, but this time it was because of the cold granite countertop against her bare butt.

"We're not taking a shower?" she teased. "I thought you soiled me?"

He wiggled his brows again. "Oh, baby, we're going to have a shower, and I'll get you all soapy and make you come. But since I'm not a fan of risking my neck during sex, we're going to have sex right here. Brace your hands behind you, Paige." His voice had taken on a husky tone. "I need to be inside you."

Paige did as he directed and spread her legs on either side of Blake's. He watched her, maybe waiting to see if she'd protest.

Not a chance. Leaning on one hand, she put her other between her legs and ran her two middle fingers through her folds. Already soaked and ready for him, she couldn't resist egging him on. Bringing her fingers to her mouth, she kept her eyes locked on his as she sucked her fingers clean.

"Fuck." Blake grabbed her under her knees and pulled her butt forward. With just enough time to throw her hand behind her, she supported herself as he lifted her up and entered her in one thrust.

They both groaned but didn't break eye contact as he pumped into her fast and hard. She locked her legs around him and hugged her heels into his butt, finding a rhythm with him.

"Oh, god!" An intense orgasm ripped through her, taking her by surprise.

"Fuck," Blake repeated as he thrust into her again and held himself against her. He closed his eyes, and she felt his body vibrate as his orgasm crested and took him over the edge.

"Wow," he said when he opened his eyes and looked at her.

She grinned. "A new word."

He raised his brow in question. She loved when he did that. "I was just commenting that 'wow' was a new word since you seemed to be reduced to only saying 'fuck' when we have sex." She couldn't keep a straight face and burst out laughing.

"Is that right, little miss 'oh, god?'" He grabbed her around the waist, her ankles still wrapped around his butt, his softening cock still inside her, and carried her into the shower.

Twenty minutes later, they were in bed, now clean and sated. Blake's arm was wrapped around her, his front spooning her back. It was one of her favorite positions, cocooned in Blake's warmth and comfort.

Tomorrow, reality would crash in, but for this moment, she could pretend that they were more than friends. That he wanted a wife and children like they'd talked about years ago. And that she would never have to worry about losing herself while trying to please someone else.

"Tomorrow is Monday," he whispered against her neck.

"You get an A plus, Mr. Akerman. You definitely know your days of the week."

"Ha, funny woman." He tickled her waist.

She squealed, something she'd done more tonight than she had in years, until he let go and pulled her back against him.

"It just means our weekend is over."

"I know." Mondays meant sleeping in separate beds. She didn't offer to change their agreement, and neither did he. They hadn't talked specifics about how long they could continue like this. Nor had they mentioned any more about the curse, but then, neither of them seemed to know what to say.

Thursday, November 14

THE CONTROL over Blake's body released. Flopping back in his office chair, he closed his eyes. He'd been taken back to 1911 to watch Mary and John fall in love and have their first child. Two more scenes closely followed. Their life on the farm was simple, but the love between the two of them was plentiful. Blake had felt a warmth in his heart just from watching, as if their love was strong enough it could spread to others. Then America joined the fight in WW1 and John was conscripted.

Life continued for Mary as she raised their children and tended the farm. Each night she sat at her kitchen table and wrote a letter to John, telling him about her day. She spoke of her love for him and her faith that he would return to them safely. Until the day a soldier came with her local clergyman to deliver a telegram.

Her hand shook as she took the telegram. It held only one line: *Deeply regret to inform you 475677 Private John Alfred Garrow Infantry officially reported killed in action between September 26 and September 30, 1918.*

Blake didn't know if he'd ever forget the sound of Mary's scream that ripped from her as she clenched the telegram in her fist.

Dropping his hands on his desk, he sat forward and jumped when he noticed Jake sitting in the chair across from him. "When did you get here?"

"About ten minutes ago. I saw when the trance released you but figured you needed time to process." Jake lifted his chin toward the side of Blake's desk. "I got you a cold bottle of water and a root beer. Thought you might want one or both."

"Thanks." Blake uncapped the water and drained the bottle.

"You want to talk about it?" Jake asked.

"I don't think it will help."

"How frequently are you getting them now?"

"Daily." The despondency must have been obvious in Blake's voice because Chewie got up from his spot on the floor beside Jake and lumbered over to him. Blake petted the big dog almost absently as Chewie offered his silent comfort.

Jake frowned. "Once a day?"

"More than that now." He'd had one curse a day for the last two, but Mary and John were his second episode since the night before. Blake glanced at his watch to see it was four in the afternoon. The first episode had hit him at eight in the morning, eight hours before. If that timing held true for the next one, it would come around midnight. "Shit," he whispered.

"What?" Jake asked.

"I haven't been able to predict when the next episode will come because they've been random. The only thing I knew was that the times between were getting shorter. If they start coming more than once a day, could they come while I'm sleeping too?"

"Maybe they'll just feel like dreams if they do."

"Maybe… But it's not the events that worry me so much. It's the feelings they evoke."

"The sadness you've talked about?"

"That. And the despair." Blake could see the worry on his friend's face deepened, but it wasn't like he could do anything about the curses. Nor could he force himself to fall in love with Paige even if he wanted to. And that was the kicker, right there. He still wasn't sure love was in the cards for him. Every time he considered it, he remembered how Paige had left him utterly shattered. For weeks, he'd walked around with a feeling of hopelessness and loss, as if Paige had taken a piece of him with her that day and he would never be whole again.

Regardless of how busy he'd been at the time, he'd needed her. Maturity and time had given him the insight to realize that he had neglected her, but not without reason. It was on him that he'd never explained those reasons to her. Instead of waiting for him to pay attention to her, he had needed her to support him. Perhaps they had both been too young to understand what the other needed.

After Paige had left him, he'd been too caught up in his pain and responsibilities to look at the situation with an unemotional eye. Then he guarded his heart and moved on. Every now and then over the years, something would trigger a memory of Paige, and he'd think about their time together and the breakup. And those same feelings of heartbreak would resurface, making him never want to risk it again if she left a second time. Paige had told him that she never planned to fall in love again either, so they'd both be better off that way.

Blake absently ran his fingers through Chewie's fur, then met Jake's gaze. "Some days all I can think about is the suffering that love caused everyone in the episodes."

"Not everyone, and some of them chose that."

Blake shook his head. "I don't think anyone chose that heartache."

"Sure they did. Martha?"

"She loved George until the day she died."

"Exactly."

Blake stared at his friend. "I don't get it."

"Martha *chose* to love George until the end," Jake said. "If she truly loved him, she probably couldn't have just turned that off, but she could have *chosen* to love him and someone else as well. And what about the sailor?"

"His love and his brother betrayed him, but he did move on. He married and had children…" Blake recalled the final scene of Christopher and his wife. "Shit," he whispered as realization dawned. "He didn't give her his heart. He told her he had already given it to another."

"Exactly. I get that they were heartbroken. On top of that, the sailor felt betrayed too. But neither of them *chose* to look for someone else to love. It may have seemed like they moved on with their lives, but a part of them was stuck in the past."

Was he doing that? Was he stuck in the past and not moving on?

An unsettling feeling, something he couldn't quite name, stirred in him. "You think I should just walk away from Paige? Leave her in the past?"

Jake snorted and sat forward, piercing him with a glare. "Jesus, you're an idiot."

"Thanks," Blake said sarcastically.

"You couldn't leave Paige in the past even if you wanted to because she's also your present. You need to leave the heartache in the past. That's the only way you're going to be able to open yourself up to love again."

That was the one thing Blake had promised himself he would never do—open himself up again. Vulnerability had a direct path to heartache. If he let go of the past heartache, he'd open himself up to more. It could become a never-ending cycle. "And if she leaves me again?"

"Then you deal with it. But what if she stays?"

"You're not being realistic. People don't always have a choice. Look at my mom and dad."

"Your parents loved each other," he countered.

"Yes, and then my dad died. My mom was heartbroken afterward and she never moved on," Blake said, satisfied that he made his point.

"I was there too, remember? Her situation was different than Martha's and the sailor's. They were both young, but your parents had twenty years together... Yes, I get that's not long compared to some marriages, but they had a whole life together, and they raised five boys. That may have been enough for your mom. She didn't need more."

Blake scrubbed his hands over his face, frustrated. He'd already opened himself up to Paige by inviting her and Emmie into his life. If they left now, he wasn't sure how he would recover. Letting them in further could mean he'd end up as desolate as Mary after losing John in WWI. His heart might consider it a death, whether it was physical or not.

Jake stood and called to Chewie. "Blake. Don't forget I saw you with Paige too. That was the happiest I've ever seen you."

"I wasn't the one who broke it off with Paige," he said, not able to hold back the defensiveness.

"Fair. But maybe neither of you were ready back then. Now, you've been given a second chance. Not everyone gets that. Don't be like Martha and let your past block your future."

Blake wasn't letting his past block his future. He was using it to protect his heart.

CHAPTER TWENTY-ONE

Friday, November 15

"Oh, god. Oh, I..." Paige held onto the headboard as she rocked back and forth on top of Blake, grinding her hips down on him for friction.

"That's it, baby, take your pleasure from me."

"I need... ah... I'm so close." Her orgasm hovered on the edge, so intense, but not ready to let go. "I need..." she pleaded, not quite knowing what she needed.

"I've got you." Blake lifted his hips and thrust up into her. At the same time, he removed one hand from her hips and rubbed his thumb on her clit.

"Oh, god," she called out as Blake increased his pressure and her orgasm exploded, the incredible sensations shredding her.

"Squeeze my cock, baby. Fuck." Blake threw his head back as his orgasm ripped through him, pulling another smaller orgasm from her.

Her hands still gripping the headboard, she looked down at him from between her arms. "I told you..." she said, panting, "I didn't want you… to fix me, but… I think you just… broke me." She grinned at him.

Blake barked a laugh and pulled her down beside him. "Then I *will* have to fix you," he said, wiggling his brows.

She closed her eyes and snuggled into him, breathing in his fresh, citrusy scent. "Tomorrow."

"That's a promise." Blake lifted off the bed and went into the bathroom. She knew he was getting a warm washcloth because he always did, and she loved that.

When he tossed the cloth to the side, he pulled the covers up. He put one arm around her and spooned her back—another thing she loved.

"Mmmm. I love Fridays," she said around a yawn.

Blake chuckled, his breath warm against her neck. "Me too."

He'd worn her out tonight in the best possible way, and she'd lost track of the number of orgasms he'd given her. She smiled to herself, proud she hadn't been a slouch in the orgasm department either, giving him three.

Just as Paige felt sleep start to take her, Blake jerked behind her. His arm stiffened under her.

"The cur—"

Paige pulled herself from his arms and turned around, sitting up on her knees.

"Blake?" His eyes were closed like he might be asleep, but he didn't look relaxed. He was still on his side from where he'd been spooned up against her back. She ran her hand along his shoulder and arm, the tension in his muscles obvious under her fingers.

He'd told her the curse took control of his body, but knowing it and seeing it were two different things. When the episode had him while in the kitchen, he'd looked like he was bracing his hands on the counter while waiting for his coffee.

She sat against the headboard and scooted as close as she

could to Blake. He was too heavy for her to pull his upper body into her lap, but she needed to touch him. She ran her hand gently along his hair.

Blake told her that the episode in the strip mall had been his second, and she knew it had lasted just under ten minutes because she'd been freaking out for every one of them. The one at the coffee maker had been his ninth, but she'd left the room, so she didn't know how long it had lasted or how many he'd had since. Blake didn't tell her every time he got sucked into an episode, but she could tell from his moods that they were happening more often now. He tried his best to remain upbeat, but there were times he seemed sad or distracted without any other obvious reason for it.

She flicked her gaze to the clock on the nightstand and then back to Blake. Seven minutes already.

Time crawled as she alternated between glancing at the clock and watching Blake. Besides being stiff as a board, he didn't seem to be in any pain, but she didn't know if she'd be able to tell if he was.

Could this be just the beginning of what they were in for? What if they couldn't stop them? Would they eventually keep Blake in a constant trance? She knew that both Jake and Cade were really worried. Both of them had taken to dropping in for a few minutes every couple of nights. A couple of times, Cade brought over some paperwork for Blake, saying he forgot to give it to him earlier, even though he would see him at the office the next day. Then there were the times Cade brought something for Emmie—a game or coloring supplies—saying Malcolm had received them for his birthday, but he wasn't old enough to use them yet.

Jake had used the paperwork excuse at least twice as well, and once he said that Chewie had wanted to see Emmie.

Not once had Blake called Cade and Jake out on the

excuses. And Paige got the sense he was just as concerned but didn't want to burden her with it.

She continued to fun her hand through his hair. At twenty-four minutes, Paige began to freak out. The time she watched him in the strip mall had been a cakewalk compared to this.

She was caressing his cheek when she felt him move. "Blake?"

He groaned and rolled onto his back.

"Blake? Talk to me, please," she pleaded, hovering over him.

"I'm okay." He opened his eyes and looked at her. "How long?"

She glanced at the clock again. "Twenty-six minutes. I was—" She blinked as her eyes welled with tears, relieved that he was okay. For now.

Blake tugged her down next to him. She propped herself on her arm so she could see him to know he really was okay.

Using the sheet, he wiped her tears, then took her hand in his. "I'm okay. I promise."

"I know. You were gone for so long. I—"

He kissed her forehead. "I'm here."

"Will you tell me what you saw?"

"You sure you want to know? It was tragic."

His voice held so much sorrow, but she wanted to help in any way she could. If listening lessened his burden even a little, she would listen to him tell her what he saw as many times as needed.

"Yes, tell me."

"It was 1704. I'm not sure exactly where, but the man was only a few generations removed from Eamon, the ancestor the curse originated with."

Blake shifted onto his side. "Roll over," he said softly. "I need to hold you."

Paige moved and settled her back against Blake's chest as he once more cradled his arm under her and held her close. As much as she wanted to see his face, she knew what he needed was more important right then.

She ran her fingers along his forearm and closed her eyes.

As he spoke, she tried to picture exactly what he was describing.

The room held a large wooden bed, a chair, and a stool with a single candle flickering—the only light in the room.

A man lay on a quilt-covered bed. Resting on one forearm, he ran his hand over the sweat-slicked hair of a woman lying beside him. She was buried beneath blankets, the edges pulled up to her chin.

The man leaned forward and placed a kiss on the woman's forehead.

"If it is time, my love, you can let go. I—" The man choked on his words as he swallowed a sob.

He seemed to be gathering his emotional resolve as he took a big breath and looked at the woman tenderly. "You have fought so hard, Bethany. I... will always... love you." He paused between words as he drew in shuddering breaths. "You are my life... and soul... Seeing you this way for so many months..."

His words trailed off again, and tears slipped down his cheeks. Using his shoulder, he wiped them away and leaned over once more, kissing Bethany's forehead. "One day we will be together again, my love... You do not need to be strong for me anymore."

A moment later the woman expelled a long breath as if her lungs were emptying of all oxygen.

The man fell over the woman; his body shook with silent sobs.

Just like he knew the year, Blake knew Bethany had been the man's wife and that they'd fallen in love very young and had been married for ten years. Their lives hadn't been easy, even with his family's wealth.

They'd tried for many years to have children, but Bethany had become sick a year ago. They'd sought doctors, but all had said there was nothing they could do. Their lives had become a waiting game as they spent every moment they could together.

When the man finally lifted his head, he picked up his wife's hand and brought it to his lips. "I will never—" he choked on a sob "—love another. That is my promise to you, my love."

A breeze rushed through the room, blowing out the candle, and time moved on. Blake could see Thomas through the years, sometimes in the bedroom and other times in what looked like a large living area with a fireplace and a long wooden table. People came and went, talking to Thomas and taking care of him. He responded and interacted, but it seemed as if by rote.

Thomas aged—his hair turned gray, his skin wrinkled—but his posture was the most alarming change. His spine curved in as if there was no reason to ever look up again.

The film of Thomas's life continued to run. His visitors dwindled year upon year as his grief enclosed him in a cocoon of his own suffering.

"I'm coming, Bethany," Thomas whispered, the sound a low rasp, as he lay on the same bed where his wife had died. He closed his eyes and exhaled as his wife had done. His body went limp.

"That was it," Blake said, his voice husky. "He died brokenhearted like all the others."

Paige rolled over to see Blake's face. "He may have been heartbroken, but he loved her so much."

"He died a lonely man because he chose not to love again."

"Maybe he couldn't."

He frowned. "Couldn't what?"

"Love someone else. Maybe Thomas had already loved the love of his life, and he didn't want to love again."

"So he chose to live alone." Blake scoffed as if the thought was ludicrous.

"It could be he didn't look at it like that. We don't know, but maybe he had no regrets."

Blake fiddled with a curl of her hair as he looked at her. "Jake and I were talking about this yesterday. I thought they were all heartbroken, but Jake said for a lot of them it was their choice. They chose not to look for another love and instead held onto a love that was gone. You think it's the opposite?"

"It was for Thomas. He had the love of his life, and she loved him back. It wasn't either of their faults that their life together was cut short."

"What about Martha and the sailor?"

"I agree with Jake about Martha. First, she chose not to tell George she loved him until it was too late. Although if he didn't feel the same about her, there wasn't anything she could do about it. Then she chose not to try to find happiness with someone else."

Paige thought back to the sailor and what Blake had said about him. "I think the sailor's situation is a little bit different since his girlfriend thought he was dead. But once she was married to his brother, instead of finding someone to love him, the sailor convinced himself he didn't have any love left to give. Maybe if he had opened up to his wife, he could have loved her and been happy."

Blake was quiet for a moment as he looked down at his fingers that were playing with her curl.

Paige wasn't really sure what the curse was trying to tell him. Was the message saying to open his eyes so he could grab onto love? Or was he destined to have the same fate as those he saw in the curse because he was too scared of the other option?

"Do you think it's too late to stop it?" she whispered, worried if she said the words too loudly that they could come true.

Blake lifted his eyes. "I don't know."

She cared for Blake deeply. It felt deeper than what they'd shared eight years ago.

Paige parted her lips, wanting to tell him she loved him. "Blake. I—"

"No," Blake said softly. He put his finger on her lips. "Don't say the words, Paige. I don't know if a confession of love will break the curse or not. But…" His eyes held sadness. "If we say them and one of us doesn't believe them, the curse probably won't break anyway. Then we'll be worse off because we hurt the other person with a lie."

She nodded, her throat too tight to speak. Her brain told her Blake was right, that they couldn't rush into this. She'd also made a promise to herself, as had he, that they wouldn't fall for anyone again, that friendship would be enough. It was her heart that didn't care about logic and whether he was right. Was this love? In her heart, she *wanted* to love him, whether she was ready or not. A shiver ran through her at the hopelessness of it all.

"You're cold," Blake said. "Roll over again. Let me get you warm."

Paige did as he asked, not correcting him on the reason for her shiver. He kissed her shoulder before tucking the blankets in around them.

A few minutes later, she heard his breathing even out with sleep. He hadn't reassured her that they would figure out a way to stop the curse, or that everything would be alright.

She held onto his arm that he'd wrapped around her. She needed his strength as an anchor because neither of them had any idea what kind of storm they were in for if the curse's episodes increased.

CHAPTER TWENTY-TWO

Sunday, November 17

"I've got it," Jake said when the doorbell rang.

Blake was about to stand but Cade waved him down. "I'll get the plates and napkins. Ford, grab some more drinks."

Jake and his brothers had come over to watch a hockey game. They had it on in the background but weren't sitting around the screen. Less than five minutes after Paige left the house to take Emmie shopping, Jake showed up with Chewie. Then, one by one Cade, Dane, and Ford stopped by.

Blake got the feeling Paige didn't want him to be left alone. He knew that seeing him go into a trance on Friday night and not being able to help him out of it had freaked her out. Yesterday hadn't been any better. When he'd been working out, another had hit him, but luckily he'd been in the basement on his own. It was the hit during dinner with Emmie that bothered them the most.

Paige said she'd picked up Emmie and made an excuse about making dessert. When she'd told him that she kept

Emmie busy in the kitchen for twenty-five minutes making a batch of cookies and constantly looking out the passthrough to check on him, he wanted to smile. At the look of worry on her face, he pulled her into his arms instead.

Later that night, he told her he didn't want to be alone with Emmie anymore. They couldn't risk it. Sooner or later, he would have to be on his own at times—it would be unavoidable—but he couldn't put Emmie at risk.

"Dig in," Jake said, setting the pizza boxes on the coffee table as Cade and Ford walked back into the living room.

He knew Dane had stayed in the living room to keep an eye on him. Blake looked over at him. "I'm okay."

Dane didn't say anything, just nodded and reached for a piece of pizza. The rest of them did the same.

"How often are you having the episodes now?" Cade asked after finishing a slice.

Blake put his plate on the table and sat back. "Daily."

Cade frowned. "Once a day?"

"No. Twice, sometimes three times." He told them what happened at dinner the night before.

"Please let Paige know that if she needs help with Emmie to call me or Jessica," Cade said.

"Thanks." He swallowed the feeling of helplessness that had become a common companion in the past week and met the gaze of each of his brothers, including Jake. "I've decided I'm going to work from home for a while. And I'm not going to drive."

"Shit," Ford muttered. "If you need to go somewhere, one of us will drive you."

"I know." He did his best to give Ford a smile just as he felt the telltale stiffening start. "Curse," he managed to force out, before falling back against the couch.

Blake heard them call his name, but it was too late. His

eyelids had closed, and images swam in his mind. The scene in front of him quickly came into focus.

A man sat hunched over a small wooden table. The flames in the fireplace a few feet away showcased his image. A draft seeped in from under the door and around the small window; the smell of the burning wood was familiar and comforting in this strange place.

The room and the man's presence, even the contrasting cool air and heat from the fireplace, felt real like all the other episodes. And like those, he knew the time and place.

It was 1617, and the man was one of Eamon's sons, the original ancestor cursed by the spirit.

The man dipped his quill in the ink and wrote a few more words before repeating the process. Blake couldn't see what he wrote, but he could feel their depth. The man loved someone with his whole heart. A soul-wrenching kind of love.

After several moments, the man stood and walked the short distance to the fireplace. He added another log before picking up his letter by the edges and holding it up.

"My dearest Margaret," he read, his tone filled with love.

"I pray these words find you well, though I wish I could speak them in person as I hold you in my arms. I yearn for the sight of your beauty as a parched man yearns for a drop of rain. You are ever in my thoughts.

"This distance between us grieves me, yet remembering that fateful day in the garden when we first met warms my soul. I fell in love with you in that moment, and every day henceforth you have owned my heart.

"Soon, my father's lands and holdings will pass on to me, and I will be worthy of your station. Then we will be free to love to our hearts' desire, as you are the one soul mine was made for. Until that time, I will live for the stolen moments we have, as brief as they are.

"I know, Margaret, my love, that one day we will walk hand in hand, and you will be mine as I am yours.

"*Yours always and forever, Colm.*"

Blake felt a shift in the air, and he now stood on a dirt road. Trees lined the road, their leaves bright and new. The warmth of the summer sun beat down on his face, melting away the draft from the small room.

Colm leaned against a barn off to the side of the road. He pulled away from the structure and walked forward a few steps before he began to run.

Blake looked beyond him to see a woman running toward Colm. When they reached one another, Colm picked her up and swung her around, their laughter like joyous music on the otherwise quiet road.

Once more, Colm's love for Margaret enveloped Blake like a swelling of comfort in his chest. Their love was so strong he could feel it.

As the corners of Blake's lips tipped up into a smile at seeing them, the air moved again.

The sun's rays disappeared, as if a cloud blocked its strength. Blake now stood beside the barn, the grass beneath his feet brown, signaling the end of summer.

A woman's cry caught his attention. He looked up to see Colm and Margaret only a few feet away. The shadows from the barn cast them in partial darkness.

Margaret took a step back from Colm and wiped her eyes with a lace-trimmed handkerchief.

"Please, my love," Colm pleaded. "This mustn't be."

Margaret sniffed, her eyes welling with unshed tears. "It must. It is my duty. He is a wealthy landowner, and I cannot go against my father's wishes. We will be married soon."

Colm dropped to one knee and took Margaret's hand in both of his. "I love you. Do you not love me?"

"I do," she said quietly. "But duty is more important than love."

Blake felt a sudden ache in his chest and knew he was feeling Colm's heart shattering.

Colm got to his feet as the air swirled around them and became colder.

When the scene changed again, Blake stood at the front of the barn, facing the road. Only a few leaves clung to the trees, most of them covering the dead grass, waiting to become one with the earth.

Dark gray clouds covered the sky, threatening rain and obscuring the sun, casting an ominous pallor over the landscape. The wind whipped up, tossing leaves in the air and chilling Blake to the bone. He only wore the T-shirt and jeans he'd had on in his house. Giving his arms a brisk rub to combat the cold, he glanced around, looking for Colm.

Both the road and field were devoid of people, but Blake felt another ache in his chest, like the one he'd felt earlier from Colm. Only now the ache felt deeper. Dread filled him. He turned toward the barn and realized time had passed. The wood was more weathered, and spaces had appeared between some of the boards.

Not seeing Colm, Blake pulled open one of the barn doors and stepped into the dim light. Before his eyes could adjust, the ache in his chest magnified, throwing him off guard. He stumbled, his shoulder hitting the doorframe of the barn, and he caught himself from falling to the ground.

He rubbed his other hand against his chest, trying to relieve the pressure, but to no avail. It wasn't sharp like an injury, but it was familiar. He'd felt it recently whenever he thought of his mom. The anguish and fatigue that lingered, mixing with feelings of anger and sadness—grief.

Straightening, he stood and looked around the barn. Beams of light shone between the wooden slats, giving him enough light to see.

Bales of hay and hand-held farm equipment covered in dust were strewn around the barn, indicating they hadn't been used for some time. Blake felt his chest constrict again as feelings of sadness and isolation surrounded him. The emotions weighed him down like they were his own.

He looked up and his breath hitched.

Colm hung from a single rope tied to the rafters. A wooden crate lay on its side below him.

Knowing that Colm had died over four hundred years ago didn't lessen the torment Blake felt being a witness to his death.

Tearing his eyes from his ancestor, Blake felt a compulsion to look around again. When he spotted a piece of paper lying on some hay, he knew he was meant to read it.

Each step he took toward the paper felt like he was walking closer to his own death, but he couldn't stop his forward movement.

He picked up the paper and looked down at the writing as a deep sadness took hold of him.

My Dearest Margaret,

For six years now I have watched and loved you, the joy of my life, from afar. I have seen you with your children, your laughter ringing out like sunshine on a stormy day. It is my greatest wish that you stay happy.

My love for you is eternal and it has kept me afloat during many a dark day. You are the soul made for mine, and I vowed that I would not rest until the day we are together. Alas, with great sadness, I must say it will not happen on this earth.

Two cycles of the moon after I became ten plus twenty years, the same curse that destroyed the souls of my oldest brother and sister descended upon me. I have fought against it with all my might, and I have lost.

One day we will be together again.

Yours always and forever,

Colm

Blake lowered his hand to put the paper back—a profound sorrow in his heart—as the air shifted and the hold on his body released.

He dragged his hands down his face, as if that would remove the image of Colm's lifeless body hanging from the rafters from his mind.

"You're back. Thank Christ," Cade said.

"I'm okay." That was a lie; he wasn't sure he'd ever be okay again.

"You were out of it for thirty minutes," Jake said, almost like an accusation. "They're lasting longer each time."

Blake often brushed off Jake's concerns, but he couldn't this time. He was worried too, but he didn't say anything. There weren't any words that could make this better, and he couldn't reassure his friend because Blake couldn't predict what was going to happen next. None of them could, not even if he and Paige did fall in love.

He did his best to shake off the thought. Without waiting for them to ask, because Blake knew they would, he described what he'd witnessed.

Although Colm and Thomas had been related to him, not everyone in the episodes were. Some were just tragic stories the curse chose to show him. And out of all the heartache and sorrow the curse had shown him, this one had been the worst. He wasn't sure if it was because Colm had taken his own life or because Blake knew Colm was his ancestor and the curse had driven him to commit suicide. As he described the events, a deep sense of helplessness settled inside him. Could this be his own future?

When he finished his story, Jake narrowed his eyes, and looked at Blake with a piercing stare. "Is that what you want? To be so lonely and miserable that you take your own life?"

"What the hell, man?" Dane asked, glaring at Jake. "How can you even ask him that?"

Blake held up his hand to calm his brother. "It's okay, Dane."

He turned back to his best friend. If he hadn't been so shaken coming out of the trance, he wouldn't have told Jake what Colm did. Jake's past had made him overly protective of everyone he cared about, and that was on a normal day.

Seeing Blake endure the episodes and not knowing how to fix them was a kind of torture for his friend that few would understand. "I'm sorry," he whispered. Jake would know he was apologizing for describing what Colm had done.

"If you don't want that, you have to stop hiding," Jake said and gave him an almost imperceptible nod.

Raising his voice to a normal level he told Jake, "I haven't said the words yet, but I'm not hiding. I can't force Paige to love me."

Ford elbowed Cade on the couch beside him. "I'm lost. You get that?"

"Yeah. Jake thinks Blake should fight harder for Paige and open himself up to love so he doesn't end up like Colm," Cade said, either ignoring Blake's quiet apology to Jake or not having heard it. Likely the former. Cade wasn't that much younger than Blake and Jake, so he'd been around to know what Jake's family had gone through.

Cade raised his brows at Blake. "Am I correct?"

"Yes." Blake didn't know what else to say. No one could force Paige to love him, but he was pretty sure he was on his way to loving her. If he confessed his love now, she might think he was saying it because of the curse. The problem was he still worried about her leaving. She'd done it once, so there was nothing to stop her from doing it again. And that was under normal circumstances. Having to deal with him and his trances made their lives anything but normal. The only thing he could do was give her time. If only he knew how much of it he had left.

CHAPTER TWENTY-THREE

Wednesday, November 20

Paige came awake slowly, enjoying Blake's warmth wrapped around her. When she finally opened her eyes, she checked the clock on the nightstand. Seeing they had plenty of time before they had to get ready for work and get Emmie up, she pushed back into him, feeling his hard length against her butt.

They hadn't made love since Friday night because Blake didn't want a curse to take him in the middle of it. She'd tried to lighten the mood by teasing him that if a curse did come over him during sex, he would stay stiff for a long time. Even though he'd laughed with her, they'd both known his situation was becoming more dire each day. Blake could get sucked into a trance at any time—no matter what he was doing—leaving him wide open to danger.

He had stopped driving for now, but what if that wasn't enough? Even daily activities could become dangerous if he suddenly lost control of himself. Going into a trance while he was walking down the stairs meant he could fall and hit his head. It would be worse if he had Emmie in his arms or she was anywhere near him.

Cooking was another risk. The episodes were lasting longer than a half hour now. If Blake had something on the stove and an episode froze him for over thirty minutes, it could go up in flames and start a fire.

Dozens of possible situations had gone through her mind over the last several days. She'd become a walking encyclopedia of worst-case scenarios.

On Saturday morning, with the image of Blake frozen and helpless stuck in her mind, they'd sat down and talked about what they could do. They'd focused their conversation on safety, avoiding any talk of love. While they'd talked, she had wanted to squash her determination to stay self-reliant—at least as much as she could considering she was living in his house—and confess her love. If that was even what she felt, because she still wasn't sure. Nor did she know how Blake felt, and the last thing she wanted was for him to feel obligated to say he loved her too only for the curse not to break. She also feared that a false declaration of love could worsen the curse somehow. There were too many unknowns for them to take chances.

Because of that, she had stayed silent about her feelings and concentrated on ways to keep them all safe. That had included her suggestion of Blake sleeping in his bed with her —all week, not just on weekends. Even knowing she wouldn't be able to do anything for him if he went into a trance while in bed, she felt better having him with her.

But her plan was backfiring because sleeping next to him every night and not being intimate was driving her crazy. She'd been so horny she had considered whipping out her battery-operated boyfriend when Blake had fallen asleep before her the previous night. Then she worried that if he woke up and caught her he would feel bad about denying her.

Going by his hardening length pressed against her, he was just as horny as she was. She wiggled her butt against him, knowing she would be able to weaken his resolve.

"Paige," he warned, his voice raspy with sleep.

She bit her lip to stop a laugh from bubbling up and rubbed against him again.

Blake used his arm across her to pull her onto her back, then hovered over her.

He kissed her softly. "I would love to mak—fuck you until we both forget our own names, but we can't."

Paige hadn't missed his slip. He'd been about to say make love, and he would have been right. Even though they weren't ready to say the three little words to each other, the act of what they were about to do would be more than just fucking.

Not that anything was wrong with a good fuck. She loved it as much as the next woman, but she knew that today it would be more than that. And they would make love—regardless of what they called it—because they both needed to feel close to each other. Maybe she shouldn't guess what Blake was feeling, but she'd wager she was right on this one—he needed the connection with her as much as she needed it with him.

Relieving some sexual tension wouldn't hurt either.

Paige planted her hands on Blake's chest, pushing him off her and onto his back as she rolled over onto him. She straddled his hips and grinned down at his wary expression.

"Paige," he warned again, but it held less conviction than the last time.

When she ground her groin into his, he let out a long groan. Knowing his resolve was almost gone, she did it again.

She kissed his lips, then ran her tongue along them. "If a curse hits, I can jump off," she whispered, teasing his lips.

"Okay," he said before his mouth captured hers in a kiss that sent tingles all the way to her toes.

He cupped the back of her neck with one hand, his other gripping her hip, as they continued to devour each other. When they came up for air, Blake dragged his lips along her jaw and down her neck. The scrape of his stubble on her skin added fuel to the fire already growing inside her.

"I need you in me," she panted, rubbing herself along his length.

He flopped back onto his pillow. "I'm yours. Take me."

Placing one hand on the headboard, Paige used it as leverage to lift herself as she reached for his cock. She positioned it at her entrance, then braced her hands on his chest as she slowly slid down onto his length. The fullness of him felt amazing, her body acclimating to him right away, as if he'd been made purposefully for her.

As she rocked against him, giving her clit the friction it craved, Blake's hands roamed over her hips before moving upward. He pinched her nipples, igniting another flame.

She rocked faster on him. "Harder," she pleaded.

"I love watching you like this," he said, sounding breathless. "I want to see you come."

Blake's hands lit up her skin, but it wasn't enough. Frustration built in her as she chased her orgasm, never quite reaching it. Climaxing a few times didn't mean it would always happen, but she wanted it to.

Tilting her hips, she tried to get closer, worried her body would soon shut off. "Ugh!"

"Tell me what you need, baby."

"I need you on top and pounding into me."

A worried look crossed his face, but before she could tell him to forget about her orgasm, he'd flipped their positions.

With his elbows on either side of her, he tilted his hips to give her the friction she needed.

He pressed his forehead against hers. "I'm not going to last long. Rub your clit."

She hesitated for a moment, then reminded herself that this was Blake and he wanted her to do whatever brought her pleasure. It didn't take long, and she felt her body stiffen as her orgasm rocked through her.

Blake thrust several more times before he vibrated with his own climax. He'd barely finished when he pulled out and rolled off her, taking her into his arms.

She cuddled into him. They were sated for now.

THE CURSE LET GO of Blake. He scrubbed his hands down his face in an effort to relieve his internal tension. Knowing it was useless, he stood from where he'd been working at the dining room table and walked into the kitchen for a bottle of water.

He glanced at his watch. It was five minutes past two, and he'd already had three episodes today. The first came a few minutes after eight in the morning, not long after Paige had left to take Emmie to daycare before heading into her office.

At eleven o'clock the second episode had frozen him while he'd been walking into the kitchen to refill his coffee. The last one had come over him while he was reading through some documents Jake had emailed him.

The episodes were coming every three hours now. As much as he didn't want to imagine them getting worse, he expected they would. They'd grown closer together until he was experiencing them daily. From daily, it hadn't taken long until he was getting several a day. He could only guess that the frequency would continue to increase.

Uncapping his water, he drank it all before throwing the bottle in the recycling bin. Would he soon need to hurry and refuel his body in the precious minutes he had between episodes? Or would that time dwindle too until he spent all his time sitting stiffly in a chair, no longer aware of the outside world?

He could see Colm hanging from the rafters in his barn, and he wondered if Colm had decided to kill himself before he was no longer able to. Blake's mom had said in her letter that the curse affected each person differently, so maybe Colm had been driven out of his mind in a different way.

Blake walked back to his dining room but couldn't sit. He was too restless, thinking that one day all he might be able to do was sit. Deciding to go for a walk, he reached for his phone. It rang in his hand, startling him.

The call display showed that it was from Akerman Contracting. Probably one of his brothers checking in on him. "Blake Akerman," he said.

"Blake, I'm so glad I got you," Denise, his office manager, said in a rush. "I know you're working from home this week, but Jake went to the city office to check on a permit, and Henry is with the senior commercial project manager at the strip mall project. Cade and Ford both have appointments."

Blake waited patiently as Denise gave him the whereabouts of his entire staff; she would eventually get to the reason for her call.

Denise took a big breath before letting it out. "Wayne is on a job—that new house reno on Arrow Street—and he's having a problem with something he needs help with. He said something about the plans not being right. Could you call him?"

"Sure. Thanks for letting me know. And Denise… you can call me anytime."

"I know… it's just with everything you're going through, I…"

He and Cade had made the decision earlier in the week to tell the senior staff that Blake was dealing with an illness. They'd said it wasn't serious but made him dizzy and prevented him from driving for a while. The story would have to do for now, and when Blake's condition worsened, they'd figure out what to do then. He wanted to say *if* it worsened instead of *when* but he couldn't lie to himself.

"It's okay," Blake said gently. "I'll give Wayne a call."

Once they'd said their goodbyes and hung up, Blake called up Wayne's number in his phone.

"Hey, Wayne," he said when the project manager answered. "Denise said you've got a problem?"

"Yeah. I need a second opinion on the plans because something doesn't look right."

Blake wouldn't risk driving, but it wasn't far away. He would be able to walk there, take a look at the problem, and walk back well before another curse hit him.

"Give me twenty minutes and I'll meet you at the property," he told Wayne as he grabbed his coat.

"Great. See you soon." Blake zipped up his coat and locked the house behind him. The weather had been mild, and luckily they hadn't had any snow yet, so the walk was pleasant. The trees had all lost their leaves, their dark branches looking stark and lonely in the overcast sky.

Leaves swirled around him as he walked, reminding him of Colm and his desolate surroundings. It had been late fall then too, the leaves already lying dead on the ground.

His latest episode had taken place in the fall. In 1672, Winifrid and Giles, madly in love, eloped, defying her wealthy family. They considered Giles to be beneath her, and once they married, cast her out. Winifrid and Giles struggled financially but were happy in their love. Several years after they wed, Giles died in an accident, leaving Winifrid alone and destitute. Too proud to return to her family, she lived the rest of her days alone and in poverty. Everyone abandoned her because of the love she had risked everything for.

Even knowing that Giles hadn't meant to die, just like Blake's dad hadn't, they had left their widows alone and grieving the loss of the one they loved. Something Blake never wanted to experience.

Pushing the thoughts aside, he turned onto Arrow Street as his phone rang. He pulled it from his pocket and saw Wayne's name on the call display. "Hey, I'm only a couple of houses away."

"Sorry, I should have called you sooner. My wife was supposed to drop off my oldest son's equipment bag before football practice, but she forgot my other kid had a dentist appointment, so she asked me to. I'm on my way to the school now. It will probably take me another twenty minutes to get back."

"I totally get it. I grew up with four brothers, remember?"

Wayne laughed. "Right. Man, I'm glad I've only got three sons; that's enough."

"We had our parents running all over the place. Why don't you take a break and watch your son's practice? I've got the code for the keypad so I can let myself in. We can talk about it in the morning."

"You sure?"

"Yeah. I'll be fine. Talk to you tomorrow." Judging by the episodes he'd already had that day, he figured he had another two hours before he had to get home. It should give him plenty of time to check out the house.

"Tomorrow," Wayne said and disconnected.

Blake looked up the code for the door before shoving his

phone in his back pocket. He walked around the large dumpster sitting on the property's driveway and up the steps to the front door. Using the keypad, he unlocked the door and let himself into the house. A strong, musty smell assaulted him.

He looked around, finding a light switch by the door. Nothing happened when he flipped the switch, but that wasn't a surprise. Wayne's crew had probably turned the power off already. There would be a portable generator around somewhere since they used them to power portable light towers they had for job sites.

Blake didn't want to bother with a generator, nor did he want to be away from home any longer than absolutely necessary. He'd find the plans and take them home to look at there.

The late afternoon winter sun streamed in through the windows, providing enough light for him to make his way around. It highlighted the dust he kicked up in the air as he walked through what had once been a large front parlor.

He spotted a couple of sawhorses standing at the back of the room with a sheet of plywood on top, acting as a makeshift table. He strode toward it, guessing the plans would be there.

As he walked further into the room, the musty smell became more pungent. Most people probably hated the mildewy, stale smell, but it conjured good memories of all the times his dad had taken him and Jake, and later his brothers, to a job site. His dad had been so patient with them, teaching them how to demolish a room and ready it for new construction. No matter how many projects he worked on, sawdust would always remind him of his dad.

Blake smiled as he absently reached for the plans sitting on the plywood. A shadow crossed his hand. He wasn't alone.

Rearing sideways, he looked up to see who was there and

stumbled. Flailing, he gripped onto the plywood to steady himself. He'd grabbed too close to the end of the board, his weight tipping it, snapping the board upright like a wall. With no way for Blake to stop his forward momentum, he crashed to the floor.

"Fuck!" His obscenity rent the air as a jarring pain ripped through his shoulder.

Panting through the pain, he rolled onto his back just in time to see the plywood teeter and fall toward him.

Whipping his uninjured arm up and across his face for protection, the top end of the wood slammed into him.

Stunned, he lay with the weight of the board on his arm as he caught his breath. At three-quarters of an inch thick, the full board weighed over sixty pounds. Luckily only the top couple of feet rested on him. It still hurt like fuck, but he didn't think he'd broken anything.

Since no one would know to come to help, he'd have to get himself out of the mess. Just then, he remembered the reason for his calamity of errors to begin with. Someone had been in the room with him.

If they had seen him fall, he figured they would have already tried to help. Holding still, he listened but didn't hear anything except a car pass on the street out front. He was going to have to save himself. Maybe what he'd seen had just been a shadow.

With one arm holding the board off his face, he moved his other, testing to see if he could lift it. Again, nothing felt broken, but his shoulder still hurt like hell. He lifted his hand to the edge of the board and sucked in a sharp breath.

Bracing himself, he placed his palm on the side of the wood to push it off. If he could get it even partway off, he'd be able to lift up his other arm to help, hopefully avoiding dragging the wood over his face and tearing the shit out of it.

Pushing the board slowly, it scraped across his arm. He

could feel his skin tear, but the hurt was a minor discomfort compared to the painful aches already throbbing in his arms.

A couple more small shoves and he figured the board would be far enough to the side to use his arm under it to lift it off. As he pushed the board, his entire body stiffened.

Fuck.

His arm struck his forehead with the full force of the plywood behind it.

CHAPTER TWENTY-FOUR

*P*aige had wanted to leave the office early to get home to Blake but had been waylaid by a last-minute request. Now, driving home with Emmie, it was just after five o'clock, and she felt a sense of relief that she would see Blake soon.

She'd worried about him all day. A hundred times she'd reached for her phone to call or text him, putting it down each time. After Craig accused her of being a nag for years, she fretted each time she reached out to Blake with something that wasn't urgent. Letting go of past habits would take time, but since she still wasn't quite sure where she stood with Blake, she was erring on the side of caution.

She'd convinced herself that one call during the day wouldn't be too much, so she called him during lunch. Blake sounded happy to hear from her, relieving some of her tension. But then he told her about the two episodes he'd had that morning.

Hearing the despair and exhaustion in his voice was like the trip through the supermarket all over again—a much-needed wake-up call. Only this time she was choosing the opposite path.

Hanging up after talking to Blake, she had an epiphany. She wasn't wrong in wanting to please her husband, but it couldn't be one-sided. It wasn't solely her responsibility to please him. You had to give to yourself first, and once you were happy, you could do things to please your partner, as long as they do the same for you.

No relationship could be exactly equal one hundred percent of the time because there would be situations where one person would give more than the other. Like Blake did with opening his house to her and Emmie.

For almost two months she'd been so concerned about not relying on Blake that she hadn't bothered to see what was right in front of her face: the proverbial peanut butter staring at her.

She was relying on him already for more than just a place to live—for companionship and someone to listen and be there. He helped out with Emmie too, but it was more than picking her up from daycare or doing the laundry; he'd been the father figure that Emmie needed. Blake's family had been there for her and Emmie as well.

Choosing to receive didn't mean she'd lost her independence. It gave her options, which was what having independence meant. She could choose what she wanted to accept and what she didn't. *God.* She'd been such an idiot.

On Friday night, she'd been about to tell Blake she loved him even though she still had doubts, but he had stopped her. Even while needing her love to break the curse, Blake's main concern was her. He didn't want to pressure her into anything. Instead of only looking out for himself, he was looking out for her too—wasn't that love?

Blake didn't need to say the words for her to know he loved her. He had shown her in a hundred different ways…

with friendship, with Emmie, with his body. With his putting her first.

That morning, he had wanted her pleasure to come before his own. What she hadn't realized until their phone call was that he wasn't trying to please her in spite of his own happiness. He could give her pleasure and also have his own. She'd given to Craig for years until her own happiness no longer mattered. Blake was showing her that they could both choose happiness.

Again, she'd been so stupid. Why was it so easy to see something happening to someone else but not yourself? She'd agreed with Jake that Martha, the sailor, and so many of the others in Blake's episodes *chose* not to love again. They could have opened themselves up to a new love, but instead, they let their past hurts stop them from finding happiness.

That's exactly what she was doing. She was so worried about losing control over her life that she wasn't *choosing* to love. Loving the right person meant they *chose* your happiness as much as they did their own. Craig hadn't done that. The only person Craig cared about was Craig. Their love—if it had even truly been that—hadn't been what either of them needed. Just like Martha and the sailor. They may have each loved someone, but it wasn't reciprocated the way they needed.

Blake's mom had said that in her letter. Not only did Blake need to find love, it had to be reciprocated. Because loving without having it returned wasn't enough.

Now it was her turn to step up.

She pulled into the driveway behind Blake's truck, excited to see him.

"Hey, sweetie, we're home." She smiled at Emmie in the rearview mirror as she turned off her SUV.

"Is Blake home?"

"Yes. Start unbuckling and I'll come around." She grabbed her bag and went around the vehicle to get Emmie out.

Hand in hand, they walked up to the front door while Emmie chatted about the game she wanted to play after dinner.

Paige reached for the front door, surprised to find it locked. She dug in her bag for the keys she'd just thrown inside and unlocked the door, pushing it open for Emmie to enter first.

"Blake, we're home!" Emmie shouted.

Paige dropped her keys on the side table and hung her bag on a hook by the door. "Let's get your coat and boots off. Then you can go see Blake."

"Okay." Emmie shrugged out of her coat and kicked off her boots, leaving them in the middle of the floor.

Paige cleared her throat, eyeing her daughter.

"Oops. Sorry, Mommy," Emmie said with a sheepish look. She hung her coat on one of the low hooks Blake had put by the door and placed her boots neatly on the rack before running off to find Blake.

Paige looked down at Emmie's coat on the low hook, realizing it was another sign of love. Not long after they'd moved in, they'd come home to find Blake in a crouch, putting away his toolbox. He showed Emmie the brightly decorated wooden row of hooks at just the right height for her. Emmie had launched herself into Blake, knocking him on his butt, his arms around her as they laughed.

Paige had thanked him, appreciating that Emmie had a place to hang her coat. Blake had done more than give Emmie coat hooks; he'd given her independence. She no longer needed to rely on an adult to put her coat away.

As Paige took off her own coat and hung it on a hook, she wondered how many other things Blake had done to give both her and her daughter independence. She would have to pay better attention.

She turned away from the hooks, then swung back. Blake's coat wasn't hanging where he usually put it.

"Mommy," Emmie said, coming down the stairs, frowning. "Blake's gone."

"He's probably working out downstairs. Let me go check."

Emmie waited in the kitchen while Paige checked the basement. When she couldn't find him, a sense of dread settled inside her. All she could think about was the story Blake had told her about Colm ending his life. She knew that Blake wouldn't do that, but it didn't stop her thoughts from heading in that direction.

"Where's Blake?" Emmie asked when Paige reached the kitchen and locked the basement door behind her.

"I don't know. Maybe he walked to the supermarket. I'll call him."

Paige grabbed her phone from her bag. It rang five times before it went to voicemail. "Hi, Blake. Uh... just wondering where you are. Can you please call to let me know you're alright?"

After she hung up, she kept her phone in her hand so she'd hear if Blake called. "I'm going to go upstairs and change out of my work clothes," she told Emmie. "You want to play with your dolls in the living room?"

Emmie held out her hand. "No. Me too."

Paige smiled to reassure Emmie, because she expected her daughter was picking up on her worry. Taking Emmie's hand, they went upstairs.

Hoping Blake would return at any moment, Paige hadn't gotten dinner ready, but by six o'clock Paige couldn't wait any longer to feed Emmie. She made her a grilled cheese sandwich and heated up a can of minestrone soup. Needing to occupy herself, she gave Emmie an early bath.

As far as distractions went, it hadn't been enough. She constantly pulled her phone out of the pocket of her yoga pants to make sure she hadn't missed a text and that her battery hadn't died.

By seven-thirty, Paige was ready to jump out of her skin. Emmie was settled in front of the TV watching a movie, but Paige couldn't sit still. For the last ten minutes she'd been pacing in the foyer with her phone clutched in her hand.

Unlocking her phone, she looked at her contacts. Jake had exchanged phone numbers with her on Sunday when she and Emmie had gotten back from shopping. Blake's brothers had too. They had tried to play it off as nothing, but none of them could hide their concern about Blake. He'd stayed silent during the number exchanges but had confessed later he was glad she had them.

She pressed Jake's. It only rang twice before he answered.

"Paige? What's wrong?"

"I can't find Blake. Emmie and I got home just after five, but he wasn't here. Only his truck. I left him a voicemail, but he hasn't called me back." She could feel her hysteria rising.

"Have you tried his brothers?"

"No. I've just been waiting, hoping he would come home, but now I'm beyond frightened for him."

"Let me call around and see if anyone has heard from him."

Hearing the worry in Jake's voice amped hers up even higher. "Okay."

"We'll find him, Paige. I'll call you back as soon as I know something."

Jake hung up abruptly. She didn't mind the lack of the usual goodbye because she just needed to know that Blake was alright.

She went back to her pacing. When someone knocked on

the door she sprinted to it, flinging it open without looking to see who it was.

"Did you find him?" she asked Jake and Cade as they walked in.

"Sort of. We know where he was last," Jake said. He glanced into the living room.

Emmie was standing up, her movie forgotten behind her. Paige rushed to her and picked her up. She'd done a lousy job of hiding her fears in front of Emmie.

Cade approached them. "Emmie, would you like to come to my house and help me read Malcolm a bedtime story?"

Emmie glanced between her and Cade, probably sensing Cade's and Jake's worry as well.

Paige forced a smile. "That's a great idea. You go help Cade read Malcolm a story and Jake and I will go get Blake."

Cade took Emmie and helped her put her boots and coat on as Paige shrugged into her own coat and grabbed her purse.

Cade had left with Emmie and soon Paige was in Jake's truck as he drove down the street. "Where is he? Is he alright? What happened?" she spewed the questions, then bit her lip to stop her question vomiting so Jake could answer.

"One of our managers needed help at a house project and called Denise because I was in a meeting. Wayne, the manager, said that while he was waiting for Blake to show up, his wife called to say they'd had a mix-up and he had to take something to one of his kids. Wayne called Blake to let him know he would be about another twenty minutes, but Blake told him not to bother. Blake said he'd look at the plans Wayne had questions about and they'd talk tomorrow morning."

"What time was that?"

"Two forty-five," Jake said, giving her a quick glance before looking back at the road.

"Five hours ago," she said more to herself than Jake. That was enough time for something to have happened.

Jake slowed down and pulled over to the curb in front of a house with a dumpster in the driveway.

As they walked up to the front porch, Jake unlocked his phone. "I'm just looking up the code for the door."

Paige reached the door first and turned the knob. "It's not locked," she told Jake over her shoulder.

Not waiting for Jake, she opened the door and stepped inside. "It's so dark, can—" She turned back to Jake to ask him to use the flashlight on his phone right as a gust of wind knocked her backward onto her butt. The door slammed shut, enclosing her in complete darkness.

CHAPTER TWENTY-FIVE

lake opened his eyes slowly and blinked to clear his vision. The edge of his arm and a sea of beige from the sheet of wood pinning his arm to his forehead, greeted him.

Forcing himself to tamp down his panic, he assessed the situation as best he could. Besides the pounding in his skull threatening to blind him, he couldn't sense any other injuries.

A couple of thoughts slammed into him. His muscles had locked like they did before each episode, but it was too soon for another one because it hadn't even been two hours since the last one. Secondly, since the curse had taken control of his body, why hadn't he been transported into a scene?

Enduring another episode wasn't on his list of favorite activities, but at least he would regain control of his body when it finished. Unlike his current frozen state.

Seconds ticked by, then minutes.

Swallowing down the bile threatening to crawl up his throat, he waited for the moving pictures that always appeared first.

When nothing happened, he concentrated on his hand at his side, trying to move his fingers.

Nothing. The curse still had control of his muscles.

As more minutes passed, he had nothing to focus on but the pain.

Blake swallowed down more bile. The pounding in his head had become relentless, battering him from the inside with every beat of his heart. Looking on the bright side, the pressure in his head was so all-encompassing he couldn't feel his other injuries. He let out a small snort at the thought, then groaned from the pain.

Time lost all meaning as he continued to swallow, forcing back bile. As bad as the shredded, raw feeling of his esophagus was from all the swallowing, he figured it was better than choking on his own vomit since he couldn't turn his head. If he wasn't pinned down like a bug, he would have patted himself on the back for being Mr. Positive.

He heard a sound and hoped it was someone coming to help. Holding his breath, he strained to see if he would hear it again.

Someone was crying.

"Help!" he attempted to yell but choked on the word. Swallowing to clear his throat, he tried again.

"Help!" His voice came out louder that time. Loud enough to be heard through his wood barrier? He could only hope.

A breeze fluttered against his cheek as images flashed in his mind.

He welcomed the scene, knowing he'd be free when it finished.

The scent of flowers hit him first. Then the timbre of organ music reached him just as his vision focused on the scene in front of him.

Blake stood in the vestibule of a church in Blue Mountain, Colorado, in 1975.

Four women stood in front of him in long, seafoam green

dresses, wearing broad-rimmed floppy hats. Each of them held a small bouquet and stood in a line, one behind the other.

The bride wore a high-necked white gown and the same floppy hat as the others, but in white. She brought up the rear of the line and held a small bouquet in one hand while her other clung to the arm of an older man—likely her father.

The woman in the front of the line nodded to an older woman in a pantsuit off to the side as two young boys opened a set of large double doors. With a big smile on her face, the first woman in seafoam green began a slow walk up the aisle.

When the woman next in line began her trek up the aisle, the man turned to the bride. "Are you ready, Carolyn?"

She beamed up at him. "Yes. I can't wait to be Mrs. Keith Merrill."

Ms. Pantsuit gestured to the bride and her father to come forward. They paused for a moment until the music changed, then walked toward the altar.

Blake followed them, stepping to the side when the bride's father handed her off to her groom.

The groom's smile looked forced as he faced his bride, sweat dotting his forehead. He and his bride turned to face the minister.

"Welcome, loved ones," the minister addressed the crowd. "We are gathered here today to join Keith Andrew Merrill and Carolyn Jane Engles in holy matrimony."

The groom held up his hand. "Wait."

Carolyn's eyes widened as Keith turned to face her.

"I'm sorry, Carolyn, but I can't do this. I don't love you."

"What? You're telling me that now?" she hissed just louder than a whisper.

"I'm sorry," Keith said again. He turned his back on her and walked away down the aisle. The groomsmen followed.

"How dare you?" Carolyn screamed. She lifted the hem of her dress and raced after Keith. She was halfway down the aisle when her hat flew off, but she didn't stop to retrieve it.

As Carolyn disappeared through the large doorway, the air shifted.

Blake didn't get a chance to look at his new surroundings before Carolyn walked right through him. He shivered at the encounter and moved off to the side to avoid it happening again.

"How could he do that to me?" Carolyn shouted, the ribbons in her hair moving with her long tresses as she paced back and forth. "He embarrassed me in front of everyone we know! I hate him. I can't believe he did that to me. How could he?"

Carolyn continued to rant. Her four bridesmaids, all dressed similarly in wide-legged jeans, sat on two couches with patterned paper covering the walls behind them. They looked uncomfortable as Carolyn paced in front of them. One of the women sat forward and looked at the others before standing.

"Carolyn," the woman said softly as she took a step forward and stopped.

She reminded Blake of a person approaching an animal without knowing how they would react.

"It's been six months. Keith has moved on. Uh. Maybe you should start dating again. Find someone new."

Carolyn spun toward the woman. "Move on?" she screeched. "Do you not remember how Keith embarrassed me? Everyone saw him walk away from me. He made me a laughingstock."

The other women stood and joined the first. "Carolyn," one of them said. "That's on Keith, not you. Amy is right; you should start dating again."

"How can I?" Carolyn yelled. "He embarrassed—"

The air swirled around Blake and the scene changed, but he still stood in the same living room. The wallpaper had been removed and replaced with tan paint that matched the slipcovers on the couches.

He did a slow 360, realizing it was the house on Arrow Street. In the dim light with the demolition underway, he hadn't gotten a good look when he had walked in. Then he'd been distracted as Carolyn paced back and forth in the last scene.

His body was trapped in the same house Carolyn was in.

This time, she sat on one of the couches, her hair now parted down the middle and tied in two braids.

Only three of her four former bridesmaids were present—two sat on the opposite couch, one of them rubbing a hand over her swollen belly. A third took small steps in the middle of the room, bouncing a baby on her hip. "Carolyn, how was your date last night?"

"He walked out of the restaurant and left me with the bill."

The women on the couch frowned, and a strange look passed between them. The woman with the baby perched on the edge of the couch beside Carolyn, bouncing the baby on her knees. "That's weird. Uh... What were you talking about before he left?"

Carolyn hesitated, then waved her hand in a dismissive manner. "The usual getting-to-know-you stuff."

"Did you mention Keith?"

"Not at first."

The woman cradled the baby against her chest and shot to her feet. "For goodness' sake, Carolyn. It's been two years. You've got to get over Keith."

"How can I? I was going to be his wife, and he humiliated me."

The air shifted to a new time, but Blake, still stuck in the house, stood in Carolyn's living room. He watched her as the scenes shifted again and again.

Instead of seeing a snapshot of her life through the years, he endured listening to her bemoan her fate year upon year. Her bridesmaids dropped off one by one over the next decade until new friends came and went. Her clothing and hairstyles changed with the times, and every five or ten years, the furniture and accessories in the room were updated.

By the time the scene switched to 2007, Carolyn's whining grated on him like an itchy tag that needed to be ripped out of the *back of a shirt. He felt like he was losing his mind. Thirty-two times he'd been transported into her living room to listen to her complain about dates who didn't understand, badmouth Keith, yell at her friends, and lament her lot in life.*

"Get over it already!" Blake yelled at her, throwing his hands in the air. He didn't care that she couldn't see or hear him; his patience had shriveled up and died.

Unaware of Blake, Carolyn held the phone to her ear and continued to rant to the poor soul on the other end about her latest failed date.

He walked over to the large front window, doing his best to block out Carolyn's whining, and looked out at the street. The weather looked the same as it had in his own time. Someone bundled up against the wind in a coat and scarf hurried by on the street as leaves blew around them.

The air shifted again, and for the first time in thirty-three time changes, Blake found himself in a different room. Carolyn lay in a double bed, her eyes closed and skin pale. Her breathing alternated between deep breaths followed by shallower ones with pauses in between.

A woman reading a book sat beside the bed.

Blake knew he had only transported one year ahead in time to 2008. He didn't know what had happened in the past year, but the sound of Carolyn's breathing told him she had something she wouldn't be recovering from.

Carolyn was only fifty-eight years old and dying. And unless she had changed in the last year, she was dying bitter and loveless.

The woman in the chair looked up when the pause between Carolyn's last breaths extended for much longer. Holding her book in one hand, she reached over and patted Carolyn's shoulder softly. "You're not alone; I'm here. It's okay for you to let go," she said quietly.

Blake stood at the end of Carolyn's bed as the pauses between her breaths continued to grow in length. With each new scene he'd been forced to endure as Carolyn refused to let go of her past, he'd become more and more frustrated, even though she had died years ago.

Keith had done the right thing by walking away, although his timing had sucked. He had freed Carolyn to find happiness, because without him loving her, they would have ended up miserable in their marriage.

Blake remembered what Jake and Paige had said about needing to choose love. He scoffed. Carolyn definitely hadn't chosen love. Instead of seeing that Keith had done them both a favor, she'd worn her embarrassment like a blanket wrapped around her, choosing to wallow in that one misfortune and be wretched and resentful for her entire life.

Blake wasn't an idiot; he didn't need to be hit over the head to see the parallels between himself and Carolyn and all the other people whose heartbreak he'd witnessed. Instead of looking for love, he'd chosen to guard his heart to avoid having it broken again.

In his own defense, he wasn't bitter like Carolyn had been, or wasting away like some of the others had. Neither did he want to take his own life like Colm had. And he wasn't settling for less than love like the sailor.

Or was he? Was he so guarded that he wasn't choosing to love Paige? He loved the friendship they had. The benefits were great too. But he wasn't opening himself up to love either. He wasn't choosing to love again.

His mom, like their ancestor Thomas, had loved with all her heart. Their loves had been taken from them far too early, but he'd bet his mom had no regrets. Thomas probably didn't either.

Would opening himself up to love—making himself vulnerable—make that much of a difference?

Fuck. He was such an idiot. He'd been waiting for Paige to decide to leave him, almost positive that she would. Love wasn't going to give him a guarantee that she wouldn't, whether by her own choice or not.

Love was a risk, but not choosing it could mean ending up like Carolyn or Martha, or Colm, or all the others who had chosen not to pursue it.

Maybe he had needed to be hit on the head, and the plywood he was currently trapped under was that proverbial knock on his noggin, even if it had been more literal. Could the curse be trapping him in this episode until he realized that he had to choose to love Paige?

Since the curse started, he'd wondered if the episodes were telling him he had waited too long to choose love, or if there was still time and he needed to hurry up. He still didn't know the answer, but he was going to take a chance and choose the latter.

Carolyn let out a long breath like her body was expelling all its air, bringing him out of his head and back to the vision. Blake looked up at the same time as the woman in the chair. He waited to see if Carolyn would take another breath, but deep down, he knew she wouldn't.

The woman patted Carolyn's shoulder. "Rest in peace, dear," she whispered before pulling her phone out of her pocket.

When the air shifted this time, Blake was ready for it.

The pain hit him all at once, although he suspected it had never left. The curse had likely made him unable to feel it while he was trapped in an episode.

His original plan, before the curse showed him Carolyn, was to push the board partway off and then use his right arm under it to help lift it off. That wouldn't be possible now because his arm was numb from bearing the wood's weight for so long.

Pushing the wood all the way off was going to tear the shit out of his already bruised and scraped skin, but unless he wanted to die in this house like Carolyn had, he didn't see another option.

Breathing out against the pain, he strained to lift his left arm that lay limp at his side, positioning his palm flat against the edge of the board. He took one more deep breath, then shoved the wood as hard as he could.

Almost simultaneously, he felt the flesh on his arm shred and the plywood tip down. He rolled onto his bad shoulder to get out of the way.

The plywood clamored to the ground behind him. Adrenaline and pain coursed through him as he struggled to his knees, then his feet. Nausea assaulted him, causing him to sway, his shoulder hitting the wall. "Fuuuuuuuuck."

Blake closed his eyes and focused on slowing his breathing. When the nausea receded, he opened his eyes, pulled away from the wall, and stood still. Once he knew he wasn't going to fall over, he checked his watch, straining in the darkness to see the time.

"Seven-thirty. Shit." He'd lost almost five hours.

Knowing Paige must be frantic, he reached back, his muscles protesting, as he pulled his phone from his pocket.

"Shit." The battery was dead. He just couldn't get a break today.

He looked at the floor to make sure he wasn't going to step on anything and took a careful step. His muscles protested again, but at least they worked.

Keeping his gaze on the floor for potential hazards, he had taken two more steps when he heard crying. He knew that sound. "Carolyn?" he called into the dark house.

"You can hear me?" Carolyn asked.

When her voice sounded closer, Blake took another couple of tentative steps until he stood in the center of what used to be Carolyn's living room.

She hovered near the front door, not standing, but not really floating either. Her hair was parted in the middle and tied in two braids like she'd worn it in the late 1970s. He'd always imagined that ghosts would be see-through, but Carolyn appeared more opaque than translucent.

If he wasn't in a rush to get to Paige—not to mention tired and in pain—he probably would have marveled at seeing a ghost. Instead, he had to hold back his irritation.

"Yes. And I can see you."

She came closer. "How do you know my name?"

Blake didn't know how to answer her. If he told her he'd seen flashes of her life because he was cursed, she might think he was lying. On the other hand, if he said he was the one who now owned her house, she might do something to his crew. He wasn't sure she *could* do something, but he didn't want to chance her hurting anyone, so he went with the curse option.

"I'm cursed and my mind gets transported back in time to see people's lives, including yours."

She frowned. "You saw my entire life?"

Blake hesitated, then decided to tell her the truth. Maybe it would give her some peace. "No. Parts of your life after Keith."

"Keith?" she asked, her tone wistful. In the next second, her expression changed, and he saw the bitter woman she'd been in all the scenes he'd witnessed. "Did you see what he did to me? Did you see how he embarrassed me?"

That was a loaded question and he had to be careful how he answered it. "I think Keith didn't want to trap you in a loveless marriage. He was trying to set you free to find a new love."

"How could I?" she screamed. Carolyn lifted her hands, palms facing Blake, and shoved them toward him.

A tornado-sized blast of air hit him. It threw him backward, his head hitting the hardwood floor. Carolyn hovered over him, her features pinched in anger.

True fear slithered down Blake's back as he looked up at Carolyn. He couldn't move, but his muscles weren't stiff and locked like they were during a trance. Instead, an invisible weight pinned him to the floor.

"Carolyn, please, let me go."

"No."

Blake tracked her image as she paced back and forth across the room. He'd seen her bitterness and anger over the years, but he couldn't understand how trapping him would help her.

"Carolyn, please," he pleaded again. "I'm so sorry Keith hurt you, but keeping me here won't change that."

In an instant, she was above him, hovering less than a foot from his face. Sweat popped out on his upper lip, but he was unable to wipe it away.

"I know *that*," she spat in a tone that implied he was stupid. "For decades I tried to get people to understand how Keith embarrassed me and made me feel worthless. No one understood."

Blake let out a slow breath of relief when Carolyn moved away to take up pacing once more. Hands on her hips, she continued her rant about Keith. If it wasn't so sad, he'd be amazed that she'd managed to rant about the same thing for over thirty years.

Since the moment Keith turned his back on Carolyn at the altar, every word had been about how he'd embarrassed her. Blake tried to remember if she had ever said she loved Keith, but he couldn't think of a single time through all the years he'd witnessed that she had. There were times he did his best to tune her out, but he didn't think she'd ever said she'd loved him. Not even when her dad asked her if she was ready before he walked her down the aisle. When she'd smiled up at her dad, she'd told him she couldn't wait to be Mrs. Keith Merrill. She hadn't said she couldn't wait to marry the love of her life.

Paige was the love of Blake's life. He'd denied it for a long time, but not anymore. Once he found a way out of Carolyn's clutches, he'd tell Paige he loved her. Even knowing there was a risk that she didn't feel the same wouldn't stop him from telling her.

"Carolyn," he said, interrupting her tirade. "I do understand how Keith embarrassed you. If he had loved you, how would you have felt if someone kept you from him?"

"But he didn't love me."

Blake wanted to roll his eyes. "I know, but if he had and someone tried to keep you from him, you'd be angry, right?"

The front doorknob rattled.

Carolyn spun toward it.

Paige opened the door and stepped inside. "It's so dark, can—"

"Noooooooo!" Blake yelled as Carolyn knocked Paige backward into the room, the front door slamming shut behind her.

His eyes already adjusted to the darkness, Blake was able to see Paige as she got up off the floor and took a tentative step toward him. He could hear Jake outside, pounding on the door, calling Paige's name.

"Paige! Get out of here!" Blake screamed.

"Blake? Where are you? It's so dark, I can't see you."

"Paige, you have to leave!" Blake yelled at her, his panic rising as he feared what Carolyn could do to Paige. He had to get her to leave. "Paige, bang on the door! Tell Jake to break it down."

She hesitated, half-turned back to the door. "What?"

"Leave!" he yelled again.

"Too late," Carolyn said in a sing-song voice.

Paige's eyes widened as she looked up to where Carolyn hovered above her.

"Carolyn," he pleaded. "Please don't hurt her."

Ignoring him, Carolyn lifted her hands, palms toward Paige, and sent a gale-force wind her way. Completely helpless, Blake watched in horror as the wind knocked Paige backward. Her upper back hit the floor, and the momentum slid her forward until she came to a stop beside him.

Blake couldn't turn his head, but he could see Paige from the corner of his eye. She wasn't moving.

"Paige? Are you okay?... Baby, answer me." Blake blinked several times to ease the strain of shifting his eyes so far to one side. "Paige." He continued to call her name, and it felt like ages before she answered.

"B-Blake? Wh-What's going on? How'd she do that?" Paige asked, her voice unsteady.

"I got stuck in a—"

"I'll explain," Carolyn said, moving to hover over Paige.

"W-who are you?" Paige asked.

"I'm Carolyn. This is my house. Well… it was."

Fear had laced Paige's every word and he wanted to tell her that everything would be okay. He didn't know if he believed it himself, but he also feared saying something that would anger Carolyn.

"What do you want?" Paige asked.

Paige drew in a breath when Carolyn moved and hung only inches above her.

"I want people to understand what Keith did to me," Carolyn spit out before moving back into the middle of the room.

"I don't know who Keith is," Paige said. "But I'm sorry he hurt you. Will you tell me what happened?"

Carolyn hovered high enough in the air that Blake had a perfect view of her features. Her eyes widened at Paige's question and a dreamy look came over her. "It was 1975, and I had the most beautiful wedding dress," Carolyn said as she launched into her story.

If Blake hadn't already loved Paige, he would have in that moment. She was one of the most caring people he'd ever met. He had known that eight years ago, and yet he'd allowed his pain to overshadow that truth. Only now could he look back and realize that Paige hadn't meant to crush him back then. She was loving and caring, but she'd also been young and looking for attention. Craig had taken advantage of that, and Blake hadn't stepped up like he should have.

Now, an angry ghost pinned Paige to the floor, and she was listening to the woman's selfish tales of woe like she mattered. At one time Carolyn should have mattered to someone, but Blake didn't have any empathy for her. While she'd been alive, she had chosen to wallow in her self-pity instead of getting on with her life.

Blake only listened with half an ear, not wanting to hear the same complaints he'd heard Carolyn spew dozens of times already. He focused on Paige's voice, her curiosity and compassion as she asked Carolyn questions.

"I'm so sorry he did that to you," Paige said with sincerity when Carolyn finished her story.

"You understand why I was so embarrassed?"

"Of course. He should have told you how he felt long before that."

Carolyn moved closer, her attention focused on Paige.

"No, you don't get it." Carolyn shook her head. "He shouldn't have told me at all. He should have married me! I was supposed to be Mrs. Keith Merrill. He promised to look after me in the manner I deserved. Not embarrass me in front of everyone I knew."

It wouldn't matter how kind and sympathetic Paige was. Carolyn hadn't changed her mind in thirty years, so he didn't expect her to change it now. If they had any hope of getting out of this, it was going to have to come from an outside source. He couldn't hear Jake yelling anymore, but he expected his best friend was working on a way to save them.

He didn't want to think about the consequences if Jake didn't come through, but he couldn't ignore the possibility either. Because of that, he couldn't wait to tell Paige how he felt.

Telling her he loved her while they were both stuck to a floor in a darkened room with a ghost hovering over them wouldn't have been his first choice, or even in his top ten. But he had to believe what he felt meant more than the setting.

Looking out of the corner of his eye, all he could see was her cheek as he spoke to her. "Paige?"

"I'm here," she said quietly.

"I love you, Paige. I think I've loved you since the very first time I laid eyes on you. Dancing on that table, even out of rhythm to the music, you enthralled me. I'm so sorry I didn't get my head out of my ass earlier to tell you."

Paige sniffed. "I love you too. I don't think I ever stopped loving you, Blake. I want to spend the rest of my life with you."

He wished he could hold her. "You and Emmie are my life."

Carolyn scoffed. "Paige, he's lying to you. Can't you see that? Men can't be trusted. They'll say they love you, and when they get to the altar, they walk away."

"I know that's what Keith did to you, but not all men are like that. I love that Blake told me he loved me, but I didn't need to hear the words to know," Paige said calmly.

Carolyn pursed her lips, eyeing Paige skeptically.

"He shows me with the little things he does every day. Like when he makes my favorite breakfast. Or when he lets me win at backgammon so I don't feel like a total dummy. When he takes my vehicle and fills it with gas so I don't have to stop on my way to work. Every time he walks by me and brushes his hand along my back because he doesn't want to miss an opportunity to touch me, he's showing me his love. He plays dress-up and tea party with my three-year-old because he loves us. When we make love, I feel—"

"Stop!" Carolyn screeched. "It's not fair. I hate that you get all that when I didn't." She lowered herself over Paige. "I should have had that and instead I was used and discarded like old trash. I want you to feel what I feel."

Paige gasped before going completely silent.

"Paige? Paige? Paige, talk to me!"

When she didn't answer, he glared at Carolyn. "What did you do to her?"

Carolyn floated over him, a smug look on her face. "I've tied her life force to mine. It's a handy little trick I learned from my home's last owner. She was a witch who loved to leave her grimoire lying around. You know all about witches and curses, don't you, Blake?"

It dawned on him why his last episode came so close after the previous one. "You triggered my curse today, didn't you?"

She grinned. "Yes. That was clever of me, wasn't it? I sensed something different about you when you arrived. I just didn't know that you'd be able to see my life or me."

Paige's breathing became deeper and then sped up. After a few moments, it paused before starting again.

The sound of her breathing pattern turned his blood to ice. Blake thought he'd felt ultimate fear earlier when Carolyn had trapped him, but it paled in comparison to the terror coursing through him now.

"You're killing her," he yelled through his panic. "Stop. Let her go. Please, Carolyn, don't kill her."

"No. Life isn't fair!" she screeched again. "It's not fair that you do all those things for her and no one did anything for me. And now I'll get even by tying her life force to mine. Since I'm dead, she'll be dead soon too."

"Take me," he said quietly.

"What?"

"Take me instead. Let Paige live and you can have my life force. I'm sure you can figure out how to keep me here with you so I'll be tied to you for eternity."

Carolyn eyed him with suspicion. "Why would you do that?"

"Because I love Paige so much that I want her to live and be happy, even if I can't be with her. She's also a great mom to a beautiful little girl, and I want Paige to be able to continue showering her daughter with love."

Paige's breathing paused again, and Blake held his own breath, waiting for Paige's to start back up. When it did, he exhaled, but with his growing terror, it felt like his lungs couldn't get enough air.

"I can't believe you'd willingly sacrifice your life for hers."

"Of course I would; I love her. Carolyn, don't you see that Keith lied to you?" Blake asked.

He did his best to make sure his tone didn't hold resentment as he looked at the bitter woman hovering over him. He had to get through to her.

"Keith couldn't have loved you. If he truly did, he wouldn't have walked away. He would have wanted to make you happy every single day. I'm truly sorry he wasn't what you deserved."

Paige's breathing paused again, but for longer. She was running out of time.

He looked at Carolyn and tried to feel something, anything, for the ghost who was killing the woman he loved. If he could empathize with her, maybe he could get through to her.

"Carolyn, I wish you had experienced the kind of love that Paige and I have. Maybe..." He purposely let his voice trail off.

"Maybe what?"

"Maybe if you let go and move on to the afterlife, you'll still be able to experience love there."

"I don't know…"

"Then please, please take me, Carolyn. Let Paige go so she can keep loving her daughter."

"You love her that much?"

"Yes, I do."

Carolyn looked down at Paige. "I just wanted—" She choked on the last word as tears welled in her eyes. "I'm sorry… so sorry," she whispered, then vanished.

"Carolyn?" Blake yelled as he struggled to release himself.

The invisible bindings on him snapped. He was free.

"Paige?" He rolled toward Paige, pulling her into his arms. Her face was pale as she gasped a breath—a normal breath— and opened her eyes.

Her hazel eyes were the most beautiful sight he'd ever seen. Tears leaked from his own as he leaned down and kissed her, too overwhelmed to speak.

The sound of wood cracking split the air. He held Paige tighter to his chest as he whipped his gaze toward the front of the house.

Jake kicked aside a piece of broken door, an ax in his hand. Dane, Ford, and Cade tumbled in next. His brothers all held industrial flashlights.

"Whoa, lower those things," he said, bending further over Paige to shield them both from the blinding light.

His brothers aimed the lights at the ground, and Jake passed the ax to Cade. "Are you guys okay?" he asked as he approached them.

Blake looked at Paige. "Yeah. A little worse for wear, but we'll be okay."

"I love you," she whispered.

"I love you too." He gave her a quick kiss and looked up at Jake and his brothers. "I'm going to need a hand up."

Cade crouched down beside him. "What the hell—"

A starburst of light exploded around them.

Instinctively, Blake tucked Paige in closer, shielding her with his arms.

"I won't harm you, my child," an angelic voice said as the bright lights softened to a soft glow that blanketed the room.

A woman with long, silky black hair and petite features floated several inches above the ground. Light emanated from her skin and spilled out from under her billowy robes as they fluttered about her body, as if caught in a gentle wind.

"Are you a ghost?" Paige asked.

"No, but I am a spirit."

"You're the one who cursed my ancestor, aren't you?" he asked the spirit.

"Yes. He was a horrible man who had no love nor empathy for those around him. He needed to be taught a lesson."

"But you didn't teach him a lesson," Jake said in a harsh tone.

The spirit shook her head. "No, I'm afraid I didn't. He died just as arrogant and lacking in empathy as when I cursed him."

Blake wanted to point out that the spirit had to have been full of arrogance herself to think she had the right to make generations suffer because of one man. Her one action five hundred years ago had hurt and maybe killed countless people. He and Paige were only two of her victims. As much as he would have liked to call her on her actions, he'd had enough of angering spirits tonight. "Are you the witch that used to live in this house?"

"No. Spirits aren't the same as witches. You're referring to the witch whose grimoire Carolyn read?"

"You know about that and yet you did nothing?" Blake spit out, his patience completely gone.

"I couldn't interfere," the spirit told him in a tone that said Blake should have known that. Yet this spirit had been interfering in his family's lives for hundreds of years. Deciding the witch wasn't important for now, he asked, "What happens now?"

The spirit smiled. "Thank you for embracing love. The curse is broken."

"That's it?" Dane asked.

"For them," the spirit said, gesturing to Blake and Paige. "The curse was cast centuries ago, and I cannot undo the past. The curse will continue for each person in Eamon's line unless they find love and have it reciprocated by their thirtieth birthday."

She faded away, leaving her legacy unchanged.

Christmas Day

*P*aige stopped at the bottom of the stairs to admire Blake. He stood in front of the fireplace as he stared at the lit Christmas tree. In the five weeks since the curse had broken, she and Emmie had permanently moved in with Blake. They'd gotten all their things out of storage, and there had been more than a few moments when Paige had needed to stop and take everything in. She'd never been happier, and she didn't ever want to take a moment for granted.

When she'd been younger, the big events had held all the attraction. She used to count down the days until birthdays, Christmases, and summer vacations. Then it was graduations, a wedding, the occasional vacation, and Emmie's birth. All those things were still important, but they were few and far between.

It was the tiny little everyday joys she consciously registered and appreciated now. She'd been truthful when she'd told Carolyn that she knew Blake loved her because of his actions.

She and Blake said they loved each other every day, but she also made sure she showed him as well. Sometimes it was a little gesture like getting up first to make him coffee or folding all the laundry because he hated folding. Or she would make his favorite dish without mushrooms, even though she loved them, so he wouldn't have to pick them out.

In the past, she would have just skipped the mushrooms altogether, but she'd been learning to please herself too. Cooking mushrooms separately so they could both enjoy what they liked was an easy thing to do.

Turning away from the tree, Blake noticed her and smiled. He held out his hand to her. "Any troubles getting Emmie to sleep?"

Paige took his hand, and he led her to the couch, pulling her down to sit beside him. "Not a one. She almost fell asleep in the bath."

"She didn't get a second wind, did she?"

"Nope. Didn't even last through one book."

He wrapped his arm around her, cuddling her into his side. The only sound in the room was the crackling of the fire, and after the noise of the day, that was enough.

"Was today too much?" he asked as if reading her thoughts.

"No, it was perfect, but I won't complain about the quiet."

"I agree. Who knew three little kids three and under could make so much noise?"

Paige snorted a laugh. "That's what you're going with? You think Emmie, Malcolm, and Jake's sweet little niece made all the noise?" She poked him playfully in his side.

"Ow," he mocked. "Okay. Maybe my brothers and I contributed a little."

Paige pulled back so she could see his face. "You knew

what Jake was bringing over, didn't you? I bet you even helped him buy them."

"Me?" he asked in a too-innocent voice.

"Okay, you go with that," she said, laughing and snuggling back against his side.

Jake had arrived with Hungry Hungry Hippos and two Rock 'Em Sock 'Em Robots. As soon as Malcolm and Emmie unwrapped the games, it became an all-out competition between the brothers and Jake, who was just as much of a brother, even if not by blood. No one could have said there was a dearth of cheering and trash talk, but somehow they'd managed to keep it clean because of the impressionable little ears around.

The day had been everything they'd planned and more, but she knew it had still been tough on Blake and his brothers—today had been the first Christmas without their mom.

While they'd been putting up the tree a few weeks ago, he had regaled her with stories of Akerman Christmas traditions. Some of the stories were from when his dad had been alive, and others from when they'd been forced to make new ones without him. She had laughed hard enough to get a stitch in her side. Emmie had loved hearing the stories too, even if Blake had exaggerated some of them. After getting to know his brothers again, Paige expected he might not have embellished them too much, but he probably made a few of them a bit more PG than the original events.

They'd started the day off opening presents with Emmie before the hoard descended for her and Blake to host brunch. For dinner they'd all gone to Jake's parents' house, something Kelly had approached her about the week before. She and Alex had taken turns hosting Christmas brunch and dinner over the years. Paige hadn't minded being asked after Jessica declined. She'd been honored to pick up the mantle.

"What are you thinking about?" Blake asked.

"Just about today." She turned around and straddled his lap, placing her hands on his chest. "You okay?"

"Yeah, I'm good." He leaned in and pressed his mouth to hers, just a soft brush of his lips.

Wrapping her hand around the back of his neck, she parted her lips, her tongue seeking his to deepen the kiss. It didn't last long, but Paige recognized the kiss for the distraction it had been. No matter how much he and his brothers had enjoyed the day, laughing and horsing around, every so often she'd seen Blake take a wistful look at the Christmas tree. His brothers did too, where they'd hung so many of his mom's ornaments.

He rotated on the couch, scooting back into the corner so he could stretch his legs out, and pulled her down beside him. She snuggled into him, her hand on his chest.

"Cade had some news," Blake said quietly as if he was reluctant to share what he'd heard.

"You don't have to tell me if it's too hard right now."

"No… that's not it." He linked his fingers with hers on his chest. "When Cade and I found the old letters and journals, we also found two old photo albums. Nothing was dated, which was really odd for my mom, as she labeled everything."

"I know," she said softly. "Remember when we were dating and I gave her flowers? And what she did to the card?"

"Right, she dated the back of it. I'd forgotten about that. Well… then you'd know why Cade and I thought it was funny that none of the photos had dates on them. Cade and I were in a few of them with Mom and her sister. Our aunt Chrys. But the crazy thing is Mom told me that Chrys died when I was a baby."

"How old was Cade in the pictures?"

"Maybe one or two."

"So either your mom lied or she couldn't remember when her sister died, although that doesn't seem likely."

Blake sighed. "That's what we thought. Kelly looked through the journals, but nothing stood out to her, so Cade hired a private investigator. She, the PI, found my aunt."

Paige turned in his arms so she could see him. "She's been alive all this time? Do you think she and your mom had a fight and that's why she said she died?"

"I don't think so. She's in a facility."

"Like a senior home?"

"No, a psychiatric hospital. Cade got an appointment for us to go tomorrow. He took the first available one, but he won't be able to go because he and Jessica are taking Malcolm to spend Christmas with her parents."

"Do you want me to go with you?"

"It's right when your parents will be getting here. I'll be fine, and Jake already said he'd go with me."

Blake lifted her off him and took her hand. "Enough depressing stuff for now. Come here."

He took her over to the Christmas tree and reached around to the back, pulling out a small wrapped box he must have hidden in the branches. "I have one more present for you."

"You've already given me so much." She went onto her toes and kissed him.

"Just one more," he said.

Taking what was obviously a jewelry box, she expected it was the earrings she'd mentioned. She pulled off the ribbon and opened the lid. Tears sprung to her eyes and she looked at Blake.

He was on one knee in front of her. "I know we haven't been back together long," he said as he took the box from her and pulled out the ring. "And proposing on Christmas is probably cliché, but if the curse taught me anything, it's that I need to cherish every moment with you, and I don't want to wait to make you mine. Paige, will you marry me?" Not waiting for her answer, he slipped the ring on her finger.

"Yes." She threw herself at him, but she knew he'd catch her.

"I love you, Paige."

"I love you more."

He frowned. "No, you can't say that."

"Why?"

"Because then you're saying the love I feel for you is less than what you feel for me, and that's not possible." He used his thumb to wipe away the tear that slid down her cheek.

"I love you, Blake."

"I love you too," he said, and then he kissed her with everything he had.

Thursday, December 26

"She's in this room," the nurse said. "Let me know if you need anything."

"Thank you," Blake said and turned to Jake as she walked away. "Ready?"

"I was going to ask you that."

Blake didn't know what to think or expect, but waiting wouldn't help him figure it out. He pushed open the door and walked in, Jake behind him. A woman sat in a rocking chair facing a window, her back to the door. Her view consisted of the low winter sun shining on barren trees.

"Aunt Chrys?" Blake asked softly, not wanting to frighten her, as he walked around to face her. Her eyes were closed, and except for the flutter of her lids, like she was in REM sleep, she didn't move a muscle.

His aunt was eleven months younger than his mom, but he hadn't expected them to look so much alike. Looking at her was liking seeing his mom again. He swallowed against the sudden emotion clogging his throat. Even understanding his aunt's life was a shadow of what it should have been, it was difficult seeing her sitting there while knowing he would never see his mom again.

"Aunt Chrys? It's Blake, Alex's oldest son." She didn't respond.

"Aunt Chrys? Can you hear me?" he asked again as he lightly laid his hand on top of hers where it rested on the arm of the rocker. Her skin felt cool to the touch, too cool for the warmth of the room.

He didn't even know if his aunt knew about his mom. Turning to Jake, he told him, "I feel out of my element."

"Do you want to stay or go?" Jake asked.

"I don't know." He turned back to his aunt and picked up her cold hand, rubbing it gently in both of his. "Yes, let's stay," he said, changing his mind. If she was having an episode similar to Blake's, maybe she'd come out of it.

Jake pulled over the spare chair from the corner and pushed it at the back of Blake's legs. "Thanks," Blake said, giving Jake a quick glance.

Looking at his aunt's hands in his, he could see how similar they were to his mom's. "Do you think my mom knew she was here?" he asked Jake without looking up.

"I don't know. Maybe the nurse would know if your mom visited, or we can ask Cade to get the PI to look into it."

"Maybe." Blake wasn't sure it would make a difference to his aunt, but it would be nice if they could shed some light on why his mom had lied to them.

"Do you know this girl?" Jake asked, showing him a

framed picture. "It was on the nightstand and it's the only photo in the room."

"I don't, but she could be the little girl from the photo album we found. If she is, then that picture is old because the girl should be about our age. How old do you think the girl in that picture is?"

"Fifteen, maybe. With her dark coloring, I don't see any resemblance to you, but then, you look more like your dad."

"Do you think she looks a bit like Ford and Gage?"

Jake pulled the picture back and studied it. "Maybe. If she does, it's the eyes."

As Blake lifted his hand from on top of his aunt's to take the photo from Jake, he felt his aunt's hand move. "She moved. Aunt Chrys? Can you hear me?"

Searching his aunt's face, he looked for any sign she'd heard him, but without knowing what could constitute as a sign. Rubbing her hands in his again, he figured it must have been an involuntary muscle reaction.

"Let me see," Blake said and lifted his hand off his aunt's again but kept his gaze on her hand. It twitched, but like last time, he expected that it was involuntary.

As he pulled his other hand out from under hers to put her hand back on the arm of the rocker, her fingers moved again. His eyes glued to the movement, he realized it was deliberate. She moved her index finger back and forth. It was too steady to be a twitch.

"Shit." He glanced up at Jake. "She knows I'm here. What should we do?"

"I guess we wait."

Clasping his aunt's hand in both of his, he looked at her face. "Aunt Chrys. I hope you can hear me."

Knowing her life had been stolen from her by a curse made him angry at the spirit's arrogance all over again. Did she even care how many lives she'd destroyed?

As the minutes ticked by, it reminded Blake of all the times he'd been locked in an episode. If he and Paige hadn't fallen in love, or it had happened too late, would he have been stuck like his aunt?

Was she aware of her surroundings, just unable to do anything, like he'd been when trapped in his episodes?

His aunt's finger moved again and her eyelids popped open. She blinked before her gaze focused on him and she gripped his hand. "Blake?"

"Wow, you recognize me? How? Did my mom come to visit?" He sounded like Emmie, throwing out questions one after the other.

"I only have about two minutes before the curse takes me again. I realized a long time ago that my version of the curse is reality distortion…" She looked startled for a moment. "What day is it?" she asked, panic in her voice.

"December twenty-sixth," he answered. She didn't ask what year, so he didn't offer that information.

"You're thirty now. The curse?"

"It started, but I fell in love and broke it. I'm so sorry that you can't—"

She waved her hand at him in dismissal. "Don't worry about me. It's too late now. Find your cousin. Her name is Maeve Montgomery, no middle name. The last time I saw her, she was fifteen. She was in the foster care system. I should have let your mom raise her like she wanted to, but I was too arrogant and stubborn. I thought the curse wouldn't affect me. Maeve was born the same year as you, on November sixteenth. She was my life, but I—"

Her eyelids fell closed and her hand went limp in his once more.

"Aunt Chrys?" he asked even though he knew it was too late. She'd been sucked back into another episode. They'd waited thirty minutes for her to come out of her last one, and they had no way of knowing how long she'd been in it before they'd gotten there.

When Carolyn had triggered Blake's curse, he'd been stuck in it for over four hours. Since his aunt had been living with her curse for decades, this might have been the only time she would be aware the entire day.

Blake placed his aunt's hand back on the arm of the chair. "I'll come again, Aunt Chrys. And we won't give up on finding a way to break this curse for good."

Leaning over, he placed a kiss on his aunt's forehead.

When he straightened, Jake was taking a picture of his cousin's photo.

They walked out of his aunt's room, and Blake stopped to speak with the nurse. "My aunt's hands are really cold. Could you please give her a blanket or turn up the heat in her room?"

"Sure. I hope you had a good visit."

"We did, thank you."

Walking back to his truck with Jake, Blake wondered if he'd given his aunt false hope by saying they were looking for a permanent cure. Or maybe he didn't need to worry about it at all since he had no way of knowing if she had even heard him.

Once in the vehicle, he glanced over at Jake. "You're going to look for her, aren't you?"

"You know I have to," Jake said quietly.

"I do. And of course I'll help. Maeve is family. But... one of these days you're going to have to accept that you can't save everyone." Blake knew it was futile telling Jake that, but just like Jake hadn't given up on him, Blake wouldn't give up on Jake.

Blake started the truck, eager to get back to Paige and Emmie.

Thanks so much for reading Cursed to Love, and you don't
have to say goodbye just yet!
Go to:
https://kjwarawa.com/cursed-to-love-bonus-scene/
to download a free bonus scene with more of
Blake's & Paige's HEA.

Then find out what happens when Mae and Jake fight the
curse and someone has to make a sacrifice that no one saw
coming, in
CURSED TO DREAM
https://books2read.com/cursed-to-dream/

IN MAGIC SERIES

Hidden in Magic

Truth in Magic

Found in Magic

Courage in Magic

Love in Magic

Forged in Magic

Forever in Magic

CURSED TO LOVE SERIES

Cursed to Love

Cursed to Dream

Cursed to Wither

Cursed to Suffer

ABOUT KJ WARAWA

Paranormal romance author KJ Warawa had worked every job under the sun, including swimwear seller, switchboard operator, legal secretary, sign language interpreter, soldier, massage therapist, and process improvement advisor, before settling into the career she'd always dreamed about: Author.

She still loves processes and spreadsheets, doesn't love massaging feet, and is currently living out her own love story in Alberta, Canada.

STAY IN TOUCH WITH KJ:
Join KJ's Newsletter at
https://kjwarawa.com/free-book/
to receive a FREE book, exclusive deals, special offers, behind-the-scenes info, and learn about new releases, plus more!
www.kjwarawa.com